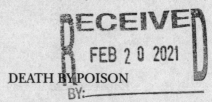
DEATH BY POISON

"I stopped by Paul's apartment a little earlier and talked to his roommate, Grace. She said the police took away the container he always used to bring home his meal from the restaurant where he did bike delivery, the Green Artichoke."

Alana blinked. "To test it for poison?"

"That would be my guess. It looks like they're treating his death as a possible suspicious one."

"Murder?" Alana gave me a horrified look.

"Maybe . . ."

Books by Maddie Day

Country Store Mysteries
FLIPPED FOR MURDER
GRILLED FOR MURDER
WHEN THE GRITS HIT THE FAN
BISCUITS AND SLASHED BROWNS
DEATH OVER EASY
STRANGLED EGGS AND HAM
NACHO AVERAGE MURDER

Collections
CHRISTMAS COCOA MURDER
(with Carlene O'Connor and Alex Erickson)

Cozy Capers Book Group Mysteries
MURDER ON CAPE COD
MURDER AT THE TAFFY SHOP

And writing as Edith Maxwell

A TINE TO LIVE, A TINE TO DIE
'TIL DIRT DO US PART
FARMED AND DANGEROUS
MURDER MOST FOWL
MULCH ADO ABOUT MURDER

Published by Kensington Publishing Corporation

Nacho Average Murder

MADDIE DAY

KENSINGTON BOOKS
www.kensingtonbooks.com

KENSINGTON BOOKS are published by

Kensington Publishing Corp.
119 West 40th Street
New York, NY 10018

All Kensington titles, imprints, and distributed lines are available at special quantity discounts for bulk purchases for sales promotion, premiums, fund-raising, and educational or institutional use.

Special book excerpts or customized printings can also be created to fit specific needs. For details, write or phone the office of the Kensington Sales Manager: Kensington Publishing Corp., 119 West 40th Street, New York, NY 10018. Attn. Sales Department. Phone: 1-800-221-2647.

Kensington and the K logo Reg. U.S. Pat. & TM Off.

First Kensington Books Mass Market Paperback Printing: July 2020

ISBN-13: 978-1-4967-2315-4
ISBN-10: 1-4967-2315-5

ISBN-13: 978-1-4967-2316-1 (ebook)
ISBN-10: 1-4967-2316-3 (ebook)

10 9 8 7 6 5 4 3 2 1

Printed in the United States of America

For my Temple City, California, classmates, then and now, who have become some of my biggest fans. We have our own high school reunion this year—number fifty—and I sure hope no murders go along with it!

Acknowledgments

I spent a week in Santa Barbara recently to soak up the sights and sounds and to refresh my memory of that lovely city nestled between mountains and the Pacific Ocean. My apologies to Santa Barbara residents for moving your Tuesday afternoon farmers' market to Wednesday morning and for adding Mama Tamale. I made up a few streets, too. I took inspiration from Madame Rosinka's palm-reading establishment on Stearns Wharf, but Madame Allegra is entirely of my own creation. Thanks, also, to the real Chumash Casino for giving me ideas. I stole the name Pause Yoga from the best yoga teacher in New England, Jennifer Walker Freeman. Because the late, great Sue Grafton lived in Montecito and set her Kinsey Millhone mysteries in a fictionalized Santa Barbara, I included various mentions of her as an homage.

No aspersions are implied on the actual Santa Barbara County coroner's office and personnel—the version in this book is entirely fictional. Author Micki Browning, a former member of the Santa Barbara Police Department, gave me help with local details about the criminal justice system, but all errors are of my own doing, including my entirely made-up interior of the station.

Thank you to D. P. Lyle, MD, for information about what a ruptured aneurysm looks like and how it is detected, and to Geoff Symon for his excellent online class about autopsies. Gratitude to Cristina Olán and my son JD Hutchison-Maxwell for checking the Spanish phrases in the book. Intrepid traveling friend Bonnie Kittle provided the inspiration to include the very odd-looking Buddha's hand citron.

While Alana wasn't the name of my high school bestie, I drew on my once-a-decade visits with Cindy Cobb Snyder—most recently during the writing of this book—for some of the scenes featuring Robbie and Alana. I'm so grateful Cindy and I can pick up where we left off, even fifty years later. I often crowd-source my punny titles, and Evelyn Dillon came up with this one. Thanks, Evelyn! I riffed on it for the name of the café.

Many thanks to Terri Bischoff and her expert editing chops for giving the book a pre-submission read and for helping me improve it in all kinds of ways.

My gratitude, always, to my family, to the fabulous team at Kensington Publishing, to my agent, John Talbot, and to the Wicked Authors. Please join Jessica Ellicott, Sherry Harris, Julie Hennrikus, Liz Mugavero, Barbara Ross, and me on our blog and our Facebook group. I never stop learning from these ladies, who provide ongoing inspiration, a sounding board, and fun.

Don't worry, fans. Robbie will be back in South Lick for the next book. But wasn't it fun to take a trip to California?

Chapter 1

Like Dorothy in Oz, I definitely wasn't in Indiana anymore. At least the Wicked Witch hadn't shown up. Yet.

The sun had just dipped into the Pacific Ocean, and a mild Santa Barbara breeze *shoosh*ed through tall palm trees. Mellow jazz slid out of speakers in a spacious function hall facing the water with glass doors open to a wide patio. The Chumash High School tenth reunion committee had organized every detail. I sipped a glass of pinot noir from a winery located less than an hour's drive away in the Santa Ynez Mountains behind us, and nervously adjusted my favorite turquoise shoulder bag. So far I hadn't seen anybody I really wanted to hang out with tonight. But people were still coming in, and I knew Alana Lieberman would be here, my bestie and constant companion from our high school days.

I felt a tap on my shoulder and turned to see a different former classmate.

"Robbie Jordan!" Jason Wong said. "What a surprise. I thought you moved back east somewhere."

I looked up at my slender friend. "Jason, it's awesome to see you. Indiana is east of here, for sure, but nearly half the country is beyond it." I'd had the same notion when I was growing up here on the West Coast. We all considered anywhere on the other side of the Rocky Mountains to be "back east." "I wouldn't miss this reunion for anything."

He lowered his voice. "I heard about your mom, Rob. I'm so sorry."

I smiled at the nickname he and Alana had called me by. "Thanks. It's been two years now. I still miss her, especially being back in all the familiar places." I blew out a breath and drew my light sweater a little closer around me. The sleeveless flowered dress I'd chosen wasn't quite warm enough for the evening, and I was glad I'd brought the wrap. "What are you up to?"

"I'm a proud member of the SBPD." He pushed up his glasses.

"The police department?"

"Yes. I'm kind of their tech detective. Some of the older guys, well, they're not really up on digital anything. I investigate cybercrime, Internet forensics, the works."

"That's awesome. Or what did we say? That's sick." We'd been on math team together and had been buddies all through high school.

He snorted. "Good thing that phrase went the way of the dodo. So what do you do in Iowa?"

"Jason, it's Indiana. You're such a Californian.

Anyway, I own a country store. I have a breakfast-and-lunch restaurant downstairs, B-and-B rooms upstairs, and an apartment at the back of the building. It's a pretty sweet setup."

"So the crossword queen goes all proprietor on us. I like it."

"I do, too." I glanced at the ID on his lanyard, which featured his senior picture. "Man, you look twelve in that photo."

He pointed at mine. "And you don't?"

"What can you do?" I shook my head. "Are you married? Have kids?"

"No to both. Going to college and then making it through the academy took up all my time. Still hoping to settle down, though. You?"

"I had a brief but disastrous marriage right after college. Now I've found a solid boyfriend, but that's as far as we've gotten."

"Glad you snagged a good man."

I was, too. Abe O'Neill was as good as they come. I looked around. Clumps of classmates, all of us nearly thirty, stood talking, laughing, reconnecting. Sure, people were cleaned up and in nice clothes, but everybody still seemed to be in pretty good shape. I idly mused on what we would look like in forty years at our fiftieth reunion. More paunch, for sure. Plus gray, dyed, or no hair, depending.

An arm went around my shoulder. "Hey, girl-friend. Whassup?" Alana said.

I twisted to see her. "Hey, you!" I threw both arms around her for a long-overdue embrace. We pulled apart to stand grinning stupidly at each other. She'd been my puzzling friend, my biking companion, and my confidante. I'd moved east and she'd slid north to Berkeley to put her doctorate in biochemistry to good use in some high-powered lab. Despite keeping in touch online, we hadn't seen each other in person since graduation.

"You guys need to get a room or something?" Jason elbowed me.

"Shut UP, Wong." My petite friend exchanged fist bumps with him. "How you been? Keeping the city safe?" She wore her auburn hair in a no-nonsense ear-length cut, as usual, and tonight she'd dressed in a green silk top and loose dark pants. Alana had never been one for skirts.

"Doing what I can," he said. "Have you figured out a cure for cancer?"

"Working on it." Alana told him.

"Really?" I asked.

She gave a little shrug. "Robbie, you know there are all kinds of cancers. But, yes, we are micro-millimetering our way closer to—"

A fingers-in-the-mouth whistle split the air. We turned toward the side of the room where a woman stood. I looked again. It was Katherine Russom, not my favorite person from our school days. The buzz of conversation quieted.

She waved both hands in the air. "Welcome to our tenth Chumash reunion, everybody! You've all got your name tags, so don't hesitate to go find your former best friend or worst enemy and tell them how much better they look now." She paused, clearly expecting a laugh. When nothing more than a polite smattering of chuckles resulted, she flicked back shoulder-length blond hair and continued. "We did pretty well getting nearly a hundred of you here out of a class of two hundred and fifty. Who came from farthest away?"

I surveyed the room. On the other side of the crowd a man waved his hand. He was tall enough that I could see dark hair already starting to recede.

"Sydney, Australia."

"Wow. Let's give it up for Joe Abrams." Katherine clapped. "Anybody from back east?"

Jason pointed to my head, so I raised a hand. "It's only halfway back, but Indiana."

Katherine peered. "Robbie Jordan?" Her mouth twisted like she'd tasted a moldy tortilla.

"Hi, everybody," I called out. "It's great to be back." *Mostly.*

Katherine cleared her throat. "The buffet is all ready, so load up a plate. We have a killer entertainment lined up after dinner."

Jason glanced at me and murmured, "If she'd ever encountered a real killer, she wouldn't use the word so lightly."

"No kidding," I said. "Alana knows this, but you probably don't. I've been involved in solving several homicide cases in the last couple of years."

He raised a surprised eyebrow. "No way, Rob. Truth?"

"Truth."

Alana nodded. "She told me about at least one of the cases. The guy in the ice?" She shivered. "That sounded like a nightmare."

"It kind of was," I agreed. "Small-town life isn't always the quiet, cozy existence people think it must be."

"Even here in paradise"—Jason gestured to the rose-colored clouds and white sand outside the doors—"we aren't immune to crime."

I shook my head slowly. "No, I bet you aren't."

Chapter 2

The buffet food was way better than I'd expected. The chef presented a creamy lime-chili-cilantro treatment on the halibut, a light Asian dressing on a soba noodle salad studded with slivers of colorful vegetables, and flaky empanadas with a cheesy chicken filling. A perfectly Californian meal. The wines were from Los Olivos and the bartender also had two taps from the Telegraph Brewing Company on offer.

As we ate, Jason, Alana, and I caught up with several other classmates at our table, all of whom had stayed in the area. Nobody had brought spouses or significant others, and only one had started a family.

When Alana used her left hand to lift her wine-glass, I caught a flash of starlight. "Give me that hand," I demanded.

She blushed and extended it, the fourth finger of which was adorned with a fat diamond on a slender gold band.

"When?" I asked in mock anger. "Who? And how didn't I know this?"

"Hey, it's not like I've had a chance to tell you," Alana said. "His name is Antonio Lacambria, we work together, and we don't have a date yet." Her smile was sweeter than homemade peach ice cream. "He only asked me a couple of weeks ago."

"Congratulations, Al," I said with a stupid grin. "I'm really happy for you. Is he Italian?"

"Yes. His parents are Jews from Rome, but Antonio was born in San Francisco."

"Your marriage linen monogram will be perfect for both of you," I said. "A–L."

"Not that we're the monogram type," Alana scoffed. "But yeah, we happen to share initials. Kind of perfect, in my mind."

Jason lifted his drink. "To Mrs. Al."

The three of us clinked glasses and our classmates across the table raised theirs, too. Alana gave us more details about her freshly minted fiancé for a few minutes while we dined.

Katherine, making the rounds greeting each table, approached us. "How's everything, kids?" A cloud of perfume came with her, way too strong for my taste.

"The food is outstanding," I began.

"Thank you. I selected the city's hottest young chef."

Jason cleared his throat. "Katherine, I thought the committee did the selection."

She lifted her chin and waved away his correction. "Of course, of course. Robbie, I expect you don't get much of interest to eat back there in Ohio."

My new mantra seemed to be geographical correction. "It's Indiana. And we happen to have some excellent chefs in the area."

"Robbie's a chef, herself," Jason said.

"I heard you were a short-order cook." Katherine pushed a strand of hair lightly off her temple with a ring-free left hand.

I smiled at her. How else to defuse this grudge she'd apparently been harboring for more than a decade? I didn't care what she thought of me. I was happy and supporting myself doing what I loved. "And what do you do?"

"I run a wedding planning company. We handle all the details, right down to the bridesmaids' shoes."

Alana regarded her. "You'd be good at that stuff."

"I enjoy it," Katherine said. "You still burying yourself in a lab, Alana?"

"Quite happily so, yes." She tilted her head and gave Katherine a little smile. "You didn't much care for lab classes, did you?"

I shot a glance at Alana. I knew what she meant. She'd been paired with Katherine for an experiment in biology class once, and had reported back that Katherine hadn't done any of the work.

"No, I didn't." Katherine blinked. "So why didn't your buddy Zoe show tonight, Robbie?"

Right. I hadn't spotted my childhood friend Zoe Stover here. "I haven't seen her in years, Katherine. I have no idea why she didn't come."

Katherine rolled her eyes a touch, as if she didn't believe me.

"She didn't register for the reunion?" I asked.

Katherine shook her head.

"Do you still play beach volleyball?" Alana asked her. "You were pretty competitive at that, as I recall."

"Still am. Our team wins nearly every game."

Katherine mimed a serve, making the muscles in her tanned bare upper arm stand out. "We have pickup games every Friday, if any of you are interested."

I certainly wasn't. Get into a game I'd never been good at with someone who preferred to win? Not for me.

Katherine gazed at the others at the table. "If any of you need my services, you know where to find me. Enjoy the evening." She headed for the next table.

"Didn't she marry Bill Lombard?" Jason asked the group. "I wouldn't think she'd be the type not to change her name."

The woman next to him, a former cheerleader, leaned closer. "She did, with a wedding straight out of central casting and several hundred guests. But the marriage only lasted a year. She dropped Bill's name like a ghost chile and went back to Daddy's."

The strum of an electric guitar caught everybody's attention. "Good evening, Chumashers! Ready for some music?" The guitarist and his four fellow musicians had been in a garage band in high school, and it looked like they were having a reunion themselves. "We're the Boffo Barnacles and we're going to entice you onto the dance floor. Get set to pull out your best high school moves."

They launched into a song by Katy Perry.

"My best high school moves were standing with my back to the wall watching everybody else dance." Jason laughed, shaking his head.

"Mine was not even going to the dances," I said.

"Come on, Rob." He stood. "Let's give it a try, anyway."

"Sure. I'm way beyond caring what anybody thinks of my dance style."

Jason and I danced most of the next hour, with Alana joining us for a few songs. At one point the band switched to oldies and somebody brought out a limbo stick. My low center of gravity and bicyclist's power thighs got me in the final three as the stick went lower and lower, but I finally fell over sideways. I laughed and scrambled out of the way of a nimble and still-petite former gymnast who ended up the winner.

After the music switched to a more Latin beat, Hector Perez approached me, a guy I hadn't known well at high school. He'd been on the dance floor since the music started, and the dude had moves worthy of the contestants on *Dancing with the Stars*.

"Robbie, right?" he asked. His dark hair curled onto his neck, and an open-collar black shirt was snug on his uber-fit torso.

"Hi, Hector. How are you?"

"Great." He flashed me a white smile. "Would you like to dance?"

I accepted. I proceeded to have the dance of a life-time, despite never having partnered with anyone during a salsa number. The man knew how to lead. With subtle pressures of his hands on mine, gently steering me in the right direction, his gaze locked on my face all the while wearing a sweet half-smile, I felt like the modern Latin version of Ginger Rogers. I didn't step on his feet once.

After the song ended, he thanked me and gave a little bow. He went off to ask another woman for the next number. I took a deep breath and headed smiling for the drinks table to grab a glass of water.

When the band took a break, Katherine summoned us all for a class picture. "You remember the drill. Tall dudes in the back, middles in the middle row, shorties in the front. Oh, and class officers in the middle of the first row."

Jason and I exchanged a look. He rolled his eyes. "Madam former president needs to get a life."

I bobbed my head in agreement but went to claim a place in the first row, being all of five foot three when I stood up real straight. Somehow I ended up near the middle next to Katherine, despite my not having held office.

The photographer stood on a chair in front of us, calling out adjustments for people to move a little to their left or right. "Remember, if you can't see me, I can't see you."

Katherine muttered through her smile, "I've never forgiven you, you know."

I turned to stare at her. "What? Forgiven me for what?"

"Smile at the camera, Robbie."

I obeyed, but my brain was in overdrive. She couldn't still be mad about—

"All eyes up here," the photographer instructed, waving her hand next to her head. "Happy cheese!" She took a half dozen shots. "It's a wrap. Thanks, gang. The committee will have the best shot within the week."

Katherine began talking to the person on her other side. I started to extend my hand to touch her elbow, to ask her what she meant. I dropped it instead. I expected I'd never see her again after tonight. What happened back then didn't matter to me. And if she wanted to nurse an old hurt, imagined or real, it was her business, not mine.

Chapter 3

My internal clock was still set to Eastern Standard Time since I'd flown in only the previous day. I awoke at three a.m. the next morning, plagued by thoughts of what had gone down at the reunion. The only thing I could think of between Katherine and me was the time Bill Lombard had asked me on a date. I knew she'd had her eye on him because she'd talked about her crush in gym class. He and I hadn't become a thing, and she'd gone on to snatch him up. And then they'd apparently gotten divorced, which certainly had nothing to do with me. I'd gotten married and divorced myself.

I managed to slip back into dreamland after an hour, only aroused at seven thirty by the aromas of coffee, bacon, and something baking drifting upstairs to my B-and-B room. A quick shower later, I locked my room. I headed for the stairs, ready to sample whatever was on the menu for breakfast. Or inhale it, as the case may be. The Nacho Average Café was already hopping when I walked in.

"Good morning, Robbie," proprietor Carmen Perez called out from the pass-through window to the kitchen in the back. "Sit wherever you'd like."

"Thanks." I slid into a seat at a two-top near the front window. I smiled to myself at her name. Carmen was the nickname I'd given my phone.

The decor here was delightfully Cali-Mex, with hues of red, orange, and green predominating. Mexican folk-art murals decorated the walls, and a dozen papier-mâché angels and clothed Day of the Dead skeletons were suspended from the ceiling. The cloth napkin at my setting was red, too. A glass door opened onto a patio dining area, where a rosemary bush the size of a sea lion grew next to the low fence and ripe oranges hung from the glossy-leaved tree just beyond. Nope, not in Indiana. The only familiar bit was a tuxedo cat snoozing in a spot of sun on the paving stones outside. He could have been my Birdy's twin.

I perused the menu, eyes widening at the mention of avocado huevos rancheros and orange scones. My stomach growled out loud. I glanced around, but none of the other two dozen diners appeared to have heard. Some wore running outfits, and a couple on the patio had a leashed golden retriever sitting under their table.

"Coffee?" Carmen appeared at my side, pot of java in hand. "Did you sleep well?" In her fifties, she wore a long salt-and-pepper braid down her back—but with a streak dyed bright red decorating the right side. She'd tied an orange apron featuring the café's logo around her comfortable figure.

"Coffee, please. And, considering jet lag, I did all right in the sleep department."

"Good." She filled my mug. "How was your reunion last night?"

"Wonderful. Truly. I caught up with a number of old friends." I cocked my head, thinking. "Wait. Do you have a son named Hector?"

"Yes, of course." High beams had nothing on Carmen's smile. "He told me he was going."

"I didn't connect your name with him before. We weren't close in school, but man, can Hector ever dance. I have no idea how to officially dance salsa, and he made me feel like I'd been doing it for years. Best dance I've ever had."

"That's Hector's passion, but he's a chef, too, you know."

"Really?"

"He went to culinary school instead of college. He's worked a few places, but now he has a food truck at the harbor."

"Awesome. I'll have to check it out this week." I pointed to the cat. "What's his name?"

"Pajarito." She pronounced it *pa-ha-REE-toh*, trilling the *r* like the native Spanish speaker she was.

"Little bird?"

"Yes."

"I have his twin, and his name is Birdy. Does yours have six toes?

"He does. That's amazing."

"Right?" I glanced around the room. "I love the decor here, Carmen."

"Thanks. I do, too." She set one fist on her waist and smiled. "It was Jeanine who suggested decorating the restaurant like this after I bought the building."

My eyes widened. "You knew my mom?"

"I sure did. We were in the Unitarian women's book group together. I still miss her a lot, and you must miss her even more."

My throat thickened. I swallowed away the emotion. "I do."

Carmen touched my shoulder. "I'm sorry, I shouldn't have brought up her death."

"It's okay. It's just that out here there are so many reminders of her and what we used to do together." I cleared my throat and gestured at the menu. "So what do you recommend? Everything sounds yummy."

"The avocado huevos are popular. I grow the avocados out back, the eggs are from a local farmer, and my mom makes the tortillas. Mamá!" she called toward the kitchen. *"Diga hola a* Robbie.*"*

A woman's face appeared in the kitchen window. *"Hola,* Robbie.*"* So short her head barely made the window, she wore the same braid as her daughter but hers was whiter than a flour tortilla. She smiled from ear to ear and waved a strong working woman's hand.

I waved back. "You're so lucky to have her working with you," I said to Carmen. "What's her name, or should I call her Mamá?"

Carmen let out a hearty laugh. "Luisa Sandoval, but everybody calls her Mamá. She taught me everything I know about cooking."

"I can't wait to taste it. I'll have the avocado huevos rancheros, please, and an orange scone, too."

"You got it. The oranges are also my own. You want a mimosa or a bloody Mary with your meal? You're on vacation, right?"

I gave it a two-second consideration. "You're right, I am." I'd closed my restaurant so my two employees and I could have a much-needed break. Since I was already paying to fly west, I'd decided to stay a week and warm up my feet while I was here. Replenish my soul on views of ocean and mountains, and feed my body on fresh, delicious, creative meals, picking up recipes to take back in the process. "I'd love a bloody Mary." Heck, I didn't have anywhere in particular to go. And I could nurse it after I ate.

"Bueno." She looked around, then lowered her voice. "Robbie, I heard something was fishy about your mom's death."

What? "What do you mean, 'fishy'? She died of an aneurysm. Didn't she?"

"That's what they said. But—" A diner on the patio hailed her, and Mamá rang their version of a "food's ready" bell. "I'll tell you later. I need to get working."

"I know how it is. I'll be around until Saturday. Plenty of time to talk."

I sipped my dark roast coffee and watched her hurry off. What could she possibly mean by "fishy"? Sure, Mom died alone, but the death certificate had listed "aneurysm" as the cause. The medical examiner's office couldn't have gotten it wrong. Could they?

Chapter 4

Before I took the first bite, I snapped a picture of my died-and-gone-to-heaven breakfast—two fried eggs on refried black beans atop a corn tortilla covered with slices of a perfectly ripe avocado and chunky homemade salsa, with a dollop of sour cream on top and more warm tortillas on the side. I posted it to the Pans 'N Pancakes Instagram account with a message reading, "March breakfast special? Could happen." I added a hashtag of #NotInIndianaAnymoreDorothy, which made me smile. I had a pretty healthy number of followers, and they weren't all Hoosiers, either. I imagined them smiling, too. I'd thought of keeping a little notebook for meal ideas, but the pictures would jog my memory about the ingredients.

I sniffed, loving the toasty smell of the tortillas, one of my favorite things to eat. I'd savored the first bite of the dish when my phone dinged with a text. I'd been trying to reach my mom's good friend Liz Stover. Her daughter and I had been friends growing up, and the two mothers had kept up their friendship in the years since graduation. Zoe and me? Not so much. We'd drifted apart during high school, and neither of us had made an effort to stay in touch. Before I'd come downstairs this morning I'd texted Liz where I was going to eat breakfast and asked about a walk on the beach later.

Liz now replied,

On my way to NAC. Walk after sounds good.

NAC? After a second, I realized NAC was Nacho Average Café. Cool. Maybe she would know something about Mom's death. Or maybe not. What I really wanted was to simply be with Liz, reminisce about my mother, and find out what she'd been up to.

Another text dinged in. I smiled when I read Abe's message.

Got six inches of white overnight. Heading out to snowshoe. Wish you were here.

I tapped a message back.

Wearing flip-flops and shorts. Walking on the beach later. Wish you were here.

I did wish he was here to enjoy my birthplace with me, and I had invited him to come along. He'd said he didn't want to intrude on the reunion, and anyway, he was slated to teach a new-employee training during the week. I sipped my bloody Mary, which was nice and spicy, exactly how I liked it. Carmen had served it in a heavy blue Mexican tumbler. I loved the feel of those glasses, and resolved then and there to pick up a set and take them home. I swooned after I bit into the scone. The orange was tangy and sweet and the crumb perfect. Maybe Carmen would share the recipe.

By the time Liz arrived I was halfway through the huevos and slowing down. The meal was super filling. I stood to give her a hug, then sat.

"Ooh, bloody Mary?" She raised her eyebrows. "Sounds great." She pulled out the chair opposite me, her spiked silver hair catching the morning light. Her skin was the weathered brown of a sun lover, which made the blue of her eyes pop.

"I love your jacket." I admired the vertical stripes of turquoise and purple on the woven cloth. "Did you make the cloth?"

"I did, and I sewed the jacket, too. Weaving is the best antidote to lawyering I can imagine. It's very meditative to sit and combine threads into something beautiful."

Carmen approached. "Hey, Liz. We gotta stop meeting like this." She glanced at me. "We just had book club on Wednesday."

"Can I get one of those? But go light on the vodka." Liz pointed to my drink. "And the veggie breakfast burrito sounds great, with extra guac."

"Coming right up." Carmen headed back to the kitchen.

"Mamá makes the best guacamole you'll ever taste," Liz said.

"I'll have to try it this week. So how have you been?"

"Busy, good. Got a new boyfriend who's pretty awesome. He's still surfing at sixty-six. My kind of man."

"You probably haven't stopped taking a board out, either," I said.

"Of course not. It's in my blood, Robbie. I've been riding the waves since I was a toddler, almost. You never surfed much, did you?"

"No. I got conked in the head once in middle school and decided staying alive was better than drowning. That's when I started biking for real. And since Mom grew up in Indiana, she never got into surfing after she moved out here."

"I remember trying to teach her. It definitely wasn't her thing." Liz laughed. "So tell me about the reunion."

"It was fine, with only a little high-school-level drama." I wrinkled my nose, thinking again of Katherine. "Anyway, the food was fabulous, very fresh and light, and I caught up with old friends. Alana Lieberman and I were tight in school, but we hadn't seen each other in person since we both left town."

"I remember her. Super smart."

"Yep. She got a PhD and is doing pretty important cancer research already. And do you remember Jason Wong?"

"Skinny kid, brilliant?"

"Yeah. He's a police officer now," I said. "Works on cybercrime."

"I'm not surprised he's a cop. He was always a straight arrow."

"I'm sure he's good at the job."

Carmen delivered Liz's drink and breakfast. "Careful, the plate's hot. Enjoy."

Liz thanked her.

"I didn't see Zoe at the reunion," I said. "How is she? We haven't really kept in touch."

The smile slipped off Liz's face. "She's having kind

of a rough patch. She's not really in shape to hang out with a bunch of successful former classmates."

"I'm sorry to hear that."

"At least she's working, but it's only as a dish-washer at a restaurant, the Green Artichoke." She tapped her fork on her plate in a slow rhythm, not meeting my gaze.

I studied her face. "Do you want to talk about her?"

She inhaled and mustered a smile. "Not right now. Let's have a fun breakfast, shall we?" She lifted her glass. "Here's to Jeanine."

I clinked my glass with hers. "To Mom."

Chapter 5

I waited to bring up what Carmen had said about Mom's death until Liz and I were walking on East Beach. A line of tall king palms separated the road from the sand, their skinny trunks topped with tufts of swooping fronds. A paved walking and biking path wound next to the trees, but we'd chosen to tread at water's edge. It was nine o'clock by now, under a cloudless sky. Liz pulled a wide-brimmed cotton hat firmly onto her head.

"You might not know I had a brush with melanoma three years ago," she said in a grim tone. "All my years in the sun have come back to bite me. Luckily, the doc caught it early, but I don't mess around now."

"I didn't know. I'm glad you're okay." I tugged my blue Pans 'N Pancakes hat a little lower on my head. "I got this Mediterranean skin from my Italian father. I tan easily, but I still try to be careful in the sun."

Liz nodded. "Jeanine told me about Roberto a little while before she died."

I stared at her. "She did? She never said anything to me. I had to discover him on my own."

"She said she was planning on telling you the whole story in person the next time she went east for a visit."

I dragged my feet to a halt, pressing my eyes shut for a moment. "And she never got the chance."

"I'm sorry, honey." Liz threw an arm around my shoulders and squeezed. "Your mom told me she felt bad for keeping it from you."

"I met my father last year when he and his wife came to visit. I have Mom's build, but I look exactly like him, Liz."

"I expect you do."

I hugged myself, watching a half dozen pelicans beat strong wide wings in a steady horizontal line above the ocean. "Let's keep walking."

We strode in silence for a few minutes. The damp sand near the water crunched under my bare feet, and the breeze was fresh and salty. I breathed deeply, shaking out my sadness.

"Are you happy back there, Robbie?" Liz asked. "You look good, you know, like you're thriving."

"I am. My country store and restaurant are staying in the black. I like what I do. It's awesome being near my aunt Adele, and I've made some good friends."

"What about love?"

"Love, too." My cheeks warmed. "I have a great guy, Abe. Yeah, love's good, too."

"I'm glad. Jeanine would have been so happy to know you've found someone."

She would. I blew out a breath. "Liz, earlier Carmen

mentioned she'd heard something was fishy about Mom's death. Do you know what she was talking about?"

Liz waited a beat. "Did Jeanine ever tell you about the environmental group she was involved with?"

"No. I don't think she did. Did they have something to do with her death?"

"Hang on. Let me talk this through. The group—and your mom—were trying to get certain agricultural chemicals banned from the region. They made a couple of conventional farmers and the chemical company pretty mad."

A little girl of about six, bucket in hand, dashed directly in front of us toward the water, followed closely by a boy the same size.

"Kids never look where they're going." Liz gave a wry laugh. "Anyway, after your mom died, one of the guys in the group contacted me. He knew she and I were friends. He had a lot of questions about the circumstances of her death."

"What?" I stared at her. "What kinds of questions?"

She gazed at me. "Maybe you should ask him yourself. His name's Paul Etxgeberria. I'll text you his info and how to spell his name, which is Basque or something."

"Mom died alone of an aneurysm. What else is there to know?" I threw my hands open. "Would a medical examiner have gotten it wrong?"

Liz paused for a few moments. "I was the one who found her."

I nodded slowly, my eyes on the horizon. Four boxy oil rigs rose up about ten miles out. Behind them the Channel Islands were clear today, especially Santa Cruz, the largest. Its twenty-two miles of gently sloping ridges rose up like a giant blue woman sleeping on the water. Liz had found my mom lying down, too, but not asleep.

"I was supposed to pick her up for book group and she didn't answer the door or her phone." Liz's voice was low and somber. "We'd given each other keys years before, just in case. I let myself in and discovered her on the kitchen floor. She'd been gone a while, I guess."

"You told me about finding her when I came out for her memorial service, but I had forgotten until now. Or maybe I subconsciously blanked it out." I swiped at a tear. "Was there something odd about the way she was lying there, or did her breath smell funny? I mean, I thought she simply fell down dead."

"That was what it looked like. I didn't notice anything odd. But I think you should talk to Paul. Here, let me send you his info now." She sank to sit on the sand and worked her phone.

I took a few steps to the water. Nobody was out there swimming for a reason. The water lapping over my feet was frigid, but for my entire life I'd never let myself visit a beach without dipping a toe in the ocean, winter or summer. I backed up a few steps to watch a tern dive-bomb the water and come up with a fish wriggling in its black beak.

I couldn't believe my mother hadn't died of natural causes. Her death had been an enormous shock, because she'd been healthy and in her fifties. But if this guy Liz knew had suspicions about her death, that would mean murder, and I didn't want that. The thought that someone might have wanted Mom dead, that malice had dive-bombed her, made me shudder.

I tried to shake off the feeling. As I watched the ocean, a sleek body farther out dipped in and out of the water, followed by three more.

"Look, Liz. Dolphins." I pointed. "We sure don't see those in Indiana."

"Nice." She boosted herself up to stand. "I told Paul you might call him. He texted back that their group is meeting this afternoon at two, said you're welcome to join them."

"I'll contact him, thanks. I at least want to hear what he has to say." I'd planned to go for a hike in the mountains this afternoon, or maybe borrow one of the bikes Carmen had available for guests and ride up the coast a ways. I would be here all week. Such a ride could wait. And tomorrow I'd ask Jason if he could put me in touch with the person who declared Mom's death a natural one. I wished I could hire Kinsey Millhone to dig into this mystery. I'd read that the Santa Teresa Sue Grafton had invented was a thinly disguised Santa Barbara. But since Kinsey was fictional, I was going to have to do this myself.

Chapter 6

After I locked the bike I'd borrowed from Carmen for a ride around the city, I meandered toward the lake in the middle of Alice Keck Park, a green oasis downtown. I checked the time on my phone. Paul had said he would find me here at four after his meeting, so I told him what I looked like. He'd invited me to attend his gathering first, but hanging out with environmentalists wasn't what I was after. I only wanted to hear his thoughts about my mother's death. It was nearly four, and the winter sun was already on its decline. I shivered and pulled the zipper on my fleece all the way up. I hoped he wouldn't be late. The bike didn't have a light, so I needed to get back to Carmen's before darkness fell in an hour and a half.

A ratty sleeping bag stuck out from behind a tall silver maple tree, and a head of matted hair was nearly hidden in the bag. I'd seen other homeless people around town, many more than had been in evidence ten years ago. The economy was taking its toll, and in a warm climate like this one, it wasn't life threatening for them to sleep outside year-round, unlike in Indiana. Still, I felt bad that anyone had to live without a roof over their head.

I kept going until I walked over a wooden bridge spanning a burbling stream. It coursed down a few smooth stones into the small artificial lake. Mallards, seagulls, and black-and-white geese paddled around, while a cormorant perched on a rock in the middle of the water. The pond had a freshwater smell that reminded me of Lake Lemon back home.

I was watching a dozen turtles sunning themselves on a log in the shallows when a deep voice behind me said, "Robbie Jordan?"

I turned to see a tall, wiry man carrying a bike helmet. "Yes. Are you Paul?"

"That would be me." His curly black hair formed a wild nimbus around his head. He was probably ten or fifteen years older than me and wore a plaid shirt and faded jeans with the right pants leg still rolled up from his ride.

I shook his proffered hand.

"Shall we sit?" He gestured toward a bench by the side of the lake and cleared his throat after we sat. "First, let me offer my condolences on your mother's passing. She was a wonderful woman."

"Thank you. She was." I looked more closely at him. "Wait, were you at her memorial service?"

"Yes."

"I thought you looked familiar." His name hadn't rung any bells when Liz mentioned it, but I'm good with faces. I knew I'd seen him before.

"I didn't get a chance to speak to you after the service," he continued. "I had to go straight to work. I'm sorry."

"It's okay. I was pretty dazed at the time. What do you do for work?"

"I bike-deliver takeout meals for the Green Artichoke. It's a low-carbon-footprint local foods restaurant down in the Funk Zone. They make quite good food and have a philosophy I can get behind."

"Sounds interesting. It wasn't there when I was growing up." Somebody else had mentioned the Green Artichoke, but I couldn't think who at the moment.

"Liz said you were interested in my thoughts about Jeanine." His expression was intense, his dark eyebrows pulled together in the middle. His knee jittered up and down, and he seemed to be avoiding making eye contact with me.

"Everybody seems to think something was off about her death," I said slowly. "This is the first I've heard of it. What do you know?"

"She'd been active in our group for a few years. We were working hard to get some of the most toxic fumigants banned in Ventura and Santa Barbara Counties."

"What, like chemicals they use for termite fumigation?"

"No. They're used in strawberry fields, which you must know are common near the coast. There's a tiny pest called a nematode that eats strawberry roots. So the farmers essentially sterilize the soil before planting."

"Sterilizing soil sounds awful."

"It is. These chemicals are neurotoxins. They don't

get into the berries—or so the chemical companies claim. But when the fumigants are sprayed, it's extremely dangerous for the health of the farmworkers and neighbors, because it's airborne. People and animals can't help but breathe it."

"Wow. That's terrible."

"No kidding. An alpaca farmer next to one of the big strawberry farms in Oxnard says her animals got sick. The farmworkers' health suffers. It's bad news, Robbie."

Oxnard was the flat, fertile coastal plain not far down the coast from here beyond Ventura. "There must be an alternative for farmers," I said. "Something organic, maybe."

He grimaced. "The alternative is for them to rotate their crops and use organic products. They don't want to. Big farmers mono-crop as cheaply as they can. Grow the same product in the same place year-round. And strip the soil of any natural defenses so people all over the country can eat big, juicy California strawberries whenever they want."

Ouch. I'd think twice next time I was tempted to buy strawberries in February. "I don't get how this fumigant is connected to my mother's death, though." I glanced up at the mountains visible above the trees. The western sun had turned the craggy peaks from their usual sandy tone to a pinker hue.

"There's a guy who's a muckety-muck at the chemical company up in Goleta." He gestured vaguely northwest. "At Agrosafe. Can you believe that name? They make mono-cropping safe for farmers' bank accounts, but not for the workers or the neighbors."

"Is it near UCSB?" The university campus, one of

nine scattered up and down the state, had had a reputation as a surfer school in earlier years but had upped its research game recently, spawning a number of companies nearby.

"Right. Your mom butted heads with this dude, big-time. Name's Walter Russom."

My eyes flew wide. "I went to school with a Katherine Russom. I bet she's his daughter." Katherine, the reunion organizer. The one with a grudge against me.

"Could be. Jeanine called him out at a public meeting, said he was a murderer."

Wow. "She never told me about him. I mean, I knew she was getting interested in environmental questions, but I never heard about her passion getting to that level."

"Yeah." He nodded. "Russom didn't much like it."

When was Paul going to get to the point? "And?"

He gazed at a couple of coots paddling across the lake, their white beaks striking against their black heads and bodies. He twisted to look into my eyes. "I think Russom poisoned your mom."

Chapter 7

Paul had said he needed to split and left abruptly. I couldn't get his words out of my head, and I longed for a quiet place to sit and think. I walked across the street to the Unitarian church Mom had started attending after I'd moved to Indiana. Once, when I was back for a visit, I'd attended a service with her. I remembered how peaceful I'd found the church. A lovely example of Spanish architecture, the large building was a hundred years old and on the National Register of Historic Places. From the outside it had the classic mission look, with curved red tiles on the roof, light-colored stucco walls, a long main building with narrow arched windows, and a dome-topped bell tower stretching above at the end.

I pulled at the handle on the left-hand door but it didn't budge. *Rats.* I peeked in through the crack between the doors. Light shone through a round, multicolored stained glass window under the arched ceiling at the front. Being Unitarian, the window design didn't depict religious symbols but rather resembled a geometrical flower.

In lieu of sitting inside, I slipped into a quiet courtyard on the church grounds instead and eased onto a bench, gazing at a calla lily about to unfold its white trumpet. In the peace and stillness I remembered it had been Liz who'd mentioned the restaurant where Paul worked. I could eat there this week and say hi to Zoe while I was at it. If she wanted to see me, that is. What had Liz meant by a "rough patch," anyway?

My thoughts drifted back to Paul. The thought of Walter Russom—Katherine's father—poisoning Mom was deeply disturbing. My mother had been a sunny force in my life and never met a stranger she couldn't turn into a friend. Who would want to snuff out the life of a person like that?

Paul hadn't been able to say how Walter Russom might have administered the poison to my mom, but he'd claimed the chemical could mimic or even cause a brain aneurysm. That would definitely be fishy, as Carmen had put it. Was Russom's company in financial trouble and Mom's public challenge to it—and him—such a threat he would kill her? Had the police investigated at the time? If they had, I hadn't heard about it. Did she have other enemies I didn't know of? I couldn't believe my peace-loving and levelheaded mother would have had enemies of any kind.

Or was Paul a nutcase extremist making up stories, and she'd died of natural causes, after all? He'd seemed nervous talking to me. Maybe he was mentally unstable. But how in the world could I find out? I snapped my fingers. I knew one avenue I could pursue. I tapped out a text to Jason, my favorite Santa Barbara cop.

Want to grab dinner in an hour or so? I have something I'd like to run by you.

A minute later his reply came in.

Sure. Casual or fancy?

I replied,

Casual's good.

K. How about Total Thai on State?

Thx. See there you at 6:30, I ended.

Good. I'd get Thai food and maybe some information, too.

I looked up at the canopy of leaves in this quiet, peaceful garden. When I was a child, Mom and I would take breakfast to the beach on Sunday mornings. A big sky, salt air, and the company of my favorite person had felt like all the spirit I needed. I still wasn't into worshiping some white-bearded, white-skinned old guy sitting on a cloud. I didn't want all the rituals and baggage most organized religions seemed to entail. But as I grew older, seeking for a connection with some kind of bigger-than-all-of-us presence was looking more attractive. Bloomington, the university town back in Indiana, surely had a church like this one. The organization, not the building, of course. I thought I'd check it out after I returned.

For now, I headed back across the park to my bike. I clipped on my helmet, unlocked the hybrid cycle—which combined traits from road bikes and mountain bikes—and headed north. If I rode up to the historic mission, a view of the city would spread out before me, ending in the great Pacific. A bit of hill work before the sun went down would clear my mind. With any luck, it would also banish any lurking demon thoughts about my mom's death.

Chapter 8

After a vigorous ride, I showered in my room at Carmen's and grabbed my car to get to the restaurant by six thirty.

The white walls inside Total Thai were covered with huge, fanciful line drawings of vegetables and cutlery with words in what must be Thai script written next to some. A grinning mushroom, two frowning slices of cucumber, a graceful clove of garlic, and a dancing sprig of cilantro indicated they'd clearly hired an artist to decorate—or had one on staff.

"I could eat pad thai for every meal," I said to Jason after I swallowed the first bite of the nutty noodle dish.

"I know what you mean. Asian comfort food, right?" He popped in a bite of his green curry and sucked in air. "Man, this is spicy."

I tilted my head. "Uh, you ordered it that way."

He mopped sweat pearls off his forehead with his napkin. "I know, and I love the pain." He lifted his beer glass. "Hey, cheers, Robbie."

"Cheers." I clinked my glass with his before taking a sip. "So where did you go to college? We really lost touch after graduation."

"I got into Cal. They have a great criminal justice program, and I double majored in computer science. What about you?"

Cal was the University of California flagship campus in Berkeley, originally the only campus. "I went to Cal Poly San Luis Obispo and majored in engineering. I got married right after I got my degree, but it didn't work out." I shrugged. "That's when I moved to Indiana, where my mom was from, and got a job as a chef. Mom's sister, Adele, lives in the same town, and I see her a lot."

"Good. You seem happy." He swallowed another bite. "Hey, fun to see Alana again, wasn't it?"

"You bet. She has some stuff to do with her parents, so she's staying down here for this week. I'm looking forward to hanging out with her again."

"So what did you want to ask me about? I mean, I'm happy to eat and schmooze, but you said you had something you wanted to run by me."

"I do." I took a moment to organize my thoughts. "A couple people who knew my mom told me today they thought something was fishy about her death. One guy even said he thought she'd been poisoned." Again a shudder rippled through me.

Jason's nostrils flared. "Poisoned? That's heavy."

"No kidding. The death certificate said the cause of death was cerebral hemorrhage caused by a ruptured aneurysm. That's all I know. I never saw the autopsy report, but I assume there was one."

"Unattended death of a healthy woman in her

fifties? They would have at least investigated, but they don't always do an autopsy. Who do these people suppose would have poisoned her, and how?"

"I have no idea. The guy who told me is an environmental activist, and I guess Mom had become one, too. He thinks Katherine Russom's father—who runs an agrochemical company in Goleta—was royally upset with my mother."

"And somehow administered some kind of herbicide to her that made her brain bleed out?"

I winced.

"I'm sorry, Robbie," he said. "Not being very gentle, am I? I put the old foot in the mouth every time. It's why I stick to cybercrime instead of walking a beat."

"Don't worry about it. But, yeah. It's what Paul suggested. Actually, a fumigant used on strawberry fields."

"Who's the dude?"

"His last name is Extraberia or something. I don't know how you spell it. Zoe's mom, Liz, told me about him, and sent me his phone number but she forgot to include his last name."

"Zoe Stover. Poor thing." He shook his head. "She's got a big-time addiction problem."

Oh. "That's so sad. Liz told me Zoe didn't come to the reunion because she's not doing well. Her addiction must have been what she meant." I levered in another bite of dinner with my chopsticks. "Remember how creative she was?"

"She snagged the Most Artistic Senior label in the yearbook."

"That's right. I'd forgotten." I took a drink of beer. "Back to my mom, I want to talk to the medical examiner. Or whoever would have determined my mom's cause of death. Maybe read the report for myself."

"We don't have ME's here," Jason said. "The Santa Barbara County Sheriff's Office handles death examinations. They have a sheriff-coroner and several investigating deputy coroners."

"Interesting. I guess every state does things differently."

"The sheriff's office has a full-time pathologist on staff, a super-competent lady named Melinda Washington. Mel's a force of nature—tall, flashy, no-nonsense—and she really knows her stuff. We're friends. I can get you her contact info." He pushed his glasses back up the bridge of his nose.

"Thanks. I would like to know how to reach her," I said. "Do you think she'll talk to me?"

"I can't say for sure, but tell her I sent you. If she won't share what she knows, you can order a copy of the coroner's report by calling the office or going in. You might want to see it even if she will speak with you."

"They must have a Web site, right?"

He grinned. "I set it up for them as one of my internships."

"You rock, Jason. I'll check them out tomorrow."

"I can poke around for you, too, if you want. I have access to all kinds of search capabilities."

I pointed a chopstick at him. "And some they don't even know you can get into, am I right?"

He cast his dark, hooded eyes right and left with a wicked smile teasing his mouth. He held a finger to his lips. "Shh, don't tell."

I returned the smile. "Cross my heart and hope to, well, live another day."

"You and me both, Robbie." He drained his glass.

The waitperson materialized at our table. "Another round?"

Jason nodded.

"Me, too," I said. "Please."

Jason leaned back in his chair. "So what do you do for fun out there in whatever vowel-initial state you live in?"

Chapter 9

I took myself for a solo walk on the beach the next morning. A brisk onshore breeze was blowing, but five years of living in a cold climate had toughened me up. I zipped my windbreaker to my neck and walked barefoot on the sand, inhaling clean salt air and the reassuring, never-ending sound of breaking waves I had grown up with. I was determined to get some answers today about what Paul had said regarding Mom's death. A squadron of long-beaked brown pelicans flew single file ten feet above the water toward the north, looking like prehistoric creatures with their wings steadily flapping. I had a purpose for the day, and they looked like they did, too. If I saw pelicans every day this week, I would fly home happy, albeit on an airplane.

Someone had drawn a huge heart in the sand and added two sets of initials joined by a plus sign. I smiled at it. Zoe and I used to come to the beach together with our mothers. Even as a child my friend was always making art in the sand, drawing huge pictures with her heel, saying the astronauts could see it if it was big enough. Or she'd collect shells and adorn an enormous dinosaur we'd formed out of the damp grains.

A heavenly breakfast burrito was my breakfast back at Nacho Average, overflowing with refried beans, peppery cheese, chunky salsa, and cubes of avocado, all wrapped around a cumin-flavored omelet and packaged in a big flour tortilla. I doubted I'd need to eat again until dinner. Carmen offered the same package I did to her B-and-B customers—breakfast in the restaurant downstairs was included in the price of the room. Unlike me, she kept her restaurant open on Mondays. I hadn't yet put breakfast burritos on the menu at Pans 'N Pancakes, but I'd already decided to after I returned. I cut this one in half and snapped a photo of it, focusing on the insides.

After she topped up my coffee, Carmen asked, "How was your day yesterday?"

"Pretty interesting." I beckoned her closer and kept my voice low. "Do you know an environmental activist by the name of Paul? Basque guy, kind of wiry, lots of nervous energy?"

Carmen nodded knowingly. "I actually dated him for a while last year."

I raised my eyebrows.

"Yeah. It didn't work out," she continued. "He was too much into his own stuff and not so interested in mine." She shrugged. "Men."

"I met him yesterday after Liz told me about him. I know you said you'd heard something was fishy about Mom's death. Well, Paul claims she was poisoned by a guy who runs an agrochemical company."

She made a *tsk*ing sound. "Why?"

"Because his group, which Mom was active in, was trying to get the company's products banned in the area. They still are. Do you know anything about that?"

"No more than what you just said. I only heard a rumor, sorry. You gonna find out the real story?"

"I'm going to do my best," I said, even though I wasn't sure how I could.

"Good luck, *hija.*"

Back in Indiana, the use of "hon" was common, even among strangers. Here, where many Mexican immigrants had been in the state for generations? Some used *hija,* pronounced "*ee*-ha," which means "daughter." Same effect, different word. I finished eating while checking e-mail and social media on my phone. Upstairs, I brushed my teeth, then headed out on the bike for the county sheriff's office about six miles away. I could have driven, of course, but I had to do something to work off the hefty burrito.

On my way I rode past Chumash High School. I slowed and watched as students moved between the buildings, books and notebooks in their arms. Some talked and laughed, many walked with their eyes on their phones, and a few loners slouched past looking miserable. I remembered an art installation Zoe had put up our senior year. It had been a seven-by-seven-foot box painted black inside and open at the front, with a sign inviting students in. She'd perched on a stool for a week, shooting photographs of all the ordinary—or crazy—poses people had struck. She'd made a video that had run on a loop in the outdoor covered lunch area the week before graduation. Zoe had excelled at creativity, while I'd aimed myself at more logic-oriented pursuits, like math team and solving puzzles.

I arrived at the sheriff's office at about nine fifteen. It was in a low building tucked under dry live oaks and a few ubiquitous palm trees. Last night I'd run across a couple of news stories from a few years ago about how the building had inadequate ventilation. One mentioned that the pathologist and anyone attending in the morgue had to wear respirators. I hadn't been able to find any recent stories about the ventilation having been improved.

I locked the bike and paused in front of the door, which was propped open under the overhanging roof. A building with air-conditioning and ventilation would not be letting air in and out through an open door. I sure hoped there weren't any lethal germs floating around. Still, I wanted to request the report and hopefully talk to the pathologist, too.

I greeted the receptionist. "I'd like to request the coroner's report on my mother's death. She died two years ago, on January sixteenth."

A small, dark-haired woman typed away without looking up. "Your name, please, and the name of the deceased."

"I'm Roberta Jordan, and she was Jeanine Elizabeth Jordan."

"I'll need to see some ID."

After I slid my license across the counter to her, she checked it and slid it back.

"That'll be ten dollars," she said. "To what address should we mail the report?"

Rats. "I'd hoped to get it now. How long will it take before it's ready?"

She glanced at me over the top of her reading glasses, as if I'd asked her to fix me lunch or something. "We're very busy here. It'll be seven to ten business days."

By then I'd be back in Indiana. I supposed getting the report by mail was better than nothing and gave her my home address. I dug in my pack, pulling out a ten-dollar bill. "I'd like a receipt, if you don't mind."

She scribbled on a receipt pad and handed me the yellow copy. Very old-school, very low-tech.

I thanked her. "Would it be possible for me to speak with Melinda Washington? Jason Wong of the SBPD said I should contact her."

"She's not here."

"Do you know when she'll be in?"

She shook her head.

Whoever thought it was a good idea to let this unfriendly woman greet the public was seriously misguided. I let out a sigh and left the building. Jason had given me the pathologist's e-mail address. I stood next to a planting punctuated with the cheery orange of California golden poppies and tapped out a message to Melinda Washington on my phone. I introduced myself, and then wrote,

> *I'd like to speak with you in person about Jeanine Jordan's death on 1/16 two years ago. My friend Jason Wong gave me your contact info. I am in town through Friday and can meet you at your convenience.*

I signed it, included my phone number, and sent the message.

Now what? I wasn't feeling as cheerful as the flowers at my feet looked. My flight home wasn't until Saturday morning. Why had I thought it was a good idea to stay out here for a week? I felt antsy with all this free time. Others with a week's vacation in paradise might take a towel, lunch, and a book—or a crossword—to the beach for the day. I'd never been good at lazing around. I had a dinner date with Alana tonight, but for now, what else could I do to follow up on Paul's allegation? I ran through what he'd said, then nodded to myself. I was halfway to Goleta now. Might as well get in more biking and pay a visit to Agrosafe while I was at it.

Chapter 10

I set one foot on the ground, straddling the bike in front of a glass-fronted two-story building in an industrial park. The name Agrosafe was scribed in a muted green, with a stylized branch winding under the name that ended in a flourish of leaves. It was a benign presentation at odds with what Paul had said about the harmful effects of the company's products. The building was flanked on one side by a software company and on the other by a medical device research lab. Several dark SUVs were parked in the lot to my right. Low beds in front featured a white daisy-type flower with a purple center.

I wished I'd spent more time running a search on Agrosafe last night. I didn't know if they manufactured the chemicals on-site or if they only handled the business end of things in this building. While I was here, I might as well ask.

With no bike rack in sight, I locked my metal steed to a sapling and headed in. But when I pulled on the door, it didn't budge. A key card swiper was fixed to the right. Maybe only employees came and went, not the public. I peered through the glass. A desk faced the door at the side of a staircase, but nobody sat at it. I spied a doorbell, pushed it, and waited, wondering if I should give up, get back on my bike, and leave. A minute later, though, a guy looking like he might still be in college—or younger—pulled open the door.

"Good morning and welcome to Agrosafe." He looked me up and down. I supposed their visitors didn't usually show up in bike shorts and a windbreaker. He himself was neatly dressed in a button-down Oxford shirt and pressed slacks, and his sandy-colored hair was neatly trimmed, too. "Can I help you?"

"Hi. My uncle owns an organic farm in . . ." *Think quick, Jordan.* "In Paso Robles. But his profits are way down and he's thinking of switching to conventional methods. He asked me if I could pick up some information for him about your products." Which was a pretty lame story, considering all this fictional relative had to do was employ Mr. Google.

"Come right in." The kid stood back and held the door for me. "I'd be happy to give you our informational brochures and put your uncle in touch with a sales representative. I'm Tommy Moore." His words came out in a rush, as if rehearsed.

Even his name made him sound twelve. "Thanks, Tommy. My name is, uh, Irene." No need to reveal who I really was. Just in case.

"Pleased to meet you, Irene. Do have a seat." He gestured to a sitting area with a couch, two upholstered chairs, and a glass coffee table covered with brochures and leaflets. The lobby had large healthy-looking potted plants scattered about. On the walls hung a big photograph of a flourishing strawberry field, another with rows of thick dark green spinach, and others of fields full of plants I couldn't identify. A large picture was mounted on the wall behind the couch, but this one featured two men in suits shaking hands in the sunshine in front of this building, with a half dozen others standing behind.

I pointed to one of the suits. "Isn't he one of California's senators?"

Tommy beamed. "Yes, with our company president, Walter Russom. We were able to work out a very nice deal benefiting the taxpayers as well as local business owners."

I peered at the picture of the men. Had I ever met Katherine's father? I wasn't sure, but they certainly shared the same toothy smile. Walter had silver hair combed back from a high, tanned brow and he looked trim, as if he played tennis or was a runner. He wore a well-tailored suit and tie.

Tommy selected several brochures from the table. "These will tell your uncle all he needs to know." He hurried back to his desk and returned with a digital tablet. "What's your uncle's name? I'll have someone contact him."

"I don't think he's quite ready to talk with a salesperson yet." I turned over one of the brochures. "But this has a number to contact. I'm sure he'll get in touch soon. I appreciate your being so helpful. Are the products made right here?"

"They certainly are." He opened a different brochure and showed me a picture of the building, which stretched way back, something I hadn't seen when I rode up. "We manufacture, package, and ship, all from here." His voice oozed with pride.

"How long have you worked at the company?" Maybe he was related to the Russoms somehow.

"I started only last month. I'm on a gap year before college. I want to major in chemistry with a minor in agriculture. My mom plays tennis with Mr. Russom, and she landed me this internship." He beamed.

Bingo on two counts. Tommy wasn't even in college, and Walter played tennis.

"I play tennis," I lied. "What courts do they use?"

"They're in Mr. Russom's neighborhood in Montecito."

I mentally whistled. Montecito was a ritzy neighborhood just east of Santa Barbara proper. "Well, it's been nice talking with you." I edged toward the door. "Thanks again for the help, and good luck with your studies."

"Thank you. It's such an exciting field. Ride safe, now."

Once outside, I glanced up at the second floor. The sun had bounced off the glass earlier. Now it had shifted and I could see into a corner office, where a man with silver hair sat at a laptop. President Walter Russom's corner office, from all appearances. Had he really poisoned my mother? Why risk all this to shut up a protester?

Chapter 11

Back in my room, changed into a casual skirt and T-shirt after my ride, I checked my restaurant e-mail and Instagram accounts. I didn't expect any issues to come up while I was gone, but you never knew. I smiled to see that Danna, my assistant at Pans 'N Pancakes, had also posted to the restaurant Instagram page. The picture was a close-up of a split baked potato on a plate in front of a snowy scene showing through the window. The potato was topped with a meaty chili, the sauce oozing down the sides. Her message read, "Next week's special. #wintereating #sticktoyourribs #notthetimetodiet #cooksofinstagram." Both my assistant and my other employee—who were also my co-chefs—had posting privileges to the account as well as to the restaurant's Facebook page. I encouraged them to go all out with alluring foodie shots.

Chili-stuffed baked potato was an invention worthy of a patent, and her photo made my stomach growl to look at it. I'd go find some lunch in a bit, but first I had a curious mind to feed.

I poked around on the Internet. Agrosafe had been in business for fifteen years. Walter Russom had founded it, and the firm was still privately held. I didn't know a lot about the stock market. It would seem "privately held" meant he made all the decisions and got all the profits—and also took all the risks on his own shoulders. Or bank account.

I paused at a news report of protestors picketing the company. A photograph showed about twelve people walking in a circle in front of the building carrying signs that read things like AGROSAFE—BAD FOR PEOPLE AND ANIMALS and CHEMICALS OUT, ORGANICS IN. Paul's tall form and dark curly hair were unmistakable. Two burly guys in sunglasses were positioned in front of the entrance, hands loose at their sides as if ready to defend the company.

The Agrosafe company ownership model reminded me of what I'd heard an author talk about one time at the South Lick Library. The presentation by a Bloomington novelist had been about self-publishing versus being published by an established firm. The speaker had said when writers self-publish, of course they get all the proceeds—or as much of them as the online distributor wants to hand over—and they also have to pay others to do all the tasks a publishing house normally handles. They take all the risk on their own shoulders.

In Agrosafe's case, Walter would be personally threatened by an effort to legally ban his major product from being sold locally. As Mom used to say in an echo of earlier activists, "Think globally, act locally."

She'd even had a bumper sticker on her truck bearing that message. If one or two California counties banned the Agrosafe fumigant product, others might follow suit. Paul had to be thinking along those lines. Was Katherine, too? Could she have had a hand in my mother's death? It made me shiver to consider the idea. I tapped my foot, wondering when I'd be able to contact the pathologist and find out the details in Mom's death report.

My phone dinged with a text, and I smiled. Danna, who'd offered to stop by my apartment every day to play with Birdy and keep him in fresh food and water, had sent me a picture of my kitty trotting toward the camera. He looked as inquisitive and alert as ever. I shot her a *Thanks* in return.

It was time for a change of scenery. I couldn't do anything about Mom's death from the confines of my room, and it was a lovely Santa Barbara midday. I tucked my hair into a ponytail, threading it through my cap, and threw on some sunscreen. I grabbed my bag, shades, and keys. I added a towel and my book and headed out for some fresh air and a bite of lunch, maybe even a snooze on the beach. What was the old saying? When in Rome, do as the Californians do?

Chapter 12

I parked near the beach. Beach volleyball was in session to my right, several co-ed games being played by fit Californians in exercise clothes. Katherine would be among them if today was Friday, or maybe she played on other days, too. Two cormorants sat on a float in a sheltered cove with their wings extended to the sides. I considered my options. I could plop down on the sand, or I could explore Stearns Wharf, the nearly half-mile-long pier stretching into the harbor.

A rumble from my stomach answered me, saying, "Lunch first." Several restaurants out on the pier were possibilities, including the iconic Harbor Restaurant. But the food trucks I spied clustered in the parking lot at the harbor to the right seemed like a more immediate—and affordable—option, and several picnic tables nearby provided a place to sit and eat.

The truck at the near end of the line sold Asian noodle bowls, the one next to it your basic hot dogs and hamburgers, and a third offered what looked like pretty ordinary tacos and burritos. I smiled at the name on the last one, Hector's Hot Bosillos. This had to be Carmen's son's food truck. I was pretty sure *bosillo* meant pocket in Spanish, and I was about to find out. He didn't have a line of customers waiting, so I approached the wide window in the side of the vehicle. An aproned Hector had his back to me, but salsa music was playing softly and he moved his hips and shoulders to the rhythm as he worked. Alluring aromas of fish, lime, and I wasn't sure what else floated out into my nose, making my stomach growl all over again.

"Hi, Hector."

He twirled with a flourish. "Robbie, what a surprise." He smiled down at me.

"I'm staying at your mom's B-and-B, and she said you had a food truck down here somewhere. When I saw the name, I figured this was yours."

"It is." He folded his forearms on the shelf at the base of the window and leaned on them. "I didn't know you were at Mom's. Nice place, isn't it?"

"It's perfect. I met your grandma, too."

"Mamá taught me a lot, as did Mom." He leaned closer. "But I'll tell you a secret. I only cook so I can dance. It's how I support my habit."

"You could do worse. Do you compete? Because, I'll tell you, you could win at *Dancing with the Stars*. You have moves like one of the show's pros."

"My buddy Paul tells me the same thing. And our teacher. But, no, I dance for the love of it. I take lessons, sure, but I also go wherever there's music."

"I heard about a Paul yesterday. My mother's friend Liz, Zoe Stover's mom, mentioned him. Does your buddy have a Basque name?"

"Exactly."

"I met him briefly downtown yesterday afternoon."

"Why?"

I wrinkled my nose. I didn't want to get into the whole Mom's-death thing with someone I barely knew. "It's kind of a long story. He dances, too?"

"He's amazing. I don't know if it's his Basque blood, but he's very talented."

"Cool. You and I didn't get a chance to talk at the reunion, but I run a restaurant, too." A gull swooped down to scavenge on the ground under one of the tables. When two more tried to elbow in on it, the first one let out a menacing cry and raised its wings until they retreated. "It's back in Indiana where I live."

"Nice," he said. "What do you feature?"

"Solid breakfast and lunch, but we offer specials every day and I try to get creative with those. Believe me, I'm taking home ideas from what Nacho Average Café offers. I want to try your *bosillos*, too. Hot pockets?"

He grinned. "Yes. Of course I couldn't call them 'hot pockets' or big, bad giant Nestlé would slap a lawsuit on me faster than a herring gull snaps up abandoned Cheetos. And each of mine has a twist."

"Well, I'm hungry. Give me two of your best twists." I checked the menu on the side of the truck. "And a Mexican hot chocolate mini-cake, too, please."

"Coming right up, *amiga*."

Three minutes later I sat at a picnic table with a

paper basket smelling like heaven. Hector's truck still wasn't busy, so I invited him to join me. He brought us each a cup of water and plopped down across from me, his eyes bright.

"This one is the Asian twist." He pointed to the deep-fried turnover to the left. "And the other one's Basque. I got the recipe from Paul."

"I know nothing about Basque cooking," I said, picking up that one. Hector had cut them in half, so I could see the contents.

"Taste it and tell me what's inside," he suggested.

The shell was light and crisp. I bit into an open end and chewed, rolling the textures and flavors in my mouth. I swallowed before speaking. "I'd say cod, olive oil, roasted sweet peppers, some potato?"

He nodded. "What else?"

I knew this was a game chefs played. I was happy to take part. "A garlic-tomato fusion." I ran my tongue around the roof of my mouth, and leaned down to sniff the *bosillo*. "Maybe the peppers are an unusual variety, and I'd say the olive oil has to be some extra-ordinary local vintage."

Hector snapped the fingers on both hands and pointed his index digits at me. "You got it, Robbie. The olive oil is made fifty miles from here on a small farm. It's out of this world." His face lost its luster and he frowned.

"What's the matter?" I asked.

"It's this cause of Paul's."

"He talked to me about his anti-fumigant campaign when I met him. My mom died two years ago, but she was working with him against the fumigant even then."

"I'm sorry about your mom." He gave me a sympathetic look.

"Thanks. So what about the cause?"

"A new strawberry farm has opened next to the olive ranch that makes the oil I use. The owners are super worried about spray drift from the fumigant Paul is fighting so hard against."

I set down the pocket. "That's bad. You can't move trees."

"No, you can't."

"Are you involved in the group, too?"

He shook his head as a couple of women on serious road bikes wearing brightly colored cycling outfits leaned their rides against the next table and stood in front of his truck, perusing the menu.

"No." He stood. "Really nice talking with you, Robbie. Duty calls." He held out his hand.

I shook it. "Same here. Watch out, I might be back. I'm around all week."

"Do it."

I bit into the other *bosillo* while it was still warm. This one was like a Vietnamese spring roll, with crunchy bean sprouts, tiny tender shrimp, and a light lime-soy flavor with an after-tease of hot pepper. Hector was a talented chef, no two ways about it. I wasn't sure I wanted to get into deep frying in my restaurant, but for now? I was in foodie heaven.

Chapter 13

I strolled out onto the pier after I ate, waving good-bye to Hector as I tossed my food-stained paper trash into the can and deposited the empty paper cup in the recycling. California was way ahead of Indiana in that regard. I wasn't sure I'd seen any public space outside Bloomington with recycling containers. I made short work of the mini-cake, a perfect small bite of spicy sweet after the savory lunch. It was like eating Mexican hot chocolate, a drink special I'd offered in my restaurant at Christmas two months ago.

Stearns Wharf had been an important addition to Santa Barbara's economy when it was built in the 1870s. Deep-water ships could dock at it and unload cargo without having to shuttle it to shore through the waves. Since the 1950s it hadn't been used for commercial fishing or trade, and now was a major tourist attraction instead. People still fished off the pier, but only for fun and their own use, and only in the prescribed areas, all of which were marked No

OVERHEAD CASTING. *Good.* The last thing strolling tourists needed was a hook in the head or worse.

I moseyed along until I came to the Blue Ocean Ice Cream Company. A tasty scoop in a sugar cone would make a perfect second dessert. The shop, which had been there forever, hadn't had the greatest reputation for flavor or service when I was in high school. But I was on the pier, I wanted ice cream, and maybe they'd improved in ten years.

I walked out empty-handed a minute later. More than seven dollars for a single scoop? Nah. I'd hit up McConnell's later. I knew they had high-quality product for less money. I popped onto a bench a little farther down and watched two men fish for mackerel over the side of the pier. Mom had brought me out here once when I was about eight and had been clamoring to learn to fish. She'd borrowed a pole from somebody and we bought a little container of anchovies to thread onto the hook. After an hour of *nada*, boredom had taken over and I'd declared I was all done with fishing.

Right now my thoughts weren't with the fishies, though, but instead on what Hector had said about the olive ranch. Those poor people. Planting trees to harvest from was a long-term proposition. It would be the same with pecan trees or peaches. Farmers were in it for the duration, especially tree farmers.

A pelican lit on the railing near the people fishing and cocked its huge head, hoping perhaps for a free snack. Such a strange-looking bird, resembling a dinosaur more than a finch. I resumed my strolling and people watching. A gray-haired couple in matching shorts and jackets power-walked past me, clearly locals on a mission to get their heart rates up in this fresh, salty breeze. Two moms pushing sleeping babies in strollers chatted as they ambled.

I slowed at the sight of a shop painted blue and white with a windowed octagonal tower, possibly meant to resemble a very short lighthouse. A cutout of a hand hung from a bracket sticking out from the wall, framed by a curvy border reading, MADAME ALLEGRA, PALM READER. PAST, PRESENT, FUTURE TOLD. The fingers and lines on the palm bore esoteric labels. I'd never been a woo-woo type, as Alana once put it. But, hey, I was on vacation. This could be fun, and nobody was in line. I pulled open the door, jangling a bell hanging from it, the sound reminiscent of the bell on my store's door back in South Lick.

Inside the tower, the room was filled with ornate statuary. Paintings of vaguely spiritual subjects filled the walls. From in here I realized the openings high up in the tower were stained glass windows, some depicting signs of the zodiac, like a scorpion and a goat. Others were harder to figure out, except one that showed a spray of cards. In a corner of the room, two chairs sat at right angles with a small table between them. A low lamp cast a warm, intimate light and the air smelled of sandalwood, as if incense had been burned in the past. Nowhere was a posted list of prices.

A woman wearing a rainbow-colored turban pushed aside a heavy curtain covering a doorway. "Welcome, friend. I am Madame Allegra." She had a vaguely Eastern European accent, which might or might not have been real, and her eyes were heavily made up to dramatic effect. She stood in front of me, a beatific smile playing around her mouth, her hands clasped in front of the white robe she wore. A heavy necklace featuring stones in all colors was her only ornamentation beyond the turban.

"Thank you. I wondered what it costs to have my palm read." Even as I spoke I noticed her gaze subtly checking out my clothes, my bag, my sandals. This woman was a detective of sorts, gathering data so she could later claim to know something about me.

She quoted me a price and gestured with a flourish toward one of the chairs. I nodded and sat, rubbing my hands on my skirt. Her first pronouncement would probably be, "You ate *bosillos* in your very recent past."

She took both of my hands in hers and examined the backs. It was an intimate act, to feel her long, smooth fingers and cool palms. I nearly pulled my hands back, but a curiosity had seized me. What would she see? Did she notice the scar from when hot oil had splashed onto my knuckles from a sausage that had exploded on the grill? Could she feel the strength in my palms from years of wielding hammers and saws, not to mention coaxing a bicycle uphill? What did she think about my only ring, an engraved silver band I wore on my right pinky?

Turning my hands palm up, she spent a long time looking from one to the other, finally laying down my left hand and taking my right in her left. "You are right-handed."

I only nodded. She'd seen that my right hand was more worn, had more calluses, was stronger.

"Your left hand indicates your potential. Your right is what you have done with it." She closed her eyes for a moment, mascara-laden lashes stark against her pale skin.

The noises from the pier were muted. I had the sense of being in a time out of time, removed from reality. I wasn't sure I liked it.

Madame Allegra opened her eyes and began tracing the lines on my palm with her index finger, another intimate gesture. Her nails didn't extend beyond her fingertips and were painted a silvery white.

I hadn't understood how sensitive the skin on my palm was before now, and I realized I'd never really looked at the spidery lines. I'd heard terms like life line and heart line, but had no idea what they meant. I supposed she would find meaning in the places where the lines crossed—and where they didn't.

"You are a visitor," she began. "You have had great pain in your life, and have survived danger." She paused.

So far? All true. And vague enough to apply to anyone. My not-woo-woo credentials remained intact.

"Your heart line is long and straight. You are in touch with your emotions and are able to have a strong love for someone."

Abe. Interesting she would say that in the absence of a ring on my left hand.

She ran her index finger across the second horizontal line. "You pay attention to detail and are organized, but sometimes you take risks."

Accurate. Still, I truly had no idea how she could tell that from lines on my hand.

She traced down the line that ran from my middle finger to the bottom of my palm. Her finger halted where it touched the line curving around the base of my thumb. "During the next few days more danger will arise, more pain." She looked up suddenly, frowning, and blinked at me. "You must be very careful, miss. Very, very careful."

More pain? I nodded slowly, feeling a chill I hadn't sensed before. "All right," I murmured.

"I believe you will survive to return to the love of your heart. But only if you take great care." She laid her other hand on top of my palm and closed her eyes again, murmuring something silently.

What could she be talking about? I was on vacation, seeing friends, trying to uncover the truth about my mother's death. How could that be dangerous?

She pressed my hand, released it, and stood. She took a deep breath, as if shaking off her trance or whatever it had been. "I take cash or credit." Woo-woo aside, this was her livelihood.

I picked up my bag and rose, too. "Thank you." I fished out the right number of bills and handed them to her.

"Thank you. And, miss?" Her accent fell away. "I don't usually say this to visitors, but I meant what I said. I couldn't discern what kind of danger will befall you. It was crystal clear that something will. You will be in great peril."

I shuddered.

Her gaze bore into mine. "Please proceed with extreme caution."

Chapter 14

Alana and I met out at Arroyo Burro Beach—or Hendry's, as locals call it—at a little before five. One of my favorite pieces of the coast, it offered a long, flat, sandy stretch to walk on. Boathouse, a foodie restaurant perched on a low bluff above the beach, was perfect for drinks and sustenance before or after a stroll. After we exchanged a hug, we sat first on a bench overlooking the ocean. Each member of a couple walked a shaggy black dog on the sand, and a kid learning to surf finally caught a wave.

"What have you been up to since Saturday?" Alana asked.

"This and that." I opened my right palm and regarded it, then looked up. "Have you ever been to the palm reader out on the pier?"

"Madame Allegra?" She hooted. "Never. I don't lean that way, Robbie. This shouldn't surprise you."

"It doesn't. And I usually don't, either, as you know. You were the one who said I was as little woo-woo prone as you were."

She laughed. "I remember."

"Anyway, I went for a meander on Stearns Wharf this afternoon."

"And for some inconceivable reason you decided to waste money on getting your fortune told."

"Actually, yes."

She gave me a classic Alana side-eye.

"Hey, don't look at me like that. I thought it would be fun, or at least interesting. Instead it was kind of disturbing." I told my friend what had gone down and about Madame Allegra's warning.

"Creepy," Alana said. "You really think you'll be in danger?"

"I sure hope not. I mean, why would I be? The woman seemed dead serious about it, though, and said she didn't usually give customers such a specific warning." I shivered again, remembering how sincere she'd been, telling me to proceed with extreme caution. I'd left the pier and ended up sitting on my towel on the beach as planned, but her warning had disturbed me too much to really enjoy it. "Enough dark stuff. Do you want to walk first or eat first?"

"Let's eat and talk, then we can walk off our drinks. The 'rents want me back later tonight for an end-of-life meeting." She rolled her eyes.

"Ouch. Is one of them sick?"

She laughed. "No, but they want to get their ducks in a row, as they put it, and make sure I know their wishes. I'm their only kid, so . . ." She lifted a shoulder and dropped it.

"Actually?" I smiled, but it wasn't a bright one. "It's a good idea, even though they aren't old. For some reason, Mom had gotten her affairs in order, too. A will, a prepaid cremation, all her account numbers and passwords in one place, her lawyer's number posted on the fridge. It made dealing with her estate so much easier."

"Do you think she had a premonition of her death?" Alana gazed somberly into my eyes.

I lifted a shoulder. "I have no way of knowing. Let's go in and not talk about dying."

"Deal." She gestured toward the restaurant. "Patio?"

"Sure."

The restaurant building had a wall of windows facing the beach, but it also included a big patio with glass walls as a shield from the sea breeze. Tall propane heaters warmed the air when needed. A ten-foot-long waist-high stone bin flamed and cast warmth around, too. All-season outdoor dining, a very California way to eat.

Ten minutes later we had drinks in hand, a blood-orange margarita for her and a honeycomb mojito for me. A blond waiter younger than us, clothed like the other waitstaff in a black polo shirt with black pants, had just brought us a plate of hot Parmesan truffle fries to start. We'd opted for the happy hour menu, from which I'd ordered Baja-style fish tacos. Alana asked for the lobster-truffle mac and cheese.

"Cheers, girlfriend." She lifted her glass.

"Here's to friendship." I clinked and sipped. "You never gain weight, do you?" She was as lean as she'd been in high school.

"Not really. I guess I have a naturally fast metabolism. You look good. Staying in shape?"

"I bike a lot. I've never had skinny hips, as you well know. But I do my crunches every morning, and my work keeps me on my feet and moving." I took another sip. "Are you going to hire Katherine to plan your wedding?"

Alana cocked her head, regarding me. "I guess I could talk to her about it. Antonio and I haven't started planning anything yet. My mom thinks we're nuts not to have even set a date. And she's in good company. The rest of the known universe has exactly one question when they see my ring. When's the wedding?" She shook her head.

"You'll get there."

We chatted about her research, my restaurant, national politics, and movies as we sipped and munched the perfect crusty fries.

"Jason seems like he's doing well, doesn't he?" Alana asked.

"He does. I always liked him. I mean, as a friend."

"He's good people."

I savored the first of my tacos a while later, trying to tease apart the tastes and ingredients. Cilantro, certainly, and the crunch of radish and purple cabbage. Something in there was pickled, too, and a creamy sauce definitely had at least jalapeño-level hotness. I gazed toward the beach.

"Interesting." I pointed to the beach. "Katherine Russom. I wouldn't have thought she was into environmental stuff." She walked with Paul, her arms crossed over her chest, as he shook his head.

"I would agree. She always seemed very much the consumer, and from what I saw at the reunion, she hasn't changed much. Who's the dude?"

"His name is Paul something, an environmental

activist. Whom my mom apparently knew and was in the same group with."

"What's the group?"

"They're trying to get a certain fumigant banned from this county and Ventura County, too. It's airborne when farmers apply it and really toxic to people and animals who breathe the stuff. I met with Paul yesterday. He thinks the guy who owns the chemical company poisoned Mom." *Oops.* We were talking about dying, after all.

Her nostrils flared. "You're kidding me. What's the company?"

"Agrosafe. They're up in the industrial park in Goleta."

"I've heard of them." She peered at the beach, too. We'd sat on two adjacent sides of the table so we could both watch the ocean. "Katherine's dad owns it, right?"

"Exactly. What do you know about the company?"

"Lemme think." She tapped a blunt-trimmed unpainted nail on the table. "I read about a fumigant made by Agrosafe in one of the research journals I subscribe to, but I can't think where."

"Let me know if you come up with it."

"Of course. But poisoning Jeanine? That seems like an extreme solution."

"No kidding," I agreed. "Also—how? How would anyone slip a toxin into her drink or her coffee? Would they have sprayed it into her house? It seems crazy."

"It does."

"Alana, you know about chemicals and stuff."

She threw back her head and laughed. "You are so not a scientist, girlfriend. Chemicals and stuff. But yeah, I kind of do know about those things in my own small niche."

"Would something like a fumigant be able to mimic the symptoms of a ruptured brain aneurysm?"

"I have no idea, Robbie. Really. Not my field at all. You'll have to find somebody else to ask."

"It was worth a try."

The waiter returned. "Can I get you ladies something else?" He eyed our empty drink glasses.

"I'm still hungry," Alana said. "I'd like the ahi poke."

"You got it." He loaded up both empty plates.

"I'll have the popcorn shrimp, please." I took a second look at the waiter. There was something familiar about him. "Wait, what did you say your name was?"

"Cody."

"Cody Russom?" I asked.

His eyes flew wide. "That's me. How did you know?"

"We went to school with Katherine." I gestured to Alana and back to myself. "She's your sister, right?"

He nodded once, looking wary.

"Have you graduated from Chumash?" Alana asked.

He blinked. "Yeah. I'm a sophomore at UCSB."

"Nice to see you again, Cody. The last time I ran into you, you were a little kid." I smiled at him. "I'm Robbie, and this is Alana. I think I'll have a glass of the house chardonnay to chase down those shrimp."

Alana ordered another margarita.

"I'll put in those orders and get the drinks out to you right away." He hurried off.

"Did he seem a little eager to get away from us?" Alana asked, looking after him.

"Maybe. But he's probably busy. And who wants to sit and yak with a couple of older women who know his unpleasant big sister?"

She snorted. Which made me giggle, as always. Soon we were in the throes of unstoppable belly laughs until tears dripped from my eyes. The descending sun grew larger and as red as a monstrous celestial blood orange until it slipped behind the ocean.

Chapter 15

The next morning found me back at the sheriff's office. I waited outside to avoid the crabby reception-ist. Melinda Washington had e-mailed me last night and we'd arranged to meet here at nine. The sky was hazier today than it had been. I sniffed and smelled smoke. Sure enough, when I surveyed the mountains to the north, gray plumes rose up. California's wild-fire problem was getting worse and worse. When I was young we never had wildfires in the winter. Now it seemed like a year-round thing. I hoped they could contain this one soon, easily, and without any coura-geous firefighters losing their lives.

A tall woman with glowing dark skin, half-inch-long hair, and two-inch-diameter red hoop earrings matching her glasses frames and her red shirt hur-ried toward me from the parking area. A capacious red leather bag was slung over her shoulder and she carried a ceramic travel mug.

"Ms. Washington?" I asked.

"Yes. Are you Robbie Jordan?"

I stuck out my hand. "I am. Thanks for agreeing to see me."

A broad smile crept across her face as she shook my hand. "Anything for a friend of Jason's, and please call me Mel. Come on in, then." Inside, she saluted the receptionist. "Good morning, Inez."

Inez nodded without looking up. I followed the pathologist, her red heels tapping the floor, through a doorway into a big room filled with desks. Several people in dark green shirts murmured on phones, worked in front of computer screens, or did both at once. We went through another doorway into a cramped office with only a high transom window, but at least it had a door for privacy. I hoped the AC was working.

"Please sit." She pointed to a chair next to her desk and plopped down in the wheeled chair. "Wait one moment while I see if I have any fresh ones this morning." She clicked on the laptop in front of her and tapped and scrolled with red-painted nails for a few minutes.

I inwardly cringed at the words *fresh ones* as I gazed around the office. Several official-looking certificates were framed on the wall. A pair of sensible black lace-up shoes were neatly arranged next to the door. On Mel's desk was a picture of a lighter-skinned girl of about ten caught midair over a trampoline, a big smile on her face, braids flying, feet kicked up in the back. A bookshelf held tomes about pathology and forensics, as well as the complete collection of Harry Potter books on the bottom shelf. Bring Your Kids to Work Day must be tricky when the work was cutting open dead people.

She turned to face me. "Sorry about the wait. So how do you know Jason, Ms. Jordan?"

"We were friends at Chumash High together. I'm in town for our tenth reunion. Please call me Robbie."

Mel nodded. "I went to Chumash, but a dozen years before you did. Where do you live now?"

"Indiana."

"So what can I help you with?"

I exhaled. "As I mentioned in the e-mail, my mother died two years ago. They told me she had a ruptured brain aneurysm. A guy I met yesterday suggested she'd been poisoned. I wondered if you remembered the case or could check the records for me."

"Poisoned?" She brought her eyebrows together. "Did you request the report?"

"Yes. But the woman at the front said it would take up to ten business days."

She shook her head. "Don't get me started on Inez. She bears no resemblance to the saint our mountains are named for. What was the name again?" She turned back to her laptop.

"Jeanine Jordan. She died on January sixteenth two years ago." A date I would never forget, one that had irrevocably changed my life. Soon after, I'd found my country store and my new home, but I'd lost my mother, the only parent I had ever known until last year.

"Got it," she said. "Of a ruptured aneurysm?"

"It's what they told me. My mom was only fifty-three when she died." Alone. Liz's description of finding Mom dead at home tore me up. I should have been with her. Nobody should die alone. And if someone had been there, maybe they could have gotten emergency help and saved her life.

"Do you know if we did an autopsy?" she asked, tapping the keys, peering at the screen.

"No. I was a mess after she died. My aunt and I came out here together, so she might remember." I wished I could call Adele and ask, but she was off doing service work in India again. I would shoot her an e-mail, though, in case she checked. Or maybe Liz knew.

"What reasons did this person have to suggest your mother was poisoned?"

"My mom was in a group protesting the use of a particular agrochemical in the region. A guy in the group said the effects of this fumigant can mimic an aneurysm."

Mel twisted her head to stare at me. "You're talking about Agrosafe, aren't you?"

I nodded.

"I've been following the story." She looked at the laptop again and uttered a mild expletive. "Excuse my French, but this system is so slow, so old, so stupidly nineteen ninety. For some reason I can't find the report on your mom."

"What? It's missing?"

"I doubt it got deleted or anything, but nothing has been updated here for centuries." She gestured around the room, which, in fact, looked a bit worn-out. The walls were dingy and the woodwork was chipped. "Well, decades, anyway. Including and especially the software. I'd move to another county, but my kid loves her school and her friends." She gazed at the picture of the girl.

"So . . ." My voice trailed off. "There's no way to know if you did an autopsy or if my mother might have been poisoned?"

"I'll find the report, Robbie." Mel swiveled her chair to face me and leaned forward, her hands on the knees of her black pants. "If we did an autopsy, we would have seen if it was an actual aneurysm. If we didn't, but had no reason to suspect a chemical agent, we might not have tested for a toxin. Rest assured, I will search every dark corner of the system for the report until I find it."

"You don't keep a paper copy?"

"Nope. We don't have the room, plus a cost-cutting edict came down from on high four years ago. Go all-digital." She scoffed. "What could possibly go wrong?"

Chapter 16

"The veggie quesadilla sounds perfect," I told Carmen at one thirty from my table on the patio. Even in winter the California skies seemed to hold so much more light than where I lived. I'd looked up the latitudes. In latitude Santa Barbara was fewer than five degrees farther south than South Lick. Seemed like a pretty important five degrees, or maybe the ocean's reflective effect made the difference. "With extra guacamole, please."

"Coming right up, *hija*. Something to drink?"

"I think for old times' sake I'd better have a Corona with lime. Because, you know, vacation."

She smiled. "Sounds like a plan."

After I'd left Mel Washington, I'd taken the bike for a ride around the bird refuge, then come back to my room for a shower. After I made my way through a delicious lunch and a beer, a nap might be in order. If I could quiet my overactive mind, that is.

Now I tapped out a quick e-mail to Adele, asking whether she knew if they'd done an autopsy on

Mom. I texted same to Liz. She'd been Mom's bestie, after all. Something caressed my bare calf. I glanced down to see Pajarito rubbing his head on my leg.

I smiled, reaching down to pet him. "Hey, buddy. You'd get along great with my Birdy."

Carmen set down the Corona and a glass with a wedge of lime stuck on the rim. "You had a good morning?"

"Kind of." Two tables were occupied inside, but we had the patio to ourselves. "I met the pathologist at the sheriff's office, but she couldn't find my mom's death report. I don't know if they did an autopsy on her or not."

"This is not good."

"You're telling me. She said she'd find it, though. Carmen, do you know anything about a company named Agrosafe?"

She stared at me with nostrils wide and mouth pulled down at the corners. "Do I ever! They're criminals. They poisoned my cousin."

"Really?" I stared back.

"Really. He's a farmworker. He picks strawberries, lettuce, whatever is ripe. He was working at an organic farm down in Oxnard but it's next to a conventional one. They sprayed the field with the fumigant Agrosafe makes. Calling it safe is a bunch of BS. I couldn't believe how sick he got."

"Did he file charges?"

"You kidding me? He's poor, Robbie. He had to stop working, and he doesn't get any paid sick leave. He had to go on welfare. He's a proud man, and he hates it."

"Carmen," Luisa called from inside.

"I gotta go," Carmen said. "We'll talk later." She bustled off, shaking her head.

Wow. Her poor cousin. I hoped he would recover. I gazed at the brilliant magenta flowers of the bougainvillea covering the wall next to me, another sight missing from the Midwest, and one I adored. Luckily, the plant grew fine without fumigants of any kind. All it wanted was a lot of sun and little bit of water.

A small brown bird hopped around in the showy plant, and somewhere a mourning dove made its *who-who, whoo, who* sound. The ones in Indiana had a different call from these western ones. Different varieties of the same species? I didn't know enough about birds to tell.

I sipped the cold beer as I checked my phone. Liz had texted back, asking where I was. I answered,

Lunch at NAC. Join me?

She responded within seconds.

Be right there.

After Carmen brought out my quesadilla, I bit into perfection. A flour tortilla filled with roasted peppers, green chiles, and sautéed onions, topped with pepper jack, folded in half and lightly fried on both sides? My idea of heaven, especially topped with fresh salsa and a generous scoop of guacamole. It would be easy to offer this same dish at my restaurant. I took the obligatory picture before I bit into it.

I was halfway through my cheesy, crunchy lunch when Liz putted up to the curb in a classic sixties VW convertible bug. Painted a light blue, it had the rounded bumpers marking it as made in 1966 or earlier. I didn't know much about birds, but vintage cars? Bring it. California must have more old cars than anywhere else in the country. It was common to see a sixties Mustang, an early-seventies Jaguar, or a well-maintained Ford truck from the fifties on the roads. They lasted a lot longer out here in the absence of salted roads and harsh driving conditions half the year.

"I'm on the patio," I called after she unfolded her tall frame from the low seat.

She gave a wave and hurried toward the door. A moment later she'd plopped into the chair across from mine, her silver hair more flyaway than when I'd seen her before. Her whole manner seemed flyaway this morning.

"How are you?" I asked.

Carmen walked up, order pad out. "Hey, Liz. Lunch?"

"Fish tacos, please," Liz said nearly breathlessly. "And I'll have a Corona, too."

"Coming right up." Carmen peered at her. "You okay?"

Liz blew out a breath. She glanced around. We were still alone out here, and she beckoned us both closer.

"I just heard the worst news."

I put my hand to my mouth, waiting. Had something happened to Zoe? No, this was shock on her face, not grief.

"Paul is dead," Liz announced.

Carmen's breath rushed in with a rasping sound. She crossed herself.

I shook my head slowly at the news. No wonder she looked shocked. "But he's so young."

"I know." Liz nodded. "He's only forty-two, or was."

"What did he die of?" I asked.

"That's the thing. They're saying it might have been an aneurysm."

"Exactly like Mom," I whispered.

Chapter 17

"Exactly like Jeanine." Liz gazed at both of us.

Carmen looked as stunned as I felt. Could Paul's death also be murder by agrochemical?

"I need to tell my boy," Carmen said. "He's gonna be sad. They were friends."

"That's right. Hector told me yesterday he and Paul were buddies." I felt terrible for Hector. "How did you find out Paul had died?" I asked Liz.

Liz wrinkled her nose. "I have a police scanner. So I can . . ." She glanced at Carmen. "So I can keep track of what's going on."

With Zoe, I imagined, but she must not want to tell Carmen about her daughter's problem. "And what did you hear?"

"They don't say much and they have all these codes," Liz went on. "But an ambulance was sent to Paul's apartment an hour ago. I know the neighborhood he lived in, and I have a girlfriend who's an EMT. I asked her what they could find out."

"Ma'am?" a voice called from indoors. "Can we have our check, please?"

Carmen raised a finger. "You tell me everything later." She hurried into the building.

Liz continued. "My friend was on that call. They discovered Paul dead on his kitchen floor."

The same way Liz had found Mom. "Why do they think it might be an aneurysm?" I asked. "You know, not a heart attack or something?"

"I don't know." She narrowed her eyes at the bougainvillea. "Something looks different? Broken blood vessels in the skin or some other sign? I actually have no idea. They're the experts. They must have a way to tell."

"I should think so. Did you hear who found him? Who called it in?"

"No, but Paul has—had—a roommate. It must have been her." She tapped the table. "Robbie, what if it wasn't a natural death?" She lowered her voice to a whisper. "What if someone killed Paul?"

"Unfortunately, I was thinking the same thing. Liz, we have to find out more about Agrosafe. About Walter Russom. I mean, Mom died two years ago. But this is happening right now. Maybe Paul's apartment building has a security camera, or a neighbor saw somebody go in or come out who isn't normally around."

"Shouldn't we tell the police our suspicions? It's their job, no? On the TV shows they do door-to-door searches for witnesses and stuff."

I let out a breath. "Of course. But us telling the cops the head of a reputable local company might have poisoned two people sounds kind of kooky. And

I don't know a soul in the police department . . . oh, wait. Of course I do. Jason."

She frowned. "But didn't you say he's in cyber-crime or something?"

"He is, but I'm sure he knows all the detectives. He's the one who turned me on to the pathologist, Mel Washington. I'll give him a call." I sipped my beer, which was no longer particularly cold. I didn't care. "I hope you'll keep in mind coincidences do happen. Paul easily could have died of natural causes. Mom might have, too."

"I know."

Carmen bustled out with Liz's beer and tacos and set them down. "I feel like strangling that Russom *hombre*. He's a criminal." She planted her fists on her hips. "It has to be him."

"Carmen, we don't know if he's done anything wrong," I protested.

"We gotta take action," she insisted.

I made a tamping-down gesture. "Liz and I agreed I'm going to talk to my friend in the police department. See what he says." I peered up at her. "Okay? Don't do anything rash. We'll figure this out."

The ready bell dinged from inside. "All right. Maybe." Off she went.

I popped in the last bite of my quesadilla, savoring the smooth mushed avocado with it, while Liz attacked her first taco.

I tilted my head and kept my tone casual. "To change the subject, do you think Zoe would like to hang out with me? We were pretty good friends when we were young, and you said she wasn't doing too well." I didn't want to broach what Jason had told me, but if Liz needed to talk about Zoe, I wanted to provide an opening.

"That's changing the subject, all right." She took a long drag from her beer glass. "You could ask her. I'm not sure what she'll say."

"Is she living with you?"

Liz let out her breath with a whoosh. "No. She's in a halfway house, Robbie. She's addicted to opiates."

"I'm so sorry." Jason had been right.

"I've tried to help her. Got her into rehab more than once. She always relapses and uses again." She lifted her chin. "Last time she lived at my place she started stealing from me. I can't have her there."

"It must tear you up to see Zoe go through such a hard thing."

"You have no idea. I ask myself where I went wrong, even though I know I was the best mom I could be."

"Of course you were. And she was fine in high school, as I remember." I thought back. She hadn't been in the top academic classes, but she was a gifted artist, sculpting and painting as well as creating art with photographs. "It's not your fault."

"Of course it isn't. And her life is her responsibility. Still, it's not easy." She mustered a smile. "I'm so happy to see you healthy and doing well. Jeanine would be so very proud of you."

I knew Mom would be proud of me. Liz and I shared a quiet moment, during which I resolved to find Zoe and talk with her if she'd let me. For old times' sake.

Chapter 18

Jason pushed through the door at the Green Artichoke at five thirty, and I waved him over to the high-top I'd snagged. Without a reservation, I'd had to resort to a bar table, even though I preferred conventional seating because of my short legs. The place was hopping for a Tuesday, clearly a well-loved local restaurant. It helped that it was in the Funk Zone, an area between the 101 and the ocean with lots of renovated warehouses housing breweries, artists, and restaurants.

My friend exchanged fist bumps with me and slid onto the stool opposite. "How's it going, Rob?" He wore a T-shirt with multicolored discs flying through the air and the words, *Diskers Do It in Rotation*.

"Not too bad. You?"

"More of the same. Work, play, sleep. Rinse and repeat."

I pointed at his shirt. "Do you do Ultimate?"

"Yeah. I love it. I'm on a pretty competitive team, too."

A waitperson stopped by. "Good evening and welcome to the Green Artichoke. My name's Debbie. What can I get you to drink tonight?" She was an older woman whose skin looked like she walked the beach at midday on a regular basis. Her deep, raspy voice pointed to her being a longtime smoker.

"I'll have a glass of the house chardonnay, please." I smiled at her.

"Seltzer with lime for me," Jason said.

"Coming right up." Debbie turned away.

"Not drinking tonight?" I asked Jason.

"I'm on call. If I get summoned to work, showing up with even a speck of alcohol in my system is a big no-no in the force."

"That makes sense." I gazed around the spacious restaurant, abuzz with conversation. The walls were a pale artichoke green, of course, with lots of windows and the occasional painting of a giant artichoke in between. Booths lined the walls except here in the bar area, where all the tables and bar stools were full. "This is a popular place."

"With reason. The food is excellent, the waitstaff well trained, and the prices reasonable. Plus, people love the whole farm-to-table thing. So what have you been doing with yourself?"

"Hanging out. Visiting with Alana. Riding. I even took a nap this afternoon." I spotted a wicked grin on his face. "What?"

"We're getting old, my friend. Did you ever take a nap ten years ago?"

"Only when I'd been up until three drinking too much. And I was a pretty boring teenager. Hangovers didn't happen very often."

"Same here. Like never, in my case." He rolled his eyes.

When our drinks arrived, I thanked the waitperson, who wore a black armband on her white sleeve.

"What's the armband for, Debbie?" I asked.

Jason blinked, watching me.

"It's for Paul, one awesome dude and an environmentalist." She patted the armband. "He died today."

"I'm so sorry," I said, meaning it. "Did he work here?" I asked to draw her out, despite knowing the answer.

"Yes. He did bike deliveries for us." She sniffed. "May he rest in peace. The poor man, taken before his time."

I nodded. "You're right, he wasn't very old. I just met him on Sunday. Had he been ill?"

"No," Debbie scoffed. "He was the healthiest guy around. But these things happen. We never know how long we have on this earth." She excused herself and left.

Jason and I clinked glasses.

"Here's to old friends," he said.

"To old friends." I sipped the cool, buttery wine and set my glass down. "And *carpe diem,* too. Because Debbie is absolutely right. None of us knows how long we have."

"I heard about Etxgeberria's death today. You didn't seem surprised when she said he had died."

I traced the condensation on my glass for a moment. "Zoe's mother and I have had a couple meals together this week. Liz and my mom were good friends. Anyway, Liz has a police scanner. She told me this afternoon about Paul being discovered dead in his apartment."

He wrinkled his nose. "Why does she have a police scanner? Because of Zoe's habit? I thought she'd gone through rehab."

"Yeah, but she keeps using again, according to Liz. I think she wants to know if . . ." I couldn't finish it.

"If Zoe ODs." Jason kept his voice gentle.

"Right." I took another sip of the cool, smooth wine. "But back to Paul. From what Liz heard, he was found dead on the floor exactly like my mother, and an EMT mentioned the word *aneurysm*. How would they know on the spot what caused his death? I mean, as long as he wasn't shot or stabbed or something. Why did they say aneurysm?"

"I'm not sure. But I'll ask around, okay?"

"Suppose he was murdered with something that made it look like a ruptured aneurysm. Poisoned. Are your fellow officers going to ask the neighbors what they saw? Try to find a security cam?" I heard the angst in my voice.

"Take it easy, Rob. You know I deal with cyber-crime, not homicide crime scene analysis, right?"

I nodded.

"The guy was relatively young and he died unat-tended," Jason said. "Of course they'll do an investi-gation. It's due diligence."

"Will you tell them about the possibility of poison-ing by fumigant?"

"Yes, Robbie." He spoke patiently, as if to a pesky child. "I'm not sure they'll give it much credence, but I'll run it by them."

"Thank you." I flashed back to my dinner with Alana. "I saw Paul walking with Katherine Russom on Hendry's yesterday afternoon. It kind of looked like they were arguing. At least disagreeing about something."

"Does the two of them arguing surprise you?" Jason asked. "I mean, Katherine finds something to disagree about with everyone, as far as I remember."

"True. But I don't know, maybe it has something to do with his death."

He gazed at me over the top of his glasses. Finally, he spoke. "I'll tell the detective on the case. Probably a long shot, but it's a piece of information."

Debbie returned. "Did you want to order food, folks?"

"I haven't even looked at the menu," I said. "Can you give us a minute?"

"You got it. I'll be back." She bustled away.

I stared at the list of dishes. "What do you recommend?" I asked Jason.

"Everything's great, really. Fish and chips sounds ordinary, but their take on it is super good. They get fish from a local guy, too. Plus the artichokes, of course. Turn the menu over."

I flipped over the long card. "Whoa. They have a whole section only for artichokes. Deep-fried hearts? I think I've died and gone to heaven."

He laughed. "Let's split some of those, plus a whole 'choke hot with dipping butter to start."

"You speak my mind, dude. I'm so not in Indiana anymore."

Chapter 19

Jason never got to order an entree, though. The deep-fried hearts had a perfect crunchy crust encasing a creamy inside, and the dipping butter for the whole artichoke was flavored with lemon and capers. We were nearly through the delectable appetizers when his phone buzzed in the case on his belt.

He checked it and shook his head. "This is why I drank seltzer, Rob. Gotta hit the station. I'm sorry to strand you." He pulled out his wallet.

I waved him away. "Just go. I'll treat you to your very expensive drink and the apps."

"Thanks."

"What's the call?"

"Unfortunately, it's an Internet predator. A middle-aged pervert who poses as a high school boy and tries to lure underage girls to meet him in person."

"Ick. And you can track him down?"

His smile was wicked. "Better than anybody else around. We've been on the trail of this particular one for a while. Looks like we might finally have him." He hopped off his stool. "Let's get together again before you go home. Deal?"

"Deal. And Jason?"

"Yeah?"

"If you hear anything about, um, what happened earlier today, you'll let me know?"

The smile slid off his face. "If I can, I will." He cocked his head. "But you'll leave police work to the police, I assume."

"Of course." How could I not? A little unofficial investigation wouldn't hurt, though.

Another fist bump—Jason and I had never been on a hugging basis—and he was gone, off to nail a pedophile. *Good.* Monsters like that should have no place in the world.

Debbie strolled up. "Where'd your friend go?"

"He got called into work, but I'm going to stay and eat. Can I order the small size of fish and chips, and a small greens salad with the clementine vinaigrette, please?"

"Sure. Another glass of wine?"

"Why not? You know, I love that you have two choices of entree sizes. It makes so much sense."

"We aim to please."

"I have a restaurant back in Indiana where I live, but we serve only breakfast and lunch."

"Neat." She set a fist on her khaki-clad hip. "You do it all yourself?"

"No." I laughed. "I have two awesome helpers. They both cook, but don't mind busing tables or washing dishes, too. The three of us make it happen and have fun doing it."

"My hat's off to you," she said. "That's a lot of work."

"Thanks. It is a lot, but it makes me happy. And my place is nowhere near as big as this one." Speaking of washing dishes, I was about to ask her if Zoe was here doing exactly that, but Debbie was hailed by another party.

Silverware clinked and someone laughed at the bar as I slid the last artichoke leaf into the cooling butter and scraped the meaty part off between my teeth. Artichokes were the food of the goddesses, despite being merely the immature flowers of giant thistles. I popped the last morsel of deep-fried heart in next. I sat and watched other diners, drinkers at the bar, the whole California scene. Everybody was casually dressed, half in Bermuda or cargo shorts. Many were tanned and fit. It wasn't only white folks, either. Skin tones and facial features represented the world. It was the rich diversity that came with living on a coast.

What would my life be like if I hadn't fled the state with a broken heart? Would I have opened my own restaurant around here somewhere? Met a man as good as Abe? Would Mom have died suddenly if I still lived in town? I shook my head at the fruitless thought. I had moved, she had died. That was that. And I was happy in South Lick. I had a thriving business, an aunt nearby, good friends, and a wonderful man. Even a darling cat.

When Debbie returned with my wine and the salad, I thanked her.

"Debbie, I'm curious. Did Paul get along with his coworkers? I mean, was there anybody who didn't like him?"

She scrunched up her nose and stared at me. "Why are you asking?"

I lifted a shoulder and dropped it. "It was just a thought."

"Everybody here loved him." She glanced at the door, then back at me. "But his hobby, his passion? That might have made him some enemies."

"The environmental work."

"Yeah." She sucked in a breath and covered her mouth with her hand, eyes wide, as if she'd realized why I was asking. "You don't mean somebody killed him, do you?"

I held up both palms. "I doubt it. Really. Anyway, the police will look into why he died. My friend who had to leave? Jason is actually a cop, and he said they'll investigate Paul's death."

"That kid's with the police? He sure doesn't look like an officer. I mean . . ."

"He is." It was true. Jason looked nothing like the image of a muscular, gun-toting, uniformed cop. The slender Asian, glasses and all, was a textbook illustration of a smart geek. Which he was. "He graduated from the academy and everything. But he works with computers instead of patrolling the streets."

She laughed. "That fits a lot better. We need cybercops, too."

"I have another question for you. Does somebody named Zoe work here? Washing dishes, maybe?"

"She's in the kitchen right now. How'd you know?" She tilted her head.

"Her mom told me. Zoe and Jason and I all went to school together. Was she working last night?"

"Yeah, of course." Debbie laughed low. "She's my

smoking buddy. We take our breaks together and grab a cig out back."

"When do you take a break? I'd like to say hi to her. Haven't seen her in years."

"At seven. Sure, you can join us."

"I might. Thanks." After she left I checked my phone. It was six fifteen. Plenty of time to eat, pay up, and go see my old friend. Zoe must be doing okay if she could hold down a job. I didn't know anything about opiate addiction beyond what I read in the news. Maybe the halfway house was a good influence on her. Maybe she'd decided to do the work to stay clean, even though Liz hadn't sounded too optimistic about the prospects.

I shoved those thoughts aside and dug into my baby greens lightly coated with one of the best dressings I'd ever tasted. I rolled it around in my mouth. They'd mixed fresh clementine juice to perfection with a robust olive oil—made from olives grown within fifty miles of here, the menu said—and a hint of garlic, some black pepper, and a touch of what might be rice vinegar. This was one I had to re-create once I got home. Tomorrow was the midweek farmers' market. I'd get a bottle of local olive oil to take back to Indiana with me even if I had to pay to check my bag on the plane. It was totally worth it.

Chapter 20

One small portion of light, crispy fish and chips later, I headed out and along the side of the restaurant at one minute before seven, according to my phone. A dim light fell on trash, recycling, and compost bins lined up like fat silent servants near a door, with a rotten-vegetable smell coming from the compost bin. I reached the parking lot in the back. The kitchen exhaust fan whirred on the roof. No lamps on posts illuminated this area, unlike in the front of the restaurant and along the side. The sun had set almost an hour and a half ago, and the moon hadn't made an appearance. The smoky smell from the fires was everywhere.

Where were Zoe and Debbie? True, business inside had really picked up in the last half hour. Maybe the waitress couldn't get away. Maybe Zoe had already taken her break. A small bat darted through the dark sky at the edge of the parking lot. Goose bumps raised on my arms and neck. Being back here alone was giving me the creeps. I should go back to the B-and-B. I could find Zoe tomorrow. Or never.

I gave it one more minute, then started to retrace my steps, rummaging in my bag for my keys. The screen door creaked open and thwacked shut. I turned around. A light had come on above the door, and a tall, thin person in a long apron clicked on a lighter.

"Zoe?" I called, hurrying toward her.

She lit the cigarette and took a long drag before facing me. She blew out the smoke to the side, not quite meeting my gaze. "Robbie Jordan? What are you doing here?" Her skin was pale under short dark hair and her hand shook. Three tiny silver rings piercing one eyebrow matched the ones marching up the outer edge of her opposite ear.

"I came back for the Chumash High reunion on Saturday," I said. "We missed you there."

"I wasn't up for it." She shrugged, a tattoo snaking up her neck from the black T-shirt she wore under the apron. "But I meant what are you doing, like, here behind the restaurant?"

"I wanted to say hi to you. I ate dinner inside, and my waitress told me she takes a smoke break with you back here at seven."

She crossed her arms. "Right. You just happened to eat here and mention my name to Deb, your randomly assigned waitress." She puffed again and blew smoke to the side. "I call BS, Robbie."

"You're onto me." I gave a little laugh. "Your mom told me you worked here, so I asked Debbie if you were on tonight. That's all." I studied her. "You and I used to be friends. I can want to see you, can't I?"

"I guess. But we live in pretty different worlds now."

True. "Are you still doing art?"

"Not really." Her right heel jittered up and down, making her whole body vibrate.

"Sad news about Paul, isn't it?"

Her foot stilled and she looked straight at me for the first time. "How did you know him?"

"I'm trying to get more information about how my mom died. Your mother suggested I talk to him."

She stared at me, as if she wasn't sure she believed me. "Yeah, it's super sad." Her focus shifted to the far dark corner of the parking lot. "He was a cool dude. He was nice to me."

"I liked what I saw of him, too. I met with him for a bit on Sunday. He and my mom were in an anti-agrochemical group together."

Zoe let my words hang in the air for a few beats without responding. "Look, I'm not sure how much we have to say to each other."

Not that she'd asked about me. Not one question, not one sympathy extended about Mom dying. "Maybe not. Well, I'll head out and let you get back to work. Take care, Zoe."

"Yeah, you, too." Her tone was sardonic as she ground the butt under the toe of her black Doc Martens. She pulled open the restaurant door.

"I almost forgot," I said. "Katherine Russom was asking about you at the reunion."

Zoe froze. She stared at me and blinked, then spat out an obscenity. "Katherine Russom is a witch. You should keep your distance from her, Robbie. She's the definition of bad news." The screen door slammed behind her.

Chapter 21

I shouldn't have napped earlier. Back in my B-and-B room at nine, I was restless and not a bit sleepy. I opened the window for some air, but started coughing from the wildfire smoke. I shut it again and the room felt stuffy, so I switched on the air conditioner to a low cool setting. I settled on top of the bedspread with a pen and *The New York Times* crossword puzzle book I'd brought. After rereading a clue for a full two minutes, I slapped the book onto the bedside table and got up.

In keeping with the decor downstairs, the room had a cheery, south-of-the-border feel. The woodwork was painted orange, the dresser and bedside table a warm yellow, and the curtains were a zigzag pattern of reds, oranges, and greens. An intricately painted blue-and-yellow papier-mâché pig sat on the dresser. Two framed pictures on the wall showed Day of the Dead skeletons. One painting depicted them in surfing clothes; the other showed a beach cookout.

I barely saw any of it as I paced. Paul was dead. Zoe was an addict. I didn't know for sure how my mother had died. Katherine's father ran an agrochemical company. What did it all mean? What could I do about any of it?

Grabbing my iPad, I sat at the small desk and searched for news. Except I still didn't know how to spell Paul's last name. *Wait.* Liz had said she would text it to me. I searched my phone, but she'd sent only his first name and number. Back on the iPad, I found the local news outlet. I saw stories about national news. A bit about the annual restaurant week and details of a major road project starting up. An article about the baby giraffe born at the zoo. A heart-wrenching story about the aftermath of the mud slide that had covered half a town on the Pacific Coast Highway south of here. But not a single word about a man found dead in his apartment. And I couldn't search for him online because I didn't know how to spell his last name.

I snapped my fingers and grabbed my phone. There was something I could do. Mel Washington had given me her cell number. Was it only this morning? It seemed like a week ago. I texted her.

Check Paul E's body for the Agrosafe fumigant.

I hit Send. But would she check? I hoped so.

I paced some more. The room didn't have a television, which was fine with me. I'd brought a novel on the trip, but I didn't think I could concentrate on reading, either. What I really wanted to do was have this whole mess sorted out, go home, and curl up on a couch with my sweetie.

Laughing out loud, I jabbed Abe's number as I figuratively slapped my own head. What was wrong with me? I couldn't curl up with my man in person until Saturday night, but I sure could talk things through with him, and he should be home from work by now.

Except he didn't pick up. I swore to myself. He could be any number of places. Having dinner with his son, or his folks, or all three. Called on to an emergency job, the plight of an electric company lineman. Or at banjo practice with the bluegrass group he played in. I sent him a quick text, asking him to call me if he could. I shoved the phone in the back pocket of my jeans, found my light sweater and the room key, and headed downstairs. Maybe a walk outdoors would clear my brain and relax me, smoke or no smoke.

Downstairs, I paused with my hand on the cool metal of the door to the outside. The restaurant was dark, lit only by a red EXIT sign. The pass-through window was closed, but I spied a light from under the kitchen door. A peal of women's laughter drew me in, and I couldn't help tapping on the door.

"Carmen?" I called. She and her mom lived in a cottage at the back of the restaurant and B-and-B, but she'd told me they used this kitchen for their own meals as well as the café's.

She pulled open the door, a Dos Equis bottle in her other hand. "Robbie, do you need something, *hija?*"

"No, not at all. I was going to go for a walk, and I heard you laughing. I hope I'm not interrupting anything."

Luisa sat on a high stool at the stainless counter in the middle of the kitchen, the surface and her hands covered in the finely ground cornmeal called masa harina. A stainless-steel bowl held a huge lump of pale yellow dough, and a stack of disks separated by waxed paper sat at Luisa's left elbow.

"Come into our *cocina.*" Carmen stepped back. "We're making tortillas for tomorrow. We'll teach you."

Her mom smiled and clapped twice, then beckoned me toward her. *"Ven aquí."*

The simple company of women cooking? Way better than a lonely walk to soothe the soul.

"Gracias," I said.

"Carmen, *cerveza para* Robbie," Luisa said, trilling the first letter of my name.

Carmen drew another bottle of Dos Equis out of the fridge and held it up.

"Thanks, I'd love one." I sat on a stool kitty-corner from Luisa.

Carmen popped the cap and handed me the bottle. "Cheers."

Luisa raised hers, too, and we all clinked bottles. The cool drink went down as easy as Carmen's smile. And the delicious corn aroma made me feel like I had come home.

After a sip, the older woman set down her drink and scooped out a portion of dough with her fingers. She formed it into a ball smaller than a baseball but a little bigger than a Ping-Pong ball. With a minute of rapid slaps between her palms, suddenly it was a thin tortilla six inches in diameter.

"Wow, she has the technique down," I said. I smiled at Luisa and gave her a thumbs-up sign.

She smiled back as she slid a square of waxed paper onto the stack, laid her tortilla on the top, and started over.

"She's only been doing it all her life," Carmen said from the stool next to me. Her habitual cheery expression faded. "Did you hear any more news about poor Paul?"

"No. Why isn't the story on local news outlets? I checked online and couldn't find a thing."

"I don't know. Think somebody's covering it up?" Carmen leaned closer and lowered her voice. "What if somebody from Agrosafe poisoned him? Maybe they're pulling strings so the news doesn't get out."

"That's quite a set of strings, isn't it? I mean, the police were called and I'm sure his body went to the sheriff's morgue. I thought newspapers and radio stations always monitor police channels and go right to the story."

"Hey, with the devils who run that company, who knows how much power they have?"

"*¿Quién es un demonio?*" Luisa asked, eyes bright.

"Nobody's a devil, Mamá." Carmen batted away the suggestion, but she turned her face away from her mother and rolled her eyes, making me laugh.

"Robbie," Luisa said. She gestured for me to scoop a ball of dough out of the bowl.

I held a finger in the air. "One sec." I scrubbed my hands at the sink and dried them before rejoining her.

Luisa motioned for me to flour my hands with masa harina first. She scooped out a hunk of dough and made it into a ball. I dusted my hands and did the same. She slapped it flat with the fingers of her right hand into her left palm, then waited for me to do the same.

I tried, but Carmen burst out laughing. My tortilla was now the shape of a hockey puck and it had stuck to my palm. Luisa set to repeatedly slapping her dough.

"You gotta find the technique," Carmen said between giggles.

I peeled it off, floured my palm again, and slapped some more. It got marginally thinner. Luisa's was finished by now. It had joined the stack and she'd started another.

"Why don't you roll them out?" I asked. "Or use one of those presses? Mom and I had one when I was young."

"Pressing would be cheating. And Mamá's a lot faster, anyway. The texture is better this way, too."

I spent the next hour with these two sunny women, sipping beer and trying in vain to master Luisa's technique. It didn't matter. I had the balm for my soul I'd needed, and after our brief mention of Paul missing from the news, all we discussed was cooking. Recipes, ingredients, preparations, Cali-Mex and Hoosier alike. Cooking was Carmen's and Luisa's livelihood and mine, too. Who could ever tire of it?

By the time I slid into bed at ten thirty, it barely registered that Abe hadn't called or texted back. I didn't care. I was tired, happy, and distracted from the week's issues, ever so temporarily.

Chapter 22

Cloth bag slung over my shoulder the next morning and a big grin splitting my face, I stood at the entrance to a long row, spanning two city blocks, of white-and-green pop-up tents belonging to the Wednesday farmers' market vendors. The first one on my right displayed boxes and baskets overflowing with fresh vegetables in all hues and shapes. The next one sold showy, colorful bouquets of flowers. Beyond that was the Pistachio Man, with dozens of flavors of bagged nuts in their shells. After him was a goat-and-sheep-cheese seller. I adored farmers' markets, and they mostly shut down for half the year where I lived. Bloomington did have an indoor winter market, but of course any produce had to be grown in a greenhouse. It was much sparser and not lush like this one.

Abe and I had squeezed in a brief talk this morning, early for him, of course, but he was as much of an early morning person as I was. He'd been out until late at banjo practice, as I'd suspected. I hadn't gotten the chance to tell him about any of my investigations. Details about a possible murder could wait until I was home.

Now I focused on the market. Mom had taught me to make a circuit of all the stalls first to see who was there and what their prices were. She and I went together, every week, to the Saturday market. The whole time I lived in Santa Barbara, that I could remember, the market was our Saturday morning ritual.

Today's midweek market, located on State Street, had opened at eight and now at nine it was bustling, despite it being a work day. Moms pushed strollers. Senior citizens ambled with walkers. Even a banker type in suit and tie carried a full bag of produce and other foods in each hand.

At the very end was Mama Tamale, the stand selling hot breakfast tamales and burritos. It had been here even when I was a kid. Back in my restaurant I served cheesy, creamy Hoosier grits as comfort food. Here? There was nothing like a soft, *caliente* tamale to warm your insides and fill you up in the most satisfying of ways. The stand would be my last stop.

The bustling scene was also a welcome respite from all the questions running through my mind about Paul's death and Mom's, too. About Zoe's addiction and her total lack of interest in seeing me last night, not to mention her warning about Katherine. Had that been residual dislike from high school days, or some newer resentment? My mood wasn't helped by the fact that I hadn't had a word back from Mel Washington, Adele, or Liz about Mom's autopsy.

But right now I was going to luxuriate in feasting my eyes—and nose and taste buds—in all these gorgeous midwinter fruits of the land. Speaking of fruit, I paused in front of Le Citron, an organic citrus farm in San Luis Obispo, where I'd gone to college. Fat thin-skinned lemons, tiny kumquats, blood oranges, pink grapefruits, bright orange Murcotts, shiny little key limes, all were arrayed in shallow boxes tilted up at the back for better viewing. One bizarre-looking variety labeled BUDDHA'S HAND CITRON had two dozen yellow fingers with curled-in pointy tips poking up from the gnarled fruit base. It broadcast a strong lemon smell but looked menacing. I didn't need any more menace this week. The farmer offered thinly sliced half rounds of a blood orange as samples, so I helped myself, tossing the rind in the provided compost bucket on the ground. The flavor was sweet and intense, slightly more bitter than a navel orange, but also less acidic.

I walked away having bought a few blood oranges and a half dozen Murcotts. Was I going to be able to find strawberries, too? February was a bit on the early side. I'd have to make sure they were from an organic farm, based on what I'd learned about the Agrosafe business and the harm their fumigant could do.

As I strolled, I sampled a fruity olive oil at one booth, then bought a bottle to take home. I added a bag of chili-lime pistachios from the Pistachio Man and four huge artichokes—despite not having a kitchen to cook them in—from a coastal farm to the north. When I reached the end of the first block, a sand-colored alpaca with huge dark brown eyes in a white face gazed soulfully in my direction. A thick rope tethered it to a stake in a grassy area right beyond the pavement. The tent next to the animal was filled with fluffy skeins of yarn, knitted scarves, and patterned sweaters, among other handmade items. A sign reading SHATERIAN'S ALPACAS hung at the back.

"Does the alpaca have a name?" I asked the little woman who sat on a high stool in the booth.

She looked up from her knitting, smiling through a round face framed by dark hair. "This one is Baby. She's not a baby anymore, but she always reminds me of one. You can pet her if you want. She's quite docile."

I stroked the soft head, then glanced at the banner. "Shaterian's is your farm?"

"Yes." She stuffed the knitting in a bag hanging from a standing frame and stood, extending her hand. "I'm Ceci Shaterian. Alpaca tender, spinner, weaver, and maker of fine knitted objects."

"Nice to meet you, Ceci. My name's Robbie. I lived here when I was younger, but now I'm in Indiana. I'm back on a visit." We shook hands. She was probably no more than a decade older than me, with eyes almost as dark as her hair.

"Must be a lot colder back there at this time of year," she said.

"Absolutely. I'm loving not wearing a coat or hat in February." I was wearing jeans today, since the morning had been cool, but shorts or skirts and sandals had been my uniform since I'd arrived. "Where do you raise these beauties?"

"Up in the foothills, on the way to Solvang. We have a small ranch, my husband and me." A shadow passed over her expression. "We'd been in Oxnard for years, but had to move last January."

She must be the alpaca farmer Paul had mentioned. "It's nice where you are, though." I gestured vaguely toward the mountains. Solvang was a quaint tourist town settled in 1911 by Danes hoping to escape the harsh midwestern winters. Much of the architecture was the frilly Nordic decor you'd expect to see in northern Europe, not the adobe practical in the dry highlands of the northern edge of southern California.

"It is lovely, and we're making the most of it. My husband has started to plant grapes, too, and we've gone a hundred percent organic. We're taking the long view." She gazed at the wool. "Do you knit?"

I laughed. "No, never learned. I might get some of these mittens, though. For when I go home."

"They're quite warm, and not itchy at all, like sheep's wool can be."

"Perfect. My aunt raises sheep in Indiana, but somehow her yarn isn't itchy, either." I set down my nearly full cloth bag and bent over the table where the mittens were arrayed. I could get a pair for myself as a souvenir, and one for Abe, too. Heck, I might as well bring home pairs for my coworkers and Abe's son while I was at it. Adele wouldn't mind. She made hats for sale from her own wool but not mittens.

"Your aunt's animals might be a variety with a lot of lanolin in their wool," Ceci said.

"Patronizing the locals, are you, Robbie?" Katherine's voice sounded from behind me.

The "witch" herself. I turned. "Hi, Katherine. Yes, why not? Believe me, we don't have outdoor farmers' markets in the winter where I live. I'm loving all of this."

"Ceci, how are you?" Katherine asked in a casual tone.

When Ceci didn't answer, I glanced at her. She'd set her fists on her hips and glared at Katherine.

"I am fine." She nearly spit out the words. "And you can tell your father as much." Ceci turned her back and fiddled with a sweater draped on a hanger.

Katherine gave me a look signifying, *What's up with her?* "See you, girls," she said, and disappeared around the end of the row.

"Is she gone?" Ceci asked in a mutter without turning.

"She is."

The farmer faced me, blowing out a breath. "The Russom family is as toxic as the chemicals they make."

I watched her. "Agrosafe?"

"Yes, bloody Agro-dangerous." She petted the alpaca with a trembling hand. "Baby, here, she nearly died when the neighboring strawberry farmer in Oxnard sprayed his fields with the 'new and improved' chemical Russom pushes to anyone who will listen. Anyone with money, that is." She wiped her forehead. "It's why we had to move. We took a huge loss, too."

"I'm so sorry to hear that. Did you try to sue the company?"

"They have the big bucks to pay ruthless lawyers. We'd have to prove that nothing else could have made our animals sick. We'd never win." She shook her head. "That man—and his daughter—ought to be shot. Or drawn and quartered. At the very least, imprisoned for the rest of their mortal lives."

Chapter 23

After I paid Ceci for five pairs of mittens, she handed me one of her cards.

"Come on up and visit the farm while you're in town if you want, Robbie. Lots more where she came from"—she lifted her chin toward Baby—"and it's a real pretty site."

"Thanks, Ceci. I'd love to. You know, earlier this week I heard about an olive ranch also being affected by the Agrosafe product being sprayed onto a new strawberry farm nearby."

"I know those folks. It's tough. They can't move their trees like I moved my animals." She shook her head. "That company is criminal, that's what it is."

I said good-bye and strolled on, still on the hunt for organic strawberries. I didn't blame Ceci for feeling strongly about Agrosafe—and the people who ran it. Except, as far as I knew, Katherine didn't work for the company. She'd said she was a wedding planner. Maybe when your father is in charge you can't help but be involved. Or maybe something more was going on.

The kid at Agrosafe had said Walter was the president. Had he founded the company, too, or been brought in to run the business by its board of directors? Surely such information was in the public domain somewhere. No, it was a privately held company, but maybe there were news articles about the firm.

I paused at an organic farm's tent where pint boxes of plump, deep red strawberries advertised deliciousness.

"Sample?" the farmer asked. At the local summer market I always bought my June strawberries from an Amish organic farmer. This one also wore suspenders and a flat-brimmed hat, but his was straw and the T-shirt under his suspenders read, *Figueroa Mountain Brewing.* Definitely not Amish. He extended a round tray with hulled berries each speared with a toothpick, most likely to keep customers' fingers from touching the other samples.

"Thanks." I bit off half the berry, savoring the sweetness, the meaty juice, even the tiny seeds on the outside that invariably got stuck in my molars. I popped in the rest, tossing the toothpick into a little basket filled with other pink-tinged slivers of wood. I wanted to buy a flat of berries, but such a purchase would be silly, I thought. Still, it was only Wednesday. "I'd like two pints, please." I easily could finish two boxes before Saturday, considering the first might not make it back to my room.

He slid the containers' contents into two paper bags and handed them over. "These are the earliest variety around here, but they're fully as sweet as the April berries."

"I live in Indiana. We don't get local strawberries until June." I glanced again at the national organic certification label on his sign. "I've been hearing about issues with fumigant spray drift from farmers who use Agrosafe's products. Is spray a problem for your farm?"

"Luckily not. We're a small farm in the hills. I have a buffer zone of a dozen miles from the nearest conventional farm. Which is good, because Agrosafe makes some bad sh—" He cleared his throat. "Uh, stuff."

"I've heard." I thanked him. I stashed the berries, paid up, and strolled on, my stomach eager for a tamale. I couldn't carry much more, anyway.

The last booth before Mama Tamale occupied twice as much space as most of the others. No banner hung from the back wall, so I couldn't tell if the produce was organic or conventional, or even what the farm's name was. Two women wearing red aprons who looked like they might be of Hmong heritage were busy selling every vegetable and fruit grown in the state, from the looks of it. The universal farmers' market rule was everything sold had to be grown or made on the farm. The variety of things in this booth made me wonder if they followed the guideline. Could one farm really manage to grow all these fruits, from citrus to melons to pears to peaches? Pears and peaches were not in season in February, unlike citrus. If these had come out of storage, they wouldn't be very good. I gave a mental shrug. Policing farms was up to the market manager, not me.

A lean woman with a lined face and a ponytail hanging down her back also wore a red apron. She wasn't interacting with the public. Instead she scurried around, making sure the displays were full, checking on the employees, bringing them a new supply of bags when one ran out. Both employees were helping customers at the other end. I was fingering the carrots when the lean woman approached.

"They'll fill bags for you. This isn't a self-service stand." Her tone was clipped and fast.

"I didn't know." I extended my hand. "Hi, I'm Robbie. I'm a chef visiting from Indiana."

She regarded me for a moment, then shook my hand with a firm, dry grip. "Welcome."

"Thanks. Where's your farm?"

"Outside Bakersfield."

"You have a long drive." It had to be at least two hours from there to here. I gestured around. "You have quite the variety. You grow all this on the farm?"

She nodded once. "Of course. It's the rule."

A reedy voice spoke from behind me. "Good morning to one of my favorite customers."

The woman smiled at the speaker. I twisted to see Walter Russom clasping the woman's hand and pumping it. He had the same silver hair I'd seen in his photograph and through his office window, but today he wore farmers' market casual, a yellow polo and khakis with sockless dock shoes.

"How are you, Mr. Russom?" the farmer asked.

"Fine, fine. My daughter and I are picking up some produce, and where else to shop but right here?"

Katherine sidled up next to him. Her smile for the

farmer ebbed when she saw me. "Still shopping, Robbie?"

"I'm almost done. This is your father?" I smiled at him, extending my hand again. "I'm Robbie Jordan. Katherine and I went to high school together."

He shook my hand. "Walter Russom. Any friend of Katherine's is a friend of mine."

"I wouldn't go that far, Daddy," Katherine muttered.

A big man in sunglasses and a dark shirt stood at the edge of the booth, hands loose at his sides. He sure didn't look like someone out to pick up a bag of locally grown produce.

The farmer stared at me. "Jordan? Any relation to Jeanine?"

"She was my mother."

"That woman nearly ruined my life," she spat out. "I know you're not supposed to speak ill of the dead, but . . ." She clamped her mouth shut and turned away, shaking her head.

But what? I swallowed. "Nice meeting you, sir. See you, Katherine." I hurried out into the fresh air of the crowded aisle. Anywhere to escape the toxicity I'd waded into.

As I waited in line at Mama Tamale, I snuck a glance out of the corner of my eye back at the farm's double-wide stand. Walter Russom's narrow-eyed gaze at me was icy enough to send a shiver down my spine.

Chapter 24

I plopped down on a bench on the sidewalk across from the market with my tamale and my bag. The tamale, the size of three decks of cards stacked up, was served in a cardboard basket. I unfolded the corn husk it had been steamed in and used the compostable bamboo fork they'd given me to scrape some of the medium-hot red sauce I'd requested off the husk onto the soft masa surrounding the filling.

The first forkful was all I'd been expecting and more. The masa was tender and warm, firm enough from the steaming to hold its shape without becoming hard. The dark shredded beef filling had exactly the right amount of cumin and chili powder. The sauce left an afterbite but didn't kill my taste buds.

My encounters with the humans at the market? Not so satisfying. Why had Walter given me a cold look? What could Mom possibly have done to wrong a farmer from Bakersfield? Ceci's accusation of financial near ruin because of the fumigant was particularly unsettling, too.

I sniffed smoke on the air and glanced around. I didn't hear sirens, so the fire must not be right here in town. I tried to spy the mountains, but trees blocked my view from here. The wildfire must be spreading. I savored the last bites of tamale, then pulled out my phone. I wrinkled my nose at what I read. The Cachuma fire was moving fast in the area of the reservoir by that name in the Los Padres National Forest up in the mountains. Alana and I had gone to Girl Scout camp for a couple of summers in the area, swimming and canoeing in Lake Cachuma. Rainfall this winter had been minimal, and these coastal mountains never got a heavy snowpack, unlike the higher-elevation Sierras. The winter rains that formerly protected against the dry vegetation often didn't come anymore. I was lucky not to have asthma, but those who did truly suffered when the air was filled with drifting smoke.

Checking my e-mail made my heart beat a little faster. Mel Washington had written. Had she found Mom's report? I stabbed open the message but swore under my breath when the only thing it said was to call her. I checked my texts. Sure enough, she'd texted me asking the same.

When I called, it went to her voice mail. I didn't leave a message, instead texting back.

Did you find something? Tried calling but you didn't pick up. Call me back any time. Thx.

Now what? I wished I'd gotten the name of the conventional farmer who was so buddy-buddy with Walter Russom. The one who'd said Mom had nearly ruined her. The name of the farm hadn't been posted. At this point I wasn't interested in going back and asking. I checked my e-mail again. Nothing from Adele had come in, either.

I didn't know what to do next. I felt desperate to find out what had really happened to my mom, and to Paul, too. Back home I could have asked Lieutenant Buck Bird, my friend and local police contact. Back home I overheard snippets in my restaurant. Back home I . . . I blew out a breath. I wasn't back home. I was here. I stood, resolved to drive back to Carmen's, get the bike, and take myself for a really hard ride. The heck with wildfire smoke. I just wouldn't go up into the foothills. There was plenty of coast to ride along.

Maybe I'd head over to Montecito and pay homage to the late Sue Grafton's home. I'd grown up reading her mysteries. How could I not? They were essentially set right here. My mom had bought each new one as soon as they came out. I read through all the existing books when I was eleven, but I'd had to wait to dive into each new one until after Mom had finished it. The situation had reversed itself every time a new Harry Potter book came out. I hadn't let her get her hands on it until I'd read it twice.

I needed a long ride to clear and sort my brain, and I needed it now. At home I might have pulled out my graph paper, ruler, and pencil, and created a crossword about the case—or cases—to organize my thoughts. Here I didn't have those supplies, and I was antsy. A hard ride would fix that.

I'd left my rental car in the municipal lot. When I was nearly at the little red Toyota, I slowed. Katherine stood, fists on hips, talking to someone through the open driver's window of a silver Lexus. She didn't look happy. I bent down a little to see through the passenger window, then straightened. Walter sat in the driver's seat. Katherine threw a hand in the air with an angry gesture, or maybe it stemmed from frustration. I couldn't tell which.

A woman with impeccably streaked hair brushed by me, nearly colliding with the flowers sticking out of one of my bags. Katherine's face hardened at the sight of the woman sliding into the passenger seat of Walter's car. The car took off. I pointed myself at Katherine. She might want a friendly face right about now. It was worth a try.

"Katherine, would you look at this." I mustered a cheery tone as I approached. "Three times in one morning. Want to go for a coffee, catch up on old times?"

She'd been gazing after the car, but whipped her head around to look at me. "Are you following me, Robbie?"

"Not at all. I'm parked right there." I pointed at my economy rental. "I was headed back to my B-and-B, but I don't have anywhere in particular I have to be."

"Coffee, hmm. What I could use is a drink." She raised her chin, as if challenging me to say it was too early. "You game?"

"Hey, ten thirty is five thirty somewhere." So much for my bike ride, but drinking with Katherine could prove a lot more fruitful, information-wise.

She barked out a laugh. "My favorite words. Follow me."

Chapter 25

Katherine and I sat on the courtyard patio of the Mission Hotel. The ubiquitous bougainvillea crawled tenaciously over a trellis, while a little fountain burbled in the corner. The stucco walls featured inset arches reminiscent of the mission itself and were topped with curved red tiles.

A waiter, an older gentleman with a full head of white-streaked dark hair, appeared and set down two thick green-rimmed glasses of water. "What would you ladies like to drink this morning?"

I jumped in. "I'd like a mimosa, please." I figured the OJ in my drink, which the menu claimed was fresh-squeezed, was good for me. Sipping it slowly would keep me as alert as possible.

"A bloody Mary for me." Katherine omitted the "please." "And double the vodka in it."

"Very good." He disappeared through the door to the building.

Katherine drew an expertly manicured finger

through the condensation on her water glass and didn't speak.

I broke the silence. "Was that your dad's wife who got into the car?"

"No. It's his girlfriend, if people in their fifties can even be called girls. They've been an item for about six months."

"You didn't appear to like her much, back there at the car."

"I don't."

"What's her name?" I asked.

"Her name's Sydelle Moore, and she has deep pockets."

"Meaning . . . ?"

"Meaning she's rich and is an angel investor in my father's company. Sydelle is the furthest thing from an angel I can imagine."

I opened my mouth to say I'd met a Tommy Moore. I shut it when I realized she might ask me where. I hung a conversational right turn in a hurry. I'd asked too much about her father's lady friend as it was. "So how did you get into the wedding planning business?"

"I like to run things." She glanced up as if checking whether I was agreeing with her.

"That sounds familiar." I softened my agreement with a smile. Her Chumash student ID might as well have read "Controlling Kate."

"Some have called me bossy. But hey, if people want to pay me to manage their biggest life event, we're all good. I majored in business at UCSB with a design minor, so this line of work is kind of a no-brainer."

"I didn't know you were interested in studying business." I tried to hide my surprise. She hadn't struck me in high school as B-school material. Good for her for following her own talents. Exactly what I had done. Different talents, of course, but here we were, both independent business owners.

The waiter brought our drinks. "Can I get you ladies a bite of brunch this morning? We have our signature Mission Benedict, salmon-stuffed French toast, and fresh-baked apricot turnovers, among other offerings."

"It all sounds wonderful, but not for me, thanks," I said. The tamale I'd consumed with great enthusiasm was going to last me for a while.

Katherine shook her head. "I'm all set."

"Very good." He cleared his throat. "Ms. Russom, isn't it?"

She glanced sharply up at him. "Yes. Do I know you?"

"You ran the last wedding we hosted. I was lead waiter."

"Ah, yes. Good to see you again."

He turned away, but moved to each of the other tables in the courtyard, straightening silverware and adjusting chairs. Katherine had her back to him. From my vantage point, I could swear he was listening to us. Maybe Katherine had been rude to him during the wedding. Or had complained about him, neither of which I would put it past her to do. I mentally shrugged. Not my problem.

I lifted my glass. "Cheers."

Katherine clinked hers with mine and took a long drag before she set it down.

"So do you get a lot of wedding business?" I asked.

"I bet there are tons of brides and their moms who want someone to organize and run their big day."

"You bet. I recently hired a second employee to help. The city has become a wedding destination, especially at this time of year. The tourist bureau calls Santa Barbara the American Riviera."

"They do? Seems kind of exaggerated."

"You think?" she scoffed. "But, whatever. It's a fine slogan if it brings brides and their daddies' wallets. Paying my bills is all I care about."

"Well, here's to another ten years of success." I lifted my stemmed glass.

"Thank you." She clinked briefly, then took a hefty swallow of her drink, holding the stalk of celery to the side. "Now that's more like it." Her shoulders, clad in a pale turquoise shirt, dipped as if finally relaxed.

A smoky breeze blew through and I coughed. The waiter finally went into the building.

"I read that the wildfire in the mountains keeps growing," I said.

"Yeah. Gets worse every year, too. You escaped all the fires and earthquakes by moving east, didn't you?"

"I guess. We get tornadoes, though, and sometimes blizzards. Although we don't have as much snow anymore, with climate change. I'm on the southern edge of the Midwest." I took another sip. "This is nice. And the juice is fresh-squeezed."

"It should be. We're in full orange season right now."

"I know. Mom and I had a tree in the backyard growing up. I don't think I drank OJ out of a bottle until I moved to Indiana. Even in college I would bring back a bag of oranges from home." I still loved the scent of orange blossoms more than almost anything. That and the aroma of gardenias. A four-foot-high gardenia bush had grown outside my bedroom window.

"We still have a grapefruit tree, and a big lemon tree, too," she said with a wistful smile. "My mom planted them when I was a baby. She's been gone twenty years this month."

I brought my hand to my mouth. I'd forgotten her mom had died when we were in elementary school. We had being motherless in common now. "You and your father must be close."

She nodded. "Most of the time. At least since he got rid of the wicked stepmother."

"He remarried?" It must have been in the last ten years. I didn't think she'd had a mom figure around in high school.

"Yes. It didn't go well. He kind of needs taking care of, but not from her."

"Who was she?"

"Only the poster child for a second wife who wants nothing to do with hubby's children, and wants said hubby to take care of her, not the other way around. The day of their divorce was my happiest in years." She rolled her eyes. "Although now he's seeing Sydelle. I'm not sure she's much better, frankly, but at least I'm older."

"It looked like you were having a fight with your father back there outside the market." I tilted my head, mustering a sympathetic expression.

She turned down the corners of her mouth. "He

can be totally bullheaded. Especially when it comes to my brother."

"Cody waited on me at Boathouse the other night. Last time I saw him he was a bratty little kid."

"He still can be, believe me. But yeah, he's all grown up now." She smiled, more to herself than to me. "And seems to have inherited Daddy's stubborn genes."

"So what does your dad do for work?"

She blinked. "I thought you knew."

Uh-oh. Had she heard I'd been asking around about Agrosafe's products? I waited, looking curious. A friend had somewhere obtained a mouse pad from the CIA, with guidelines for agents. "Neither deny nor confirm," was the first instruction. Useful advice for life.

"He's the president of Agrosafe," Katherine said. "Making Agricultural Chemicals Safe for Farmers is their motto."

"Are you part of the business?"

"Me? No way." She drained her glass. "Man, that went down easy."

I cocked my head. "What did you mean at the reunion, that you hadn't forgiven me? For what?"

"Never mind." She swept a strand of hair back. "It doesn't matter anymore."

Oh, well. It was probably about me dating Bill. It definitely didn't matter anymore.

She gazed at the door to the inside.

Wishing the waiter would reappear so she could order another drink? My mimosa was barely a third gone.

She looked back at me. "Somebody told me you do undercover investigations these days. Like a private detective. You channeling Kinsey Millhone or something?"

"Of course not." I shook my head. "A couple of bodies have shown up back where I live in the last year or two. I've kind of gotten involved in the homicide investigations, but only to help the police. I run a restaurant, a country store, and a B-and-B. I have my hands full." A scrub jay lit on top of the wall, its azure feathers brilliant in the sunlight.

"Of course." She watched the jay. "I just wondered, because you seem to be asking a lot of questions for somebody simply out here on vacation."

"I'm trying to track down what really happened to my mom. That's all." The bird sat hunched over, intent. Its raspy, questioning *chee* seemed like a warning, as if it was cautioning me to be careful. Not the first to do so this week.

"Right." Katherine drew out the word as if she didn't believe me.

The jay, its blue tail a thing of beauty, regarded me out of a beady black eye, like it might not believe me, either.

Chapter 26

Katherine and I ran out of things to say to each other by eleven thirty. Despite her four vodkas, she said she had to get to work. I wandered around downtown at loose ends for a while. I had nothing I really needed to shop for, and I'd decided to order those heavy glasses online so I wouldn't have to haul them home in my suitcase. I supposed I could check out the historical museum, but it was some blocks away.

On a whim I texted Liz.

Send me Paul's apartment address?

I hit Send. I knew I should probably leave talking with Paul's neighbors to the police, but it couldn't hurt to go have a look at the neighborhood.

Liz's response, the address and nothing more, came back in moments. I stared at the message. Paul's place was a couple of blocks from the house I'd grown up in, which I'd sold after Mom died. Could I handle going by for a peek on the way to Paul's? What if the new owners had cut down the gardenia, with its lovely waxy white blossoms, and the orange trees? Suppose they'd done some ugly remodel to the sweet bungalow I'd shared with Mom the entire time I lived in California? I shook my head. I needed to see the house and put it behind me, no matter its current state.

Ten minutes later I turned onto Golden West Street. The neighborhood was a quiet one of modest two- and three-bedroom cottages built right after World War II. Some were of stucco, some wood-framed, all with wide, shaded front porches that would have looked at home back in Brown County. A few houses now had had second floors added, or a monstrous addition in the back. Many remained as I remembered, with tidy front yards and eucalyptus and sycamore trees shading the properties.

I rolled slowly by, braking to a stop opposite number 5031. I let out a breath. The shingled cottage with its peaked roof and porch overhang looked as I remembered it, unaltered structurally. The front lawn, though, had been dug up and replaced with native cacti and other plants that could survive on little water. Colorful small figures were tucked in here and there. A foot-tall red-and-white mushroom. A blue-and-yellow roadrunner. An orange grinning fish with black stripes. A gnome wearing a serape. And several fanciful wire creations, including one of a person on a bike and one of a humpbacked Kokopeli dancer blowing its flute. The breeze through a set of wooden wind chimes hanging from the porch played rich, resonant sounds like a marimba. Two small bikes had been dropped in the driveway.

Inching the car farther a few yards, I peered into the side yard, smiling when I saw the shiny green of the gardenia bush next to the window and a few splotches of orange against dark green leaves in the backyard. All was well with my old house. I approved of the xeriscaping in the front. From all appearances, the house had a family living in it who was benefiting from the scents and the fruits. I could move on.

Paul's address was a two-story house on Santa Catalina. The building looked a century old, with ornate woodwork, a wraparound covered front porch, and big windows. Even if I hadn't seen the four mailboxes on the front porch and four gas meters on the side, I would have said it was a rental property. The clapboards hadn't been painted in a long time, and some of the trim was either rotting or missing, which was a shame on a historic building. At least nobody had cut down a big old camellia bush, which was covered with fat pink blooms. Nope, I wasn't in Indiana, where nothing would bloom until at least April.

I parked across the street. On the porch I peered at the names on the mailboxes. Apartment 1B, which bore Paul's name, also had *Grace Fujiyama* neatly printed on the same small white rectangle. His roommate, obviously. Also a girlfriend? I hadn't heard about him having a sweetheart, but I'd barely known him. Units 1A and 2A appeared to be occupied by single men, 2B by a woman.

I pressed the doorbell with Paul's name on it. Two minutes later with no answer, I pressed 1A. *Nada.* I also tried 2A, also zilch. But 2B was actually home. Someone clattered down the stairs inside and pulled open the front door. A woman wearing an oversized shirt covered with paint smears in all colors raised light eyebrows, a smudge of blue on her cheek.

"You're not UPS," she said.

I laughed. "No, I'm not." I pulled out the slightly shaky story I'd come up with. "I'm investigating your neighbor Paul's death, though. I wonder what you can tell me about any visitors he had on Tuesday."

Her mouth pulled down. "Poor Paul. But . . . investigating?" Her voice went up. "I thought they said he simply died. What's there to investigate?" She peered at me as if the answer might be written on my person somewhere.

"His family asked me to look into it. To make sure his was a natural death, as they say." I smiled politely.

"Taylor did?"

Taylor must be a relative, maybe a brother. I waited without responding for her to go on. I couldn't very well ask who Taylor was.

"Huh," the woman said. "Anyway, I'm afraid I can't tell you a thing. I was busy painting, and my studio faces the back. I get in the creative zone and I don't even hear voices, doorbells, nothing. You're lucky I was fixing coffee just now or I wouldn't have known you were here."

"I see. Well, thank you. Enjoy your art making."

She grinned. "You can count on it. I could no more not paint than not breathe." The door clicked shut. I looked to either side. Was it worth knocking on neighbors' doors? To the right was a screen of high, thorny pyracantha shrubs between the houses, the bushes covered in the bright red berries that gave the plant its common name of firethorn. To the left every blind and drapery was drawn tight and the house had an unoccupied look to it. Strike two. I supposed I could ask across the street.

I trudged down the steps onto the front walk and was halfway to the road when I glanced to my left. A woman walked briskly toward me on the sidewalk carrying two heavily laden cloth bags. One had a baguette poking out the top and the other a dark green bunch of frilly kale. She wore tennies with calf-length yoga pants and moved with the easy grace of an athlete. I paused when she turned up the walk. Was she Paul's housemate? Would she speak to me? Or maybe she was visiting one of the other apartments and had nothing to do with Paul.

"Grace?" I asked.

She wrinkled her nose, pushing black-rimmed glasses up the bridge. "Yes. Do I know you?" She had a Japanese surname, but her Asian ancestry looked a couple of generations removed.

"I'm Robbie Jordan. I'm looking into Paul's death and wondered if we could talk for a moment."

The color drained from her face. She glanced away, then back at me. "What do you mean, you're looking into it?"

"Could we sit for a little bit? I can explain." I pointed to the two rockers and the hanging swing on the porch.

She nodded and I followed her up there. She set down the bags and plopped heavily into the farther rocking chair. I perched on the swing at the end at right angles to her.

I cleared my throat. "I met Paul on Sunday. My mother, who died two years ago, used to be in the same group as him."

"The anti-agrochemical group." She pulled up her knees and wrapped her arms around them.

"Yes. Paul said he thought maybe Mom was killed because of her activism. I live in Indiana now, but I'm out here for a visit. What he said shocked me, of course, and I've been trying to get at the truth."

"Have you learned anything?" She tilted her head, looking more normal again.

"Not yet. The pathologist in the coroner's office is trying to find my mom's autopsy report. At the time they said she died of a ruptured aneurysm."

"What does her cause of death have to do with Paul?"

"May I ask, were you more than roommates?"

"We were good friends," Grace said. "And I . . . I was the one who found him. I called 911, of course, but it was too late." She swiped at her eye.

"I'm so sorry. Nobody should have to die alone. My mom did, too."

"He was just lying there. Cold. It was awful." She shuddered.

"It must have been." I shook my head and reached over to pat her knee. "Did the police come?"

She studied her hands. A bird rustled in the middle of the long, narrow leaves of the oleander bush beyond the porch. It was a lethally poisonous plant, despite its beauty when in bloom. A lawn mower engine roared to life somewhere on the block.

Grace looked up at me. "They did, with their blue gloves and their evidence bags. I kept asking what they were looking for, but they told me to wait here on the porch. A detective came out and asked me a million questions. I'd been teaching yoga in Goleta all morning. I didn't see anybody or hear a thing before I left. I don't think I helped the dude at all."

"Where do you teach?"

"Pause Yoga. It's my studio." She frowned. "I didn't know when Paul had come home, what he'd eaten, anything. Of course I told them about his environmental activism and his complete hatred for Agrosafe."

"Of course. Did you see what they took out of the apartment?"

"His laptop. His pack. And his lunch container. That part seemed odd."

"A takeout box?"

"Sort of. It was like one of those divided Styrofoam takeout boxes except it was glass, with a tight-fitting lid. He refused to have anything to do with containers that weren't reusable, even though it was heavy to carry on his bike. His arrangement with the Green Artichoke was he could always take home a meal when he left work. I guess they thought it made up for his low pay."

And the police wanted to check the container for poison residue. *Good.*

"They took some of the oleander leaves, too." She pointed to the big shrub at the end of the porch.

I knew how toxic oleander was. When I was in high school a child had chewed on one of the long, pointed leaves while playing alone and had died of the poison. The detective must be trying to cover all his bases.

Grace gave me an intent look. "Robbie, do you think someone killed him? There was no blood or wound or anything. It looked like he'd had a heart attack or something and fell down dead."

Exactly like Mom. "I don't know. I do have an old

friend who works in the police department. I can see if he knows anything."

"Will you let me know if you hear?" she asked. "Tell me your number. I'll text you so you'll have mine."

I read off my number to her. She tapped into her phone, and I heard the *bing* of an incoming text on mine.

"There," Grace said. "You know, Paul was a really nice guy, but he was kind of a fanatic. I wouldn't be surprised if he had a lot of people angry at him."

"I guess it comes with the territory when you feel strongly about a cause."

"I guess." She studied her hands. "Thanks for coming by. I feel so lost."

I stood and held out my hand. "I truly know the feeling, Grace. I wish we'd met under happier circumstances."

She rose and shook my hand. "Me, too."

"I'll be in touch if I hear anything. I'm going back home Saturday, but I'm hoping for information before then."

"Good."

I turned before I crossed the street. Grace had picked up her bags and had her hand on the door handle.

"You have a great farmers' market here," I called.

She smiled. "I know."

I waved and headed for the car, my fingers itching to text Jason and see what he knew.

Chapter 27

"I so needed this," I said to Alana at two that afternoon. She'd messaged me earlier when I was still nursing my mimosa with Katherine, asking me about going for a walk later. After my visit with Grace, I'd stopped back by my room to drop off my purchases and give the artichokes to Carmen to use however she wanted. As predicted, I'd already made my way through one box of strawberries. I'd texted Jason but hadn't heard back.

Now our bare feet crunched briskly through the sand at Hendry's Beach, our shorts and T-shirts a far cry from winter wear in the Midwest.

"Me, too," Alana agreed. "When I'm at home working, I rarely make time to get to the coast. Plus, from Berkeley it's a hike to get to a walkable beach."

"Remember when we came here on that double date our junior year?"

She groaned. "With those twins, Whoosit and What's His Name? That was a disaster and a half."

"No kidding." I snorted. "They wanted to go on a moonlight walk with us."

"The blond one kept trying to lag behind with me and cop a kiss."

"And you finally linked arms with me so he couldn't." I laughed. "Boys who thought they could outsmart us got wise quick."

"I'll say. So what did you get up to today?" she asked.

"I was going to go for a long bike ride, but I got waylaid by Katherine Russom."

She glanced over at me. "Waylaid?"

"Actually, I saw her at the farmers' market this morning and ended up asking if she wanted to get a coffee. She suggested a drink, instead."

"In the morning. I'm guessing you went along with it."

I laughed. "It was ten thirty and I nursed a mimosa very slowly. She had the equivalent of four bloody Marys before noon by the time we were done."

"Why did you extend the olive branch to her all of a sudden, Robbie?"

I walked on a few more steps, loving the sand between my toes, the salty Pacific breeze in my hair, the sandpipers trotting along the water's edge ahead of us. "I keep running across unsettling things this week, and it's only Wednesday. You heard Paul Etxgeberria died?"

"Wait. Who is Paul, again?"

"He was an anti-agrochemical activist who had worked with my mom. We saw him walking here with Katherine Monday when we were at Boathouse."

"Right," she said. "The guy she seemed to be fighting with."

"Exactly." I nodded. "So far he seems to have the same cause of death as Mom did. And everywhere I look, I get more confused."

"For example?" Alana made a rolling "please elaborate" motion with her hand.

"For example, at the farmers' market this morning, an alpaca farmer basically said Katherine's father had ruined their lives. She told me the drift from Agrosafe's sprays made her animals sick. She and her husband had to sell out at a loss and start over up in the hills."

"Ouch. Poor alpacas, too."

"No kidding. A little while later, I talked to a conventional produce farmer from Bakersfield who seemed very buddy-buddy with Walter Russom. When she heard my last name, she said my mother had nearly ruined *her* life, or something to that effect. Both times Katherine was part of the conversation."

"Aha!" She held up an index finger. "Exhibit one. Robbie befriends the villain for the sole purpose of getting information out of her."

"A girl's gotta try, right? Katherine was surprisingly receptive to hanging out with me for an hour or two."

"You mean, as long as alcohol was involved."

"Yeah, maybe." We walked on for another minute. "This week I also learned Zoe Stover is an addict. She washes dishes at the Green Artichoke, and Paul was a delivery person."

"Poor Zoe. Is it oxy?"

"Probably. Opiates, is what her mom said." I blew out a breath.

"That stuff's brutal. A guy who attends my temple up in Berkeley has been clean for a couple of years, but it's a real struggle for him."

"I just hope she doesn't get into heroin and run into fentanyl along with it."

"Really," Alana agreed.

"I also stopped by Paul's apartment a little earlier and talked to his roommate, Grace. She said the police took away the container he always uses to bring home his meal from the restaurant where he did bike delivery, the Green Artichoke."

Alana blinked. "To test it for poison?"

"That would be my guess. It looks like they're treating his death as a possible suspicious one."

"Murder?" Alana gave me a horrified look.

"Maybe."

We walked in silence for a couple of minutes. Two lean, tanned men ran toward us, shirts tucked into the back of their shorts. Several wet-suited surfers floated astride their boards waiting for a good wave. Under a striped umbrella a white-haired woman sat in a low folding chair reading a hardcover novel while her husband did a crossword next to her. I scolded myself for not doing the same so far this week. I was in California in February. I should be on the beach working harmless puzzles instead of trying to solve a real one.

"Did you know Katherine had a stepmom for a few years?" I asked Alana. "It was after we graduated."

"I did know. My mom worked with her on some

charity board or something." Alana tapped her fore-head with her index finger. "Mom said she's a nut-case, but a very smart nutcase. She apparently soaked Mr. Russom for a lot in the divorce."

"Huh." I watched a pelican plunge nose first into the water. It surfaced with the pouch under its beak full with seawater and a wriggling fish. "I wonder . . ."

"What?"

"Maybe Katherine's dad is hurting for money. He wouldn't be able to afford a court case against his fu-migant."

"So he has to kill off the opposition?" Alana's light green eyes went wide under her black-and-orange Gi-ants cap with the intertwined *SF* on the front.

"Your guess is as good as mine. The question is, was Katherine helping her father? Did she try—un-successfully—to dissuade him and is now trying to cover up his crimes? Protect him?"

"Or is she the killer?" Alana elbowed me. "You bet-ter be careful, girlfriend. You don't want to mess with somebody like Katherine. She's never been long on scruples."

"I promise."

Chapter 28

After our walk, Alana and I agreed a late lunch at Boathouse was exactly what we needed. It was for me, anyway, as my hearty tamale was a long-ago memory by now. We settled into a table on the patio again. A young woman brought us menus and said our wait-person would be right with us. We were the only diners out here.

"I wonder if Cody is working this afternoon," I said.

"So you can grill him about his father?" Alana lifted her pale eyebrows.

"Maybe. Not grill, exactly." I picked up the menu. "Ooh, I didn't see this the other day. Chicken mole nachos." I pronounced the name of the rich sauce the Spanish way, *MOE-lay*.

"Sounds delish." She giggled. "I remember the first time I read it on a menu. I had to be all of six, and I wondered what a chicken mole was. Some kind of underground rodent with feathers?"

We'd both been big readers as kids. "I know what

you mean. I read *Ali Baba and the Forty Thieves* and had no idea why he was calling the door a see-same. Mom hadn't read it aloud to me and that was how I sounded out *sesame.*"

A gull squawked, hovering above the glass wall as if it wanted to perch. The restaurant had strung a wire above the wall adorned with colored metallic streamers. The bird had nowhere to land. Smart move. And the wall looked festive, too.

"Speaking of Cody." Alana pointed.

He hurried into the patio from the parking lot and rushed toward the restaurant, not even glancing at us.

"Somebody must be late for work," I said.

"I guess. Maybe he just came from class." She perused the menu. "I'm going for California fish chowder and more of those truffle fries. Plus a pilsner."

"Sounds good." I checked my phone. *Rats.* Still nothing from Mel Washington.

"Why the frown?" Alana asked.

"Yesterday morning I met the county pathologist. She couldn't find the death report on my mom."

Alana eyed me for a moment. "And you want the report to learn if your mom was poisoned or not."

"Right. I want to find out if they did an autopsy at the time. If they did, I assume they would have detected toxins in her. Since they called her cause of death an aneurysm, I would accept it. But if they didn't perform an autopsy, well, then we don't know."

She nodded once. "So I made an appointment to talk with Katherine tomorrow afternoon about the work her company does."

"You would hire her to run your wedding?"

"Probably not, but I'd like to see what she offers. Will you come with me?"

"I'd love to. Tell me where and when."

She'd opened her mouth to speak when Cody approached us. *Bingo.*

"Back so soon, ladies?" Cody's shoulder-length hair was tied back at the nape of his neck, as it had been Monday, but today he looked less neat than he had then, and he didn't smile at us.

"Couldn't stay away." Alana smiled up at him.

"What can I get you today?" His pencil-holding hand over the order pad shook slightly.

"I'd like the mole nachos, please," I said. "I'm back here from where I live in Indiana, and believe me, you can't get mole anywhere there."

He smiled briefly. "Yeah, mole is pretty awesome. Where are you staying?"

"I have a room above the Nacho Average Café."

"Tell Carmen hi from me. I washed dishes for her in high school."

"I will." I glanced at the beer section of the menu. "I'd like a Vat 629 IPA, too." I heard a phone vibrate but it wasn't mine, and Alana didn't move to check hers, either. Must be his.

Cody's brows lowered. He jotted down my drink without meeting my gaze. After Alana gave him her order, he hurried off without speaking.

"Does he seem nervous or upset?" She watched him go. "Like he's not dealing with whatever."

"I'd say so. But why?"

"Think something came up with Daddy? Or with big sis?"

"No idea."

"I think we need to engage him in some serious conversation when he comes back. It's not like he has anything else to do out here."

I agreed. We chatted about Alana's work until Cody returned with our drinks.

Alana thanked him. "So Cody, what's your major at UCSB?"

He blinked and gave a little frown. "Um, double major in chemical engineering and computer science. Why?"

"Those are serious majors," she said in an approving tone. "I'm in biochem myself. Are you looking to go into business with your father after you graduate?"

"What?" He stared at her. "Are you kidding? I hate . . ." He gave a hard shake of his head. "Never mind."

"You don't approve of the products Agrosafe makes?" I tilted my head.

He gazed at me. "No, I don't." He glanced over at the restaurant's building.

"I heard the sprays can really make people—and animals—sick," I continued.

"Exactly." Cody shook his head, looking disgusted. "That poor lady's alpacas."

"You mean Ceci Shaterian," I said.

He did a double take. "Yes, but how did you know?"

"I met her this morning at the market."

"Yeah," he said. "She had to move her whole farm out of Oxnard."

Alana was watching him. "I heard there's a group working to ban the stuff from the county."

I blinked. She "heard" there was a group? She knew very well there was a group, because I'd told her.

Cody's eyes widened and he gave a quick nod. "I've been going to their meetings. We're getting close."

Interesting. A rebel in the family.

"Do you surf?" Alana asked. "You look like a wave rider."

A smile finally made its way onto his face. "Whenever I can." He gazed out at the waves.

A woman stuck her head out of the restaurant. "Russom?"

Cody cleared his throat. "Gotta go. I'll be back with your food, ladies."

Once he was gone, I leaned closer to Alana. "He's gone over to the enemy."

"Very much what it sounds like. Trying to ban his father's bread and butter. I wonder if Daddy knows."

I'd had the same thought. Or was Cody spying for Agrosafe? He'd sounded sincere in what he said. Could a twenty-year-old be such a good actor? Of course he could. People younger than twenty had won Oscars, after all.

Chapter 29

Mel Washington ushered me into her office at five thirty. "Thanks for coming so promptly." Today she wore a magenta knit top that popped against her skin, with dangling earrings to match.

"I was already out with my car when I got your message." My heart was racing faster than Lance Armstrong coasting down a French Alp. "Did you find the report?"

The pathologist stared at her computer screen, then swiveled to face me. "Yes. It turns out I was away at a professional conference the week your mother passed, and my colleague filed the report using a different naming system than mine. He did do an autopsy, Robbie." She paused, watching me. "It's the only way to determine a ruptured aneurysm as a cause certain of death."

I blinked, thinking. "So a ruptured aneurysm is definitely what killed my mother."

"Yes. There aren't any external signs. The brain

ceases functioning. If unattended, the person loses consciousness, falls down, and dies. I'm very sorry."

"Thank you." I studied my hands. The weight of wondering if she'd been murdered had only half lifted. "Mel, would it be possible for a fumigant to mimic a ruptured aneurysm, or cause one? And could someone like you or your colleague miss such a toxin in a person's system?"

She rocked a little in her chair as she thought. "A toxin like that might cause a brain bleed, for sure. I am not sure about this particular fumigant."

"And if it looked like a brain bleed, your colleague wouldn't have thought to go further with tests for the chemical."

"Pretty much." She tapped the phone she'd laid on the desk. "Now, I got your message about the man who was found deceased yesterday. I have a backlog of, um, corpses right now, but I will definitely perform an autopsy and run tox screens for what you mentioned when I get to his remains."

Remains. The word sounded so clinical. Like there were only little bits of Paul remaining. Certainly his soul was gone, his essence. But his body was intact. Wasn't it?

A thought occurred to me. "Don't the police want the autopsy done as soon as possible?"

Mel cocked her head. "Why would they? As far as they know, it was a natural death. Unless you've told them your poisoning theory?"

"I suggested it to Jason, and he said he would pass it along. He also told me he wasn't sure they'd really think it credible." I wrinkled my nose. "On the other hand, Paul's roommate told me the police took a few things away from their apartment, like his takeout meal container.

"Interesting. Well, to answer your question, no one has suggested putting a rush on Mr. Etxgeberria."

"Darn." I thought for a moment. "How the heck do you spell that, anyway?" I'd seen the name on his mailbox but hadn't memorized the spelling.

She tapped the keyboard for a few seconds, then said, "E-t-x-g-e-b-e-r-r-i-a."

"Can you text it to me, please?"

"Sure." She picked up her cell phone. Her desk phone rang. Her gaze went to the wall clock. "Robbie, I have some things to finish up before I can leave. Let me know if there's anything else I can help you with, all right?"

I stood and extended my hand. "Thank you, Mel, for being honest with me, and for hunting down my mom's report."

She shook my hand. "Of course. When do you leave?"

"Saturday morning."

"I won't be able to give you the results of the Etxgeberria autopsy, you realize, as you're not family. Even if we get it accomplished before you leave." Her eyebrows gathered in and she looked sorry to have to tell me.

"Sure." I was sorry to hear it, too, but I understood. By all appearances a woman with scruples, Mel worked for the sheriff and took her job seriously.

"Have a good rest of your week out here," she said. "I'm glad we got to meet."

I thanked her and made my way out, no wiser than when I went in, really. Sure, my mother had died of a ruptured aneurysm. But had poison caused it or not?

The smoky air had thickened and now stung my eyes. My brain felt thick, too, with a haze of unanswered questions.

Chapter 30

I sat in my car outside a downtown bank for a moment at six twenty that evening checking my email. Liz had shot me a text about a gathering, open to the public, with Walter Russom as featured speaker, to be held in the bank's meeting room. It was sponsored by the Greater Santa Barbara Chamber of Commerce. The advertised title was "Local Business Initiatives," whatever that meant. I didn't have anything else on my calendar and decided to hear what he had to say.

A black SUV pulled into a space a few yards away. A beefy dude wearing a dark shirt and khakis, his eyes hidden behind sunglasses even though the sun was gone, exited the driver's door and stood with his hand on the roof, scanning the lot. Walter emerged from the passenger door, and young Tommy from the Agrosafe lobby slid out from the back seat. A shorter version of the driver appeared, too, in a similar uniform, right down to the shades. He hurried to the bank's door and held it open for Walter and Tommy. Walter had a personal driver now? Or two bodyguards, from the looks of it. *Right*. I recognized the bigger one from the farmers' market, and I'd seen both of them in the news report about the protesters in front of the Agrosafe building. Was Walter feeling threatened or was he just paranoid?

The shirts gave one more glance around, then entered the bank. I waited a minute before following them in and took a seat on the side aisle of a big meeting room. The dudes had taken up positions standing in the back corners of the room.

Most of the rest of the audience wore suits and professional clothes, looking exactly like Chamber of Commerce members. I felt distinctly underdressed in my jeans and sweater. At least I hadn't ridden my bike, so I wasn't also sweaty and toting a helmet. Walter stood at the front of the room to the side while a woman in a pale green linen pantsuit and heels fiddled with the microphone. Tommy helped her. He'd added a tie to his button-down for this evening's event.

Someone approached in the aisle at my left.

"Is the seat next to you taken?"

I glanced up to see Ceci Shaterian pointing to the empty chair. "No. Help yourself." I angled my knees so she could slide in. She hadn't seemed to recognize me, but then she talked to dozens of shoppers at the market, while she was the only alpaca farmer I'd met.

When she was settled, I extended my hand. "Hi, Ceci. We met at the market this morning. I'm Robbie Jordan."

"Ah, yes. Hi, Robbie." She shook my hand enthusiastically and smiled. "From Indiana." She pulled a knitting project using variegated yarn in the colors of the rainbow from her bag and started to click softly.

"You have a good memory. But I thought you hated this guy." I gestured toward the front. "Why are you here?"

She gave a sardonic half-smile. "It's always good to keep up with the enemy." She knitted a few more stitches. "Robbie, I was serious. You should come visit the farm. I think you'd like it."

"Thank you for the invitation. I'll see if I can stop by tomorrow."

"Perfect."

Linen Suit tapped the mic. "Good evening, everyone. Let's get started."

The woman introduced herself as the chairperson of the Chamber. "I'm glad to see so many here tonight. Everyone is welcome to join us for refreshments after the presentation. I think most of you know our speaker. For those who don't, I'm delighted to present Agrosafe president Walter Russom in our ongoing lecture series about local initiatives. Let's give him a big Santa Barbara welcome." She stepped back and clapped politely.

The audience joined in, but the sound was not rousing. As I glanced around, I noticed more than one businessperson not applauding at all. Less than well loved, perhaps, was Walter?

He approached the mic and raised it to his level. He cleared his throat. "Thank you, Madam Chair. I'm pleased to be back with our hardworking Chamber." His voice rasped on my nerves as much as when I'd heard him at the market. He pulled out a pair of reading glasses and settled them on his nose, then opened a folder on the lectern. "Tonight I would like to share what Agrosafe is doing to keep our local farms happy, healthy, and most of all, profitable."

"Healthy. As if," Ceci muttered. "His own profits are all he cares about."

A woman to Ceci's right turned her head and nodded in agreement.

Walter began to speak about working with strawberry and greens farmers to ensure the highest possible yields. His speaking style was rote, as if he'd said these words too many times in the past. I covered a yawn with my hand. The occupants of the row in front of us all gazed at their phones instead of Walter. Why had they even come? For the food, drink, and networking after the talk, probably. Certainly not for the content.

"Sounds like he's on something," Ceci murmured.

"I know. Maybe he's bored with the subject matter." He hadn't seemed like this at the market this morning. He'd been a lively Mr. Charm with the Bakersfield farmer.

When he finished, the chair stepped forward and leaned toward the mic. "Thank you, Walter. We have time for a few questions. Please identify yourselves when you speak."

Ceci shoved her knitting into her bag and stood. "Ceci Shaterian, alpaca farmer. What are you doing to ensure toxic spray drift doesn't sicken farmworkers and neighbors?" She stayed on her feet.

He peered at her, his mouth turning down in disapproval. "Ms. Shaterian, we have had these discussions before. Our products are EPA approved for use with food products." He clipped off his words like an impatient instructor.

"You nearly killed half my herd of alpacas, and you know it. Your product is lethal to any living creature within breathing distance."

A gasp went up. Several in attendance nodded as if they knew the story. One of the shirts materialized in the aisle next to me. Walter shook his head.

Ceci went on. "We had to sell out and move to get away from the Agro-so-called-safe sprays on the neighboring property. Your company offered no recompense. You're a criminal, Mr. Russom, and I want to be sure everyone here knows it. There's not one thing safe about your products." She picked up her bag. "See you, Robbie," she mouthed as she squeezed by me.

The bodyguard, if that's what he was, made as if to take her elbow.

Ceci glared at him. "Don't even think about touching me."

The guy dropped his hand. I twisted in my seat to see him follow her to the back of the room. He didn't leave, though. She was going to be fine.

Walter stood in place, arms folded on his chest. A buzz of whispered conversations floated around the room.

"Who else has a question?" Linen Suit plastered a smile on her face. Silence was the response. "Let's give Walter a big thanks for sharing. Then we'll get started on the social part of tonight." The applause this time was even fainter than at the start, although Tommy had stood. He clapped loudly, wearing a big smile for Walter. The rest of the attendees began to rise and drift toward the tables at the back.

I watched for a moment. I didn't know a soul there, but my late lunch with Alana was a while ago. I might as well stick around for a bit. I headed into the hall first and found the ladies' room. I was in the last stall when two other women came in.

"Worst talk ever," one said.

The other gave a throaty laugh. "You can say that again. Was he on something?" Her voice was low and rich.

"I heard he has an addiction issue."

"Really?" Low Voice asked as water ran.

"Yes. I don't know why he would. He seems like he exercises and keeps himself in good shape, but a friend said she saw him handing over money to a dude down by the beach."

"You mean in exchange for drugs? Heroin or crack?"

"Maybe."

"Bad stuff. I wonder how he can keep running his business."

"I'm not sure he is, at least not well," the first voice said. "Did you see their latest quarterly report? He applied for a big loan from this very bank and was denied."

Low Voice whistled. "I wonder why Madam Chair even invited him tonight."

"He's been on the schedule for months. You know how she likes to schedule a year's worth of speakers."

The door whooshed open and shut, and the room grew quiet. I finished up and washed my hands, alone with my thoughts. Walter Russom, pillar of the business community—and an addict? *Wow.* I wondered if what she'd said was true. And if he was addicted to something, did he ever cross paths with Zoe?

I headed back into the room, now awash with chatting and laughter. Walter held a small plate but wasn't eating, and he stood by himself. Somebody should remedy that, and it might as well be me. I accepted a plastic cup of white wine at the drinks table and loaded up a small plate of my own with a mini-quiche, a Buffalo wing, a few cubes of cheese, and a small bunch of grapes.

"Good evening, Walter." I smiled at him.

He gazed at me, giving his head a little shake as if I'd startled him. "Evening."

"Robbie Jordan. We met this morning at the farmers' market."

"Ah, yes. Katherine's friend. And you came to my little talk tonight."

"I did." I took a sip of wine. "What did you think of what the alpaca farmer said?" I cocked my head, watching him.

He didn't meet my gaze and lifted his chin. "She has no grounds. Our product is safe."

"Not according to Paul Etxgeberria." Should I mention my mom, too? I decided not to. "He also told me it is highly toxic."

"Then he's a damn fool."

"You mean 'was.' You didn't hear that he passed away yesterday?"

His eyes shifted left. "No, I didn't."

"It's very sad. He was so committed to improving the environment."

Walter finally looked at me. He'd narrowed his eyes and his nostrils flared. "Who are you again? Are you one of those radical kooks?"

"No. I'm just visiting. I came back for our high school reunion. The one Katherine organized."

Tommy walked up, jittering with nervous energy. "Oh, hello, ma'am. Was the information I gave you useful to your uncle?"

"Very, thank you so much."

Walter looked from Tommy to me and back. He opened his mouth.

"There you are, Walter." Linen Suit appeared at his elbow.

I took the opportunity to turn away. I'd had enough of Walter Russom. And I sure didn't want Tommy to start calling me Irene in front of his employer.

Chapter 31

Once again I found myself with an unscheduled evening and ants in my pants. When I got back to the B-and-B, the kitchen was dark, so hanging out with Carmen and her mom wasn't going to happen. I paced around my room for a few minutes. I texted Alana, but she replied she was busy with her parents. Jason didn't respond when I pinged him. I wrote to Liz and asked if she wanted to go visit Ceci's farm in the morning and she didn't return a text, either. Was this what my life had come to? Back in the place where I'd grown up and nobody to hang out with? I wasn't about to contact Zoe after the way she'd reacted to me.

"Think creatively, Jordan," I scolded myself. I snapped my fingers. I could go to the movies, something I never made time for at home. I didn't mind seeing movies alone. I wouldn't be talking to anyone during a film, anyway. I checked the local listings. An art theater downtown had a screening of an indie flick I'd heard about, and it started in twenty minutes. *Good.* I grabbed my bag and sweater and headed back downstairs.

After about ten minutes I noticed headlights close behind me. They were super bright and positioned higher than mine, like it was an SUV or another vehicle larger than my little economy rental. Somebody was hot to trot, but there was nowhere for them to pass me on the city street until I pulled into the theater's parking lot. I made a circuit but groaned to find it full. I blew out a breath and headed back onto the street. Two blocks farther, around the corner, and another block and a half down, I finally found a place at the curb. I locked the rental and hurried back toward the main drag. The moon was ascending, blood orange from the smoke that still filled the air.

Halfway down the dark block the hairs on the back of my neck rose, my Spidey sense on high alert. Was someone following me? Someone unhappy I'd been asking questions about Agrosafe? Someone threatened I was looking into Paul's and my mom's deaths? I took a quick glance around but didn't see anyone. I slid my phone out of my bag and swiped it awake in case I had to dial a quick 911. I strode as fast as I could short of jogging and heaved a deep sigh of relief when I hit the well-lit thoroughfare.

The film was only sparsely attended. My bucket of popcorn—which passed for dinner, since I hadn't finished my appetizers after the lecture—and I had the second row all to ourselves. I happily lost myself in the big screen for the next hundred minutes.

But when I emerged onto the street, it was nearly ten o'clock. The moon was higher and barely any shade of orange at all. The street was nearly deserted. The few other moviegoers turned left toward the parking lot. Music drifted out from an Irish bar across the street and two guys stood in front of it smoking, but on this side I had the sidewalk to myself. I turned to the right. As I walked I threaded my keys through my knuckles in one hand and held my phone in the other. Living here, I'd never felt Santa Barbara was dangerous. Now? I wasn't so sure.

I was nearly to the street where I'd parked when a voice sounded from a dark doorway next to me.

"Hey," a gravelly voice said.

I gasped and tripped, barely catching myself.

"Spare change?"

I backed up to the curb as I peered toward the voice. A man sat on the ground with his hand out. I shook my head.

"Sorry." I rushed on. I should have given him something. But what if he wasn't really a dude down on his luck? What if he grabbed my wrist? My heart thudded.

And now I had to traverse the dark side street once more. What an idiot I was. I should have given up on the movie rather than park there alone. I should have stayed home and read a book. Watched a flick on my iPad. Anything but this.

Still, I had to get my car. I tapped on the flashlight app to illuminate my way so at least I wouldn't trip again. Partway down the first block I thought I heard footsteps. I halted and whirled. I couldn't make out anyone. I hurried faster. At the car I fumbled with the keys and dropped them. I finally clicked the door open and slid in. Hitting the lock button had never felt so good.

Once I cleared downtown, I glanced in the rearview mirror and let out a frantic moan. Headlights, high and bright in my eyes. *Again.* I sped up. They matched my speed. This was a wider road with zero traffic on it. My hands, now sweaty, clenched the steering wheel. I didn't dare stop and use my phone to call for help. I had two miles to go before turning off for Carmen's.

My tail backed off. Maybe it was simply somebody in a big effing hurry. Maybe they weren't after me. I tried to deepen my breath, to calm myself. It wasn't working. I checked the mirror on my side and swore. The vehicle was coming up on my left—and fast. They were too close. They were going to sideswipe me! The road was elevated here with a steep drop-off to my right. I was toast.

Blue and white lights strobed toward me. A siren grew louder. The big vehicle slowed and got back behind me. It drifted back to a safe distance. I blew out a breath. I'd never been happier to see the cops.

The police vehicle drew closer. Were they after my assailant? They sped past. And when I checked my rearview mirror, all I could see were the police lights disappearing into the distance. The big vehicle was gone. Had it pulled over and extinguished its headlights or taken a side road? I had no idea.

I turned left onto Carmen's street and slowed, my

hands damp on the steering wheel and my legs shaky. I should have listened to Madame Allegra. I thanked whatever lucky stars had saved me. And vowed not to venture out alone at night again until I was back in cozy South Lick.

Chapter 32

I awoke with a thudding heart. The room was dark and I didn't feel a bit rested. When I saw that my phone said it was two twenty, I swore. I was normally a good sleeper. Occasionally, when I woke up in the wee hours, it took me some time to get back to slumberland. I'd fallen asleep at around eleven, after indulging in a little glass of whiskey, since I'd bought a small bottle at a local microdistillery after I'd arrived.

But why was my heart racing? I lay quietly on my back, trying to figure it out. I had the feeling I'd been in a dream with someone chasing me, but I couldn't . . . oh, wait. Someone *had* been chasing me, in real life, only a few hours ago. It was why I'd had the whiskey, to calm my nerves.

I sat up and switched on the bedside lamp. My heart refused to slow. I could barely swallow. Did this room have good locks? Did the building? Maybe my chaser would come after me again. I shouldn't have imagined I could go around asking questions with impunity. What had I been thinking, going to Walter's talk? Visiting Paul's apartment, talking with Grace. Even asking Zoe questions. Stupid, stupid, stupid.

Of course I wanted to get to the truth. Of course I wanted justice for Paul. But that was the police department's job, and the sheriff's—not mine. Madame Allegra had foreseen me being in danger. How could she have? But she had. And I hadn't been careful this week, not at all. It might be time for me to pay attention to woo-woo. Maybe.

My ears rang. My breaths came fast and furious. Was I having a panic attack? I'd never experienced one before. And I didn't know anyone who had. I forced myself to breathe slowly, in and out. I leaned back against the cool, smooth pillows and dropped my shoulders, letting my hands go limp at my sides. I murmured out loud, "You're safe. It'll be fine. You're safe. It'll be fine," over and over, with every exhale.

Eventually, the trick worked. I turned out the light and slid back down under the covers. I vowed tomorrow and Friday I was going to be on vacation. No snooping, no questions, *nada.* But I kept up my mantra until my eyes shut of their own accord.

Chapter 33

I trotted downstairs to breakfast at eight the next morning. I'd headed out for a sunrise bike ride at six thirty. A vacation bike ride, as I reminded myself. The air seemed less smoky at dawn, especially down by the beach, and the exercise in the fresh salt air had invigorated me. Now showered and dressed in jeans, top, and sandals, I was ready for whatever this day held. I couldn't wait for a cup of rich, dark coffee and something yummy to eat. My pursuer of the night before seemed like a bad dream in the plentiful light of a California day, and my panic attack hadn't returned, either.

Inside the deliciously fragrant café every table was taken. I headed out to the patio, waving at Carmen as I went. At the table next to the wall three women in running clothes sat perusing menus with two mutts lying at their feet. I slid into a seat at the other end of the space next to the rosemary shrub covered with tiny blue flowers. I ran my hand over the greenery and inhaled, then picked up the menu.

Carmen brought a pot of coffee. "Good morning, Robbie." She poured.

"Thanks, Carmen. How are you?" I gazed up at her. Her braid was messy and her lipstick was on crooked. She usually looked a lot more put together.

She glanced around and used a low voice. "I think a bad guy was casing the joint last night."

My mouth dropped open at the archaic phrase, but at the same time my insides chilled. "Casing the joint? What do you mean?"

"Somebody rattled our door near midnight, like he was trying to, you know, break in."

Gah. "Your door in the back?" There went my sunny balance.

"Yeah." She pulled her mouth down.

"That's terrible. Did you call the police?"

"Nah. I don't like police, and we got good locks. Did you hear anything?"

"I didn't, but I was upstairs. I went out to a movie downtown, got back a few minutes after ten, and went to sleep around eleven." Or maybe I'd heard something in my sleep, and that was why I'd awoken with a racing heart. "Do you have a security camera for the restaurant?"

She nodded a couple of times, quickly. "Out front, but I haven't had a chance to look at the pictures yet."

One of the dog women caught Carmen's eye.

She held up a "wait" finger to the woman and said to me, "We're busy this morning. Do you know what you want? I made a spinach-artichoke-egg bake casserole with the hearts of those artichokes you brought."

"Spinach and artichoke sounds good."

"It is. I also have a California Benedict special."

Ooh. "With avocado? Now you're talking. That's exactly what I want, thanks. Can I get a little plate of the egg bake, too? I'd love to taste it."

"Of course. The casserole is good, and those artichokes were outstanding, but the *Benedito* is one of Mamá's specialties." She leaned closer. "She's got something she wants to tell you, too, but I'll need to translate. When we get a break, I'll bring her out."

I thanked her and she bustled off. What did Luisa have to tell me? And was the lurker my pursuer? The thought sent shivers through me. It meant he—or she—knew where I was staying. Last night I'd been afraid my would-be attacker would follow me here. Now I was afraid they had, but in stealth.

A text buzzed in from Liz, saying she'd love to go to Ceci's with me and would pick me up at ten. I tapped back my okay and thanks. I snapped a selfie of me in front of the bougainvillea wall, the blooms a lush cloak, and texted it to Abe, saying I missed him and wished he were here. Sipping my coffee, I idly scrolled through Instagram and then my e-mail, but in the background of my thoughts was last night's would-be intruder. I hoped Carmen's security cam would reveal who it was, although any bad guy worth his stuff knew to avoid those spying eyes. Maybe I could get the story of why Nacho Average Café's owner didn't like police, too.

I set down the phone when Hector emerged onto the patio holding a mug of coffee. I waved him over. "Come for some home cooking that isn't your own?" I asked. "Please join me."

"Morning, Robbie. You got that right. When you're

a cook, it's like a mini-vacation for somebody else to prepare food for you."

"Which I have totally been soaking up all week. Plus your *bosillas*, of course. Dude, those were perfection."

"I'm glad you liked them. I love getting creative."

"Have you thought about opening a restaurant?" I asked.

"Nah. I told you, I only cook to support my dancing." The light went out of his eyes. "Paul's never going to dance again."

It hit me. How could I have forgotten he'd said they were good friends? "Hector, I'm so sorry. I should have said something as soon as I saw you. You miss him."

He sniffed and blinked. "I do, more than I even thought. The guy was so full of life. You should have seen him on the dance floor. He had style in spades. And to fall down dead like he did? It's not fair. It's not the way things are supposed to go."

I lowered my voice. "The police are looking into whether someone might have killed him. That maybe he didn't just drop down dead."

His mouth pulled down in a horrified expression. "You're not kidding, are you?"

I shook my head.

Hector narrowed his eyes. "If so, it had to have been Katherine's dad, the Agrosafe guy. He's gotta be furious about the group trying to pull his product from the market."

"I had the same thought."

He stood abruptly. "I need to make a call. I might know something. Catch ya later, Robbie."

I stared after him. What would he know? Who was he calling? I didn't even have his contact info to follow up, but I could get it from Carmen. Who somehow materialized next to me with my breakfast. I shook off thoughts of Paul's death and stared at the beckoning dish in front of me. Two mounds of English muffin, Canadian bacon, and fried egg, topped with avocado slices and dripping with parsley-flecked Hollandaise sauce over all of it. Two thin slices of orange on the plate were the perfect local garnish. I snapped a photo of the laden plate.

"Am I in heaven, Carmen?" I glanced up at her, spying her mother behind her. "Oh, Luisa, *buenos dias.* I didn't see you."

Luisa smiled, but it was a faint one. She rattled off some Spanish.

"She says her sister, my *tia* Nelinda, cleans house for Walter's ex-wife," Carmen translated.

I nodded to myself. Katherine's former stepmother.

Carmen kept her voice low. "Mamá says Nelinda overheard the lady talking about Mr. Russom's habit. She said he spends a lot of money on it." She rubbed her fingers together in the sign for plentiful cash.

"Habit like an addiction to drugs?" I asked, my gaze on Luisa. Maybe those women at the chamber event were right.

"No. Like in gambling. Apparently, it was one of the reasons she divorced him."

Gambling. *"Gracias*, Luisa.*"* I smiled at her.

Luisa shook her head and said something to her daughter.

Carmen laughed. "She says to call her Mamá."

"Gracias, Mamá.*"*

Luisa nodded and squeezed my hand in both of hers, then she pointed to my plate and made a fork-to-mouth gesture. *"Cómelo, mientras esté caliente."*

"Eat it while it's hot," Carmen translated before she and Luisa headed back inside.

Walter Russom was losing money gambling. I didn't think there was a casino nearby. At least, there hadn't been one when I was growing up. Or had there? I hadn't known about one. Maybe Walter gambled on-line. I assumed one could do so these days. I'd read about people who kept on betting even while losing huge amounts of money, sure the next game, the next card would reverse everything.

Did Walter try to eliminate anyone who threatened his company's profits—as Paul had—because he was desperate for money? Or was something else going on? And what about what the woman at Walter's talk had mentioned, that he was at the beach exchanging money for something? I blinked, thinking. Maybe he had borrowed cash and was being forced to pay it back with interest. Was there a California mafia?

My fingers itched to go online. I'd seen a few days ago that Agrosafe wasn't a publicly traded company. Still, I bet I could dig up something about their finances. Everything was findable online if you looked hard enough.

Chapter 34

Liz and I *putt-putt*ed into the foothills two hours later on our way to Ceci's farm. The road was the old stagecoach route over San Marcos Pass. It became super twisting with hairpin turns farther up, but down here modest homes were mixed with animal farms and undeveloped hillsides. She'd put the top down on the VW, and the air rushed past my face. I'd threaded my ponytail through the Nacho Average Café cap I'd gotten from Carmen, a souvenir I was going to treasure. I'd given her my Pans 'N Pancakes hat in exchange, which had delighted her.

"How do you keep this car in such good running order?" I asked. "It's really old."

"I take it down to JJ's Vintage Automotive in Las Fincas. The woman who owns it, Jamie Jullien, only works on cars made before they started putting computers into them."

"I love it. She must have a lot of business."

"She does. She's good at coaxing years out of treasures like mine." She patted the dashboard.

I sniffed the air. "The fires seem better today, don't they?"

"The air does seem more clear," Liz agreed. "I think they might have gotten the worst of the burns contained overnight."

"The wildfire got pretty bad there for a day or two."

"I know."

I waited a beat. "Liz, I have something to tell you."

"This sounds bad." She glanced over at me. "It's not about Zoe, is it?"

"Not at all."

"So tell."

"I spoke to the pathologist yesterday," I said. "She found Mom's death report. She definitely died of a ruptured brain aneurysm. The kicker is, they didn't test for a toxin that might have caused an aneurysm because nobody suspected homicide at the time. And she was cremated. We'll never know the answer."

Liz reached over and patted my knee. "It doesn't matter, Robbie. She loved you until her last breath. You hang on to that. Because it's true."

I gazed out at the hillside. "I know." I took a deep breath and swiped at the corners of my eyes. She was right. Mom's love was all that counted.

Liz cleared her throat. "Are we—I mean, you—trying to accomplish something at this farm, or is this simply a fun vacation field trip?"

Good question. "A little of both. At the farmers' market Ceci expressed quite strong feelings against Katherine Russom, and she publicly challenged Walter Russom at that Chamber of Commerce function last night, the talk you told me about."

"So you went to that? How was it?"

"I did. He didn't say anything very interesting. Anyway, I want to dig a little deeper into what Ceci said, if I can. Plus, she invited me up to her farm. And who doesn't love alpacas?" I was on vacation, after all.

"Exactly. I might check out using some alpaca yarn in my weaving, if it's thin enough."

"Perfect. I'll bet she can spin it as finely as you want. I don't know anything about turning wool into yarn, but I've watched my aunt do it a few times." I checked the GPS on my phone. "One more mile, then we turn off to the right." The phone beeped twice. "Uh-oh. I just lost the cell signal. I hope Ceci has signs."

At least the fire hadn't reached down here. Peeks into the canyons we drove through showed a green fuzz on the ground, the first results of the winter rains, sparse as they'd been. Live oaks and pinyons were their usual khaki green. I inhaled all the lovely dry smells of the region as we passed. Wild sage. Feral rosemary. Manzanita, whose fruit did look like little apples, and the healing aroma of witch hazel. Plus pungent eucalyptus trees, not native but imported from Australia in the nineteenth century. The trees thrived in dry climates and had had few diseases or pests until a few decades ago. Fires were another story. The Oakland Hills had been devastated by a fast-moving burn some years ago that devoured the sap-rich eucalyptus trunks and fragrant leaves.

We came to a sign cut in the shape of an alpaca

with SHATERIAN painted across the animal's back. The head pointed to the right. "There's the turnoff." I pointed.

Liz steered onto the dirt road past the sign. We bumped along for a quarter mile until we came to another version of the same sign, with the alpaca facing left this time.

"We should be nearly there," I said.

We rounded a bend and I pointed to a pasture on our left, where several dozen long-necked beasts grazed. A few paused and raised their heads at the sound of the car, and one trotted to the wire fence, eyes wide and curious. The sight made me smile. A low white barn had a fenced-off paddock adjoining it, where a few goats rested in the shade of a tall oak tree. and a half dozen chickens pecked in the dirt. The red clapboard house beyond was a classic ranch, with a wide porch and roof overhang. Liz pulled up and switched off the car, its engine trembling with the cut-off as only a Bug's can do.

A slender woman with curly black hair even wilder than mine walked out of the barn. She wore rubber muck boots and carried a bucket full of feed.

"Can I help you?" she asked after we climbed out.

"I'm Robbie Jordan and this is Liz Stover. Ceci invited us to visit the farm."

"Sounds good. I'm Taylor Etxgeberria. I volunteer with the animals."

Taylor, who the artist at Paul's house had mentioned. I had no idea she would be here. "You must be Paul's sister," I said. "I'm so very sorry for your loss."

She turned her face toward the field for a moment, sniffling. She faced us again wearing a grim expression. "I am, and thank you. It's been an awful week, and the animals are the only thing getting me through so far."

"Paul was an awesome guy," Liz said. "He's much missed."

"Thanks." Taylor gazed at Liz and then at me. "So you both knew him?"

"It's kind of complicated," Liz began. "Robbie's late mom was my dear friend, and she was in the anti-agrochemical group with Paul."

I nodded. "I live in the Midwest now, but I'm out here for a week. Liz introduced me to Paul because he had an idea my mom's death two years ago might have been murder, not a natural one."

Taylor's dark eyes went wide. "You're kidding."

I shook my head.

"And now my brother is dead, too." Taylor brought her hand to her mouth. "He was completely healthy and not very old. I have no idea why he died so suddenly."

"That's how my mother went, too." I touched Taylor's arm. "I spoke with the pathologist at the sheriff's office about Mom. She said she will look for toxins when she, uh, examines Paul."

Taylor stared at her boots, then spoke in a whisper. "They told me they're going to do an autopsy. It sounds awful, but if it will get to the truth, they should." She shuddered. "I'm glad my parents aren't alive to see this."

"Do you know of anyone at all who might have wanted to hurt Paul?" I asked.

"Other than the entire Agrosafe company? Not really. He was a little self-righteous about protecting the environment and not owning a car. But he was a sweet man just trying to do the right thing."

"Of course," I said. "Let me know if you think of anyone or anything that might help me figure this out."

Taylor scrunched up her nose. "Are you a detective or something?"

"Not exactly."

Ceci bustled around the corner of the house. "You came!" She walked up to us with a smile wider than the San Andreas Fault and a lot less dangerous. "And you've met Taylor, best volunteer west of the Rockies?"

"Yes, to both," I said. I introduced Ceci to Liz and they shook hands.

"Want to meet the gang?" Ceci pointed to the grazing alpacas.

"Sure," Liz replied.

"I'll get back to my chores," Taylor said. "Don't leave without saying good-bye."

"I promise," I assured her. The sun was so warm I shed the light sweater I'd slipped on before I left earlier.

Liz was already following Ceci through a gate into the field. I was about to follow when Taylor grabbed my sleeve.

"Wait," she said. "There was a girl at the restaurant where Paul worked. A dishwasher, I think."

Zoe?

"I never met her, but Paul was always trying to save her or something."

"Save her from what?"

"I don't know." She gave a sad little smile. "He was always rescuing animals when we were young. Turtles, snakes, kittens, injured birds, you name it."

"He had a kind heart."

She bobbed her head. "I'll say. Anyway, he told me this girl needed help. He asked her home a couple of times, cooked for her, that kind of thing."

"Like they were dating?" I asked.

"Not really. Anyway, I don't know anything else. And it's not like she was an enemy, but he said she wasn't warming up to him very fast."

"Name?"

She shook her head. "Sorry."

Chapter 35

"Detective Gifford?" I asked the man standing in the tie and dark blazer near the door of the Santa Barbara library. If this dude wasn't a detective, I wasn't a Santa Barbarite.

He turned and nodded.

"I'm Robbie Jordan. Jason Wong said you wanted to speak with me." Jason had texted me as I was driving back to town with Liz an hour ago and asked if I would be willing to have a chat with the detective working Paul's case. We'd agreed on the library as a neutral public space.

"Yes, ma'am. I'm Nolan Gifford with the Santa Barbara Police Department. I'm a detective sergeant in the Criminal Investigations Division. Thank you for agreeing to meet with me." His handshake was firm without being bone crushing. So far he hadn't smiled, and his manner was brisk. "I've saved us a table over here."

I followed him into the older part of the library, with its two-story-tall arched windows and an enormous fireplace a century old. A big wall clock marked noon as patrons in armchairs perused newspapers, worked on laptops in carrels, and read books at round tables. He gestured to a similar table in a corner of the room and sat in one of the chairs, laying a device half the size of a small TV remote on the table between us. I lowered myself into the other seat but perched on the edge.

"Do I have your permission to record our conversation, Ms. Jordan?"

Yikes. My heart rate zoomed into the red zone. Did he consider me a suspect? "Um, yes." I folded my hands on the cool, smooth tabletop to keep from fiddling with them.

He switched on the device, cited the date, and introduced himself. "I am speaking with Roberta Jordan of South Lick, Indiana, and am recording this interview with her permission." His voice was deep and rich, like a radio broadcaster's, even though he spoke softly. He added the date, time, and our location. "Where are you staying during your visit here?"

"In a B-and-B room above the Nacho Average Café." I told him and his recording the address.

"Thank you. Please tell me how you knew Paul Etxgeberria."

I swallowed. "My late mother's friend Liz Stover put us in touch. I only met Paul once, last Sunday."

"Why did Ms. Stover want you to meet the deceased?"

I winced at the term, accurate though it was. "My mother—Jeanine Jordan—passed away two years ago. At the time they told me it was from a ruptured brain aneurysm. My mom and Paul were in an activist group together. Liz said Paul had mentioned maybe Mom's death had been from poisoning, not from natural causes."

His eyebrows went up and he blinked. "Is that so?"

"Yes. I met Paul Sunday afternoon and we talked."

"Where did you meet?"

"In Alice Keck Park." Sitting this close I could see acne scars scattered over Gifford's face. He must have had a bad case of it as a teen.

"And?" He gestured for me to continue.

"Their group was working to get certain fumigants banned from the county. The chemicals are neurotoxins and are sprayed, so they make farmworkers and nearby animals sick. Ask Ceci Shaterian. Have you heard of her?"

"No, ma'am."

"She raises alpacas." I told him about Ceci and her husband having to sell their Oxnard property at a loss and move to the hills to escape the Agrosafe spray. "Apparently, exposure to the chemical manufactured by Agrosafe in Goleta might mimic a stroke in the brain, or cause it, I'm not sure. Paul said my mom had gotten into a public fight with Walter Russom, who runs the company. Paul thought maybe Walter found a way to administer the chemical to my mom to get her out of the way."

"Wong says you've been trying to investigate these matters yourself."

Was this meeting a scolding to leave police work to the police? "Not really. I mean, I'm curious, sure. Jason and I went to Chumash High with Walter's daughter, Katherine."

"I spoke with a lieutenant at the South Lick Police." He cocked his head. His brown hair was cut so short it didn't budge with the movement. "He said you have a knack for running down murderers."

My buddy Buck. Was this good or bad?

"I also understand you've been speaking with Mel Washington."

"Yes. I asked her to track down my mom's death report because I never saw it. It took Mel a while, but she found it. They performed an autopsy on my mother. It turns out she did die of a ruptured aneurysm, but they didn't check for poison in her system."

"Right. But you asked her to make sure to check for those agricultural neurotoxins in Etxgeberria's remains."

"I suggested she might want to, yes." I was going to go on, but shut my mouth instead. Why get any deeper in trouble than it appeared I already was? Except I couldn't help myself. "Has she found any?"

"Ah." He hesitated as if deciding what to reveal. "Actually, the autopsy is not yet complete." He watched me for a moment. "Is there anything else you've learned this week? Anything you'd like to share with us?"

I blew out a breath. "I heard Walter Russom has a gambling problem. Someone said he applied for a big loan and was turned down."

"Who was that someone?"

"I don't know. It was a conversation I overheard in the ladies' room."

"Which ladies' room?" He gave me an exasperated look.

"Sorry. I went to a Chamber of Commerce talk Walter gave downtown last evening. These women were talking in the restroom, but I have no idea who they were. One said her friend had seen Walter giving money to someone down at the beach. They thought it was for drugs."

"Duly noted."

"But—" I took a deep breath. "But the cook at the café said her sister cleans for Walter's ex-wife."

"What is the sister's name?"

"Nelinda somebody. I don't know her last name. The cook's name is Luisa Sandoval, but she doesn't speak English. Her daughter, Carmen Perez, owns the café." Was I nervous-rambling or what? "The sister overheard the ex talking to someone about how much money Walter spends on his gambling addiction. So I was wondering if he found a way to kill Paul, to remove the threat to Agrosafe's profits, because he is desperate for money."

"Interesting." Detective Gifford nodded slowly. "I assume you've checked into Walter's alibi for the day Paul died, or the night before."

"I am not free to divulge the details of our investigation. I also understand you paid a visit to Grace Fujiyama, Etxgeberria's housemate."

"Yes." The guy was good. He wasn't consulting notes and had all these names in his head. Had Grace told him I'd been there, or had he been back to the apartment? "I went to the house yesterday."

"For the purpose of?"

Should I tell the truth or fudge it? "She found Paul dead, in the same way Liz Stover found my mom. I guess I wanted to sort of reach out to her. And also find out what she knew."

"Which was?"

"Well, she said your people were there, and a detective asked her questions. Was it you?"

"Yes."

"She told me you took Paul's lunch container," I went on. "Did you find—" I stopped when he held up his hand. *Rats.* "I get it, you can't tell me."

"Precisely."

"What about the oleander leaves your team took? Are you looking for that toxin, too?" The stuff grew everywhere, mostly because it was so hardy, drought-resistant, and beautiful when it bloomed.

Gifford only shook his head.

I gazed at the tall bookshelf full of thick reference volumes behind him. It was oddly comforting to see a library still stocking dictionaries, thesauruses, almanacs, and volumes of local history printed on real paper with sturdy bindings. For people to pull down and peruse in person, rather than wandering over the Internet in search of the same information. A shame those books didn't contain the answer to who killed Paul.

"Ms. Jordan? Do you have anything else you'd like to share?"

I flashed on Cody and on what Katherine had said about him butting heads with his father. "Walter's son, Cody, is waitstaff out at Boathouse at Hendry's Beach. He's a sophomore at UCSB, and he said he's part of the group trying to ban his father's product. Earlier, Katherine had told me Cody and Walter totally butt heads. Father and son fighting because Cody is opposed to his dad's livelihood? I can see it."

He tilted his head, as if I'd finally told him something he didn't already know.

"And there's one more thing. I went to the movies last night downtown. By myself. Someone followed me back to my B-and-B when I was driving. They tried to run me off the road."

His eyebrows met in the middle and he looked sideways at me. "Did you see who it was? Could you identify the vehicle?"

"I couldn't see who was behind the wheel. I'm driving a small rental. All I know is this vehicle was bigger, like an SUV or maybe a truck, and had really bright headlights. I was only saved by a police car coming toward us with lights and siren on. My would-be attacker backed off and disappeared."

"What street was this on, and what time?"

"The movie got out at nine thirty, so nine forty-five, ten, sometime around then. I was on Del Vista at the time."

"Did you report the near attack?"

"No. I didn't have the make of car, the plate number, or anything. I know Walter owns a big SUV. Also, Carmen, the owner of the café, told me she heard someone in the night trying to break into the cottage in back where she lives with her mother."

"I'll see what I can find out."

"Thanks." I cringed at my thoughtlessness. Carmen hadn't wanted to call the police. "Carmen said she didn't report the intruder because she and her mom don't like police. I don't know if, as immigrants, they've suffered police brutality or what. But if you talk with them, please be gentle."

"I will do my best. Terminating this interview at twelve twenty-two." He clicked off the recorder and stood. "I thank you for your time. Here's my card.

You happen to learn anything new, please call or text as soon as possible." He drew a card out of his shirt pocket with two fingers and slid it across the table.

"I will."

"And, Ms. Jordan, I need to officially caution you to stay well away from anything having to do with Etxgeberria's death. We don't know if it was from natural causes or was criminal homicide. But if the latter is the case, we have a very dangerous person out there, and you have already nearly become a victim. We do not want a second homicide to occur. Do you understand?"

"Yes, sir." I stood and held out my hand. "I understand completely. I'm flying back to Indiana on Saturday morning and fully intend to make my plane, alive and well."

Gifford shook my hand. "A wise choice." He turned to go.

"Detective?" I waited until he looked at me. "Good luck."

Chapter 36

Alana picked me up for the appointment with Katherine at a little before one. Ten minutes later she parked on the street in front of a house built in a style I would call Late California Ugly: a newer-construction stucco building low in front with a second story rising up behind. The garage jutted out in front of the house, eight-foot walls surrounded the back of the property, and a deep green manicured lawn in front was wasting the region's precious water resources. An equally wasteful big honking SUV sat in the driveway. The neighborhood barely qualified as Montecito. It was so far on the outskirts of the exclusive conclave, it should have been called Montecito Lite.

"This is it?" I asked. "I don't think I ever came here while we were in school together."

"This is it. And why would you have? Katherine wasn't exactly your bestie."

"True words."

"Anyway, this is her father's house. I'm not sure if this was the family home when we were younger.

Katherine lives here and runs her business out of the spare bedroom, as I understand it."

"Gotcha. It must be where she lived when she was growing up. She told me about a grapefruit and a lemon tree her mom planted after Katherine was born, and that she still has them. I guess living here is a sweet deal for her."

"Yeah, but she's twenty-eight and living with Daddy. Not so sweet, in my universe."

"Right. Are you really considering using her to plan your wedding?" I asked.

"Probably not. But since I'm a total newbie at this, I want to gather information on the process. A friend up north did it all herself, you know, with a planning app and tons of running around. It seemed like a huge amount of work for her. I'm sure Katherine's approach is the exact opposite, with a price tag to match. It'll be a data point."

I smiled at her. "Ever the scientist."

"And why not?" She grinned back. "Shall we?"

Katherine, wearing cream-colored pants and a pale green blazer, pulled open the door seconds after Alana pressed the doorbell, as if she'd been watching out the window for us. She greeted Alana with a handshake and then spied me standing behind. "You're getting married, too, Robbie?"

I laughed. "No. Just supporting my BFF."

Katherine blinked. "Please, follow me."

She showed us into her office. Alana and I sat together on a sofa sized for an engaged couple, with Katherine in an armchair opposite. A small vanilla-scented candle burned on her desk, filling the air with a cloying sweetness. A binder lay on a coffee table in front of us, and Katherine held an iPad in her lap. The walls displayed perfect photographs of perfect weddings, except there wasn't a mixed-race or same-sex couple in the bunch, and no Asians or obvious Latinos among the brides and grooms, either. Katherine didn't exactly serve a cross-section of California's population. The only personal touch in the whole office was one of Katherine hugging a black-and-white dog.

"Is he your pup?" Alana asked her.

Katherine's mouth turned down. "He was. Topsie went over the rainbow bridge last year. I miss him like crazy." She plastered a cheerleader-worthy smile on her face and brightened her tone. "Who's the lucky man, Alana? He couldn't be here?"

Alana batted away the notion. "No, I'm down for the reunion and a visit with my folks. And to see Robbie, of course. His name's Antonio, and I'm sure he's hard at work in Berkeley."

Katherine typed into her iPad.

"Hang on, Katherine." Alana held up a hand. "I'm only gathering information. We haven't decided on our process at all, so you don't need to open a record for us or anything."

Katherine blinked, but set down the iPad. She folded her hands in her lap. "That's fine, of course. Tell me about the kind of wedding you envision. You and Antonio, naturally."

I stood. "Excuse me, Katherine. Can I trouble you for where I can find a bathroom?"

Katherine lowered her chin and would have gazed at me over the tops of her glasses if she wore any. She looked as if she didn't believe me. I waited.

She ceded. "Down the hall, third door on your left."

"Thanks." I stepped into the hallway. I doubted Alana would hire Katherine. But an opportunity had been handed to me on an abalone shell and I wasn't going to waste it, my vow to the detective notwithstanding. Surely Walter was at work and Cody at class. At least, I hoped they were both out of the house. I should be able to poke around for a moment or two with no one the wiser.

Various framed pictures lined the walls in the hallway. An entire wall on my left was covered with school portraits of Katherine and her brother on a timeline from kindergarten through senior year. The opposite wall showed them solo and on athletic teams: soccer for both, Cody on swim team, and beach volleyball for Katherine.

A doorway led into a messy bedroom, looking like it belonged to a guy. A young guy. The next door was open only a few inches. I peeked in to see a bedroom, impersonal-looking except for a makeup table littered with bottles, small brushes, and foundation sponges. Katherine's room, clearly, possibly remodeled into a guest room after she'd moved out? She must have reclaimed it for her own when her marriage dissolved.

The wall between Katherine's room and the next door seemed to be Walter's. Walter posing with colleagues in front of the Agrosafe building. Walter with the governor, the columns and dome of the state capitol building in Sacramento looming behind them. Walter shaking hands with a heavyset man in a suit in front of a glitzy building. The building's sign was above their heads in the background, but the only word in the shot was *Casino,* and the corner of the picture was signed in a scrawl I couldn't make out. I peered at Walter's companion and his high cheekbones. Maybe he was Native American. I was pretty sure most, or perhaps all, of the casinos in states other than Nevada were run by tribes on tribal land. *Huh.* There must be a casino around here. The handshake didn't look like one between owner and addicted player. Could Walter have a business interest in the casino instead of a gambling problem?

After the door to the bathroom, the hall ended in a great room facing the rear of the property. I stood at the entrance, surveying it. Another hall led off the opposite side. I was dying to snoop in Walter's office, if he had one at home. But I'd overstayed my bathroom break as it was.

A creak sounded from the far hall, or maybe from the kitchen. *Yikes.* I wasn't doing anything wrong, but I didn't want to have to explain myself to Walter, Cody, or even a housekeeper. Backing up a few quick steps, I shut the bathroom door behind me with an obvious click. I stayed in there the requisite amount of time, making sure I flushed before opening the door even though I hadn't actually availed myself of the facilities.

Before returning to Katherine's office, I snapped a quiet cell photo of the casino picture. I might have to go try my luck at the slots before I headed east, as long as this casino wasn't too far away.

The binder from the side table now lay open on the table in front of Alana. Katherine pointed to pictures in plastic sleeves. I hung over the back of the sofa to watch. The two facing pages were collages of gazebos, flower-strewn platforms, and vintage-looking arches with blooms and vines everywhere.

"These are some of the floral arrangements we can do over the nuptial arch," Katherine said.

Alana glanced up at me. If that wasn't panic in her eyes, I didn't know what "Rescue me!" looked like.

Katherine flipped the page. "Now, for the table centerpieces, we offer a wide range of choices and prices, of course."

"Of course," Alana murmured. She cleared her throat, glanced at her watch, and said, "Would you look at the time? I have to pick something up from my parents' lawyer, Katherine. I'm sorry to cut this short, but . . ." She stood.

Katherine jerked her chin back with a frown. "Oh. I guess I thought . . ." She let her voice trail off.

I straightened. Alana had made it clear at the beginning she wasn't ready to sign on to anything.

Katherine finally stood, too. "Let me send you home with some printed information. Our services really are the best. As the bride, you shouldn't have to worry about a thing." She drew four sheets, each printed on different color paper, from a rack on her desk, and topped the stack with a glossy brochure. "My personal cell is right here on the back. Talk to hubby-to-be and Mom and get back to me at any time. The earlier, the better, of course! You wouldn't want us to be out of availability for your dream weekend."

Katherine's tone was so false-cheerful brittle, I thought it would break.

"Of course." Alana's voice was her usual reasoned calm.

"Katherine," I began. "I want to change up my vacation a little. Is there anywhere to gamble around here? A casino or something closer than Vegas?" I smiled with my best innocent expression, but crossed my fingers behind my back.

Alana whipped her face toward me as if she couldn't believe what I'd asked. Katherine frowned and gazed right and left in a Where'd-the-real-Robbie-go? gesture. I didn't say anything, not daring to communicate nonverbally with Alana. Plenty of time for us to talk later. We'd be back inside her car in a New York minute.

"Well, yeah," Katherine said. "The casino is a half hour away over near Santa Inez. If you'll excuse me for saying so, it doesn't seem quite like your kind of place, though."

"Thanks. I'm all about new experiences these days." I shrugged. "I thought I'd see how the other half lives, or the other something percent, anyway. Who knows? Maybe I'll win a few bucks."

"Or not." Katherine's mouth looked like she'd bitten into the sourest of lemons. "Just don't make a habit of it, Robbie. Trust me."

Chapter 37

"You took, like, the world's longest bathroom break," Alana remarked after we pulled away from the Russom home.

"Sorry." I lifted my hand to shield my eyes from the sun glinting in.

"I thought I was going to die in there, Rob. Katherine has to learn the soft sell. She didn't listen to anything I had to say about what we want and don't want. Instead she kept showing me pictures of high-end ceremonies."

"Did you ask her what the sticker price was for any of them?" I angled sideways in my seat so I could see her expression.

"Once, when she showed me a series of shots of a wedding at the casino you asked about. As if I would want to get married at a casino!"

"I swear I can see the smoke coming out of your ears, Alana. Take a deep breath, now." I waited until she obeyed orders before going on. "Better?"

"Yes. Where did you disappear to, anyway?"

"Honestly? I was snooping."

"No, sir."

"Yes. Trying to get the dirt on Katherine's father." I didn't add, *But don't tell the detective.*

"Well, thanks for coming back to the wedding 'planning' office." She surrounded the word with air quotes. "I didn't want to have to go looking for you, but I really, really wanted to get out of there. Can you even imagine paying forty thousand dollars for the privilege of having someone like Katherine run your wedding as if it was a Vegas show in a place where people are smoking, drinking, and gambling?"

I laughed. "I can't, actually."

Alana shook her head in disbelief. "My mom said she and Dad got married on a bluff in Corona del Mar with Dad's uncle officiating. Everybody was barefoot, and Mom sewed her own white peasant dress. The reception was a potluck supper in the park overlooking the Pacific. Her parents bought champagne, and dessert was a big carrot cake my grandma made, with Snoopy bride-and-groom figures."

"I like it." Her parents' kind of celebration did seem ideal. "No fuss, no muss, right?"

"Exactly. And affordable. I mean, Antonio and I earn decent salaries, but why waste it on some extravaganza when what you really want to spend money on is your first house?"

"Of course. What do you want to bet the thought of a homegrown wedding gives Katherine heart palpitations?"

"Her bad luck. I'm totally tending toward a super-simple wedding, maybe in Santa Cruz. You would come, wouldn't you?"

"Alana, look at me." I waited until she glanced my way. "Of course I would." I opened my hands to the sides.

"I know." She smiled back, then pursed her lips. "But Antonio's Italian parents? I'm not so sure they'll go for the hippie-style celebration."

"You love him. He loves you, and he loves his parents, I assume. He'll convince them." I gazed out the windshield. "Alana, do you know a Moore family? The mom, Sydelle, plays tennis, and one son is about nineteen."

"Moore. Hmm. Does this have to do with Walter Russom and the guy you met, the one who died?"

"Maybe. The kid, name of Tommy, is an intern at Agrosafe. And Sydelle is dating Walter, according to Katherine."

She snapped her fingers. "My mom was in the garden club for a while. She got sick of all the posturing and quit. I think a Sydelle might have been one of the movers and shakers, part of the upper echelon."

"It's not a name anyone would forget."

"Right. Anyway, can you believe they even had an upper echelon? Mom just wanted to hang out with other ladies who liked to grow flowers and vegetables, maybe learn some stuff. She didn't get it with that bunch, believe me."

"Tommy Moore seems like a really eager beaver, as if he wants to impress Walter above all else."

Alana scrunched up one eye. "You don't mean he'd commit murder for him, do you?"

"I guess not. I'm sure you're right. I might be reaching a bit."

"Whatevs. I'll ask Mom what she knows about Mrs. Moore tonight and let you know, okay?"

"Thanks. So how about coming with me for a quick visit to the casino in Santa Inez?"

"What? Right now?" Alana's voice rose. "Why?"

I lifted a shoulder and dropped it. "To see how the rich people live?"

"Or the troubled and gambling-addicted. I can think of a zillion things I'd rather do." My friend shot me a glance more full of disbelief than a judge hearing a serial liar's latest case. "Seriously?"

"Okay. Truth time," I confessed. "I heard Walter is addicted to gambling. When I was dawdling on the way to the little girls' room, I saw a photograph of Walter all buddy-buddy with a guy who might have looked indigenous. What if Walter owes the casino a cow-patty load of money? What if his debts are ruining his business?" I should text Detective Gifford the picture. But he'd probably consider my even being in Walter's house a form of investigating. He might not believe I went with a friend interested in Katherine's business. Kind of interested. I decided to wait on the text.

Alana drove without speaking for a minute, but her direction was clearly northwest. That is, where Santa Inez sat in relation to Santa Barbara. "Did you notice when we left, Katherine said something about not making a habit of gambling?"

"I did."

"Sounds like she's aware her dad has a problem."

"I know." I glanced over at her. "I didn't get a chance

to tell you I was interviewed by a police detective earlier today."

Her eyes went wide. "Like, grilled at the police station in a grim room with a one-way mirror?"

"You watch too much television."

"Actually, I don't watch any. Who has the time?"

I laughed. "Anyway, I met Detective Gifford at the library. It was all very civilized. Except he recorded our chat, and I was severely cautioned not to try to investigate Paul's death."

"Which is exactly what you're doing, and carting me along for the ride."

"Sort of. But how can asking a few questions in a big public place be dangerous?"

"I don't know. Notice I'm not exactly being dragged there. A few more hours with my bestie? No-brainer." She tapped the steering wheel. "I remember hearing about the casino being built when we were kids."

"You do?" I asked. "I don't."

"They put up the fancy resort later, maybe ten years ago. I've lost track."

"How were you aware of such stuff and I wasn't?"

"Dad has a friend in real estate development." She waved a hand in the air. "The guy got the contract for the resort and was over the moon about it."

"Interesting. But, you know, simply because I want to check out a casino doesn't mean you have to go with me."

"I know, Rob. It's not like our first investigation or anything."

A snort slipped out. "You call lurking around that dude's backyard an investigation?" Alana and I had done what we called surveillance during our junior year. Mainly it consisted of sneaking into the backyard of a cute guy she had an impossible crush on and using her binoculars to spy on him. The escapades were total girl fun. And resulted in zero dates for her. "Listen, you can take me back to my room and I'll grab my car."

"And miss an adventure with my sister in crime? Not a chance!"

Chapter 38

As we drove over San Marcos Pass on a road only recently repaired from a landslide, the scenery was stunning. The Cold Spring Canyon Bridge in particular made me gasp every time I saw it. An arch bridge that ran four hundred feet above the canyon below, it had another two thousand feet of mountains stretching up on both sides. From there we wound down the mountains, ending up in an inland valley.

"Geez, what a glitzy place," I said as we pulled into the drive leading to the casino.

Alana bobbed her head in agreement. "Yeah, well, the type of people who like casinos probably expect bling on steroids." She glanced at me. "Remind me what we're hoping to accomplish here? Are we just going to go in, gamble, and hope to see Walter lose his shirt or something?"

"I'm not sure. Tell you what, I'll buy you ten dollars' worth of tokens and you can try to win a few bucks while I go snoop around."

"Tokens?" She hooted. "What century do you live in, anyway? I bet they don't use tokens anymore. It's gotta be all digital and stuff."

I laughed, too. "Color me clueless. When it comes to gambling, I'm perfectly content to stay that way."

"And you're not doing any snooping without me, girl, so get that idea out of your head." She parked between a late-model Jaguar and a dusty, dented Corolla, with a dark blue mini-van beyond on one side and a big white pickup truck on the other. "I guess all types come here."

We walked toward the casino entrance. The hotel stretched out to the left. All around both buildings were more green lawns, ponds with fountains, and plantings to make people think they were somewhere with unlimited water, rather than in a semi-arid Mediterranean climate with a years-long drought going on. I didn't understand that kind of mentality.

Inside, an over-air-conditioned foyer had walls lined with big showy pictures of happy Native people. A school filled with healthy, alert children. Senior citizens doing intricate beadwork in a community center. Attentive teens at desks with a Native elder writing words I didn't recognize on a whiteboard. And signage indicating all this was made possible by the profits of the resort.

Could it be so straightforward? I didn't know. What about the dangers of drinking and the lure of gambling the casino offered? What about the effect on the environment? Back in South Lick my aunt and others had successfully protested a resort going in, a development that had unfortunately ended up resulting in a murder. It wasn't a Native American casino, but a beautiful wild hillside would have been destroyed by a big showy vacation destination mostly for rich folks. Not so different from here.

From behind a counter to our right, a distinctly white woman wearing a lot of makeup smiled at us. "Welcome. Is this your first time here?"

"Yes." I smiled back. "How do things work?"

She handed us each a brochure. "This includes a map." She opened mine. "The slot machines are here, the craps tables there, and we have several options for poker. You can use cash, a payout card, or a ticket."

I tilted my head at Alana at the mention of cash. She rolled her eyes.

"Do you have blackjack?" Alana asked.

I shot her a glance. I had heard of blackjack, but had no idea of the rules or how to bet on it. Did Alana? This friend was full of surprises.

"Naturally. Right over there." The woman pointed a long red nail. "And of course our girls circulate taking complimentary drink orders."

Sure. Get the patrons tipsy so they'd spend more recklessly, be unable to bet clearly, and lose the ability to count cards. I'd heard of the free drinks deal in Las Vegas, even though I'd never been.

"Thank you," Alana said to her. "Shall we, Roberta?"

When we were out of the woman's earshot, I raised my eyebrows. "Roberta?"

"Seemed like a good idea to disguise ourselves a bit, don't you think?"

I narrowed my eyes. "You're one smart lady. But what's this about blackjack?"

She laughed. "We used to play it in grad school. For pennies, of course. It's kind of fun, and I know a few tricks for winning."

"Are you going to play it here?"

"I might wander over and check out the action. Meet back here in half an hour?"

"Sure. I wonder how I can find out what kind of game Walter usually plays."

"Ask one of the 'girls'—like her." She pointed to a ponytailed blonde in a short black skirt and a very snug sleeveless top with multicolored horizontal stripes, apparently the uniform for the drinks crew. "Say you're looking for him. If he's so much of a regular, everybody should know who he is. Slipping her a ten might help." Alana headed for the blackjack tables in the far corner.

To my right, the constant two-tone dinging from dozens of slot machines was about to give me a headache, as were the flashing lights and the smell of cigarette smoke brought inside on gamblers' clothing. Way across the room I spied green felt tables. Everywhere were men and women playing and betting. Women in tight short dresses with heels and women in sweat suits and tennies. Men in bespoke suits and others in jeans, cowboy boots, and snap-closure plaid shirts.

All the drinks staff seemed to have eyes only for active players. I slid into the nearest slot machine seat and fed in a ten-dollar bill. The traditional levers had ceded to a touch screen, which I was hesitant to actually touch. Did they ever disinfect these things? Less than a minute elapsed before the blond ponytail approached with a smile. She held a round tray with an order pad on it.

"What would you like to drink, miss?"

Up close I saw she couldn't be much over twenty-one. She had dark eyes, and the blond had come out of a bottle. Someone who had grown up on the reservation, perhaps. A small black half-apron was tied over her skirt. At least the servers weren't forced to wear heels to work in. Her canvas sneakers were striped to match her top.

"I'd like an IPA, please," I told her.

"I'll be right back with your drink. Good luck!"

"Thanks. But hang on a minute? I'm looking for an acquaintance, a Walter Russom. I know he comes here a lot. Older fellow, in good shape. Do you know what game he usually plays?"

Her smile flickered for a second. Had she had a bad experience with him? I hoped not.

"Mr. Russom prefers the high-stakes poker tables. I'm not sure he has come in yet today, though."

"Thanks."

She headed off for another customer who had claimed a slot machine. *Yet* today. Interesting choice of words. Did Walter really gamble here every day? Instead of playing, I watched the flow of people from all walks of life up and down the central aisle. A heavyset man in a suit but no tie made his way up the aisle from the back. He stopped and shook hands with people every few feet on both sides, so his progress was slow. As he drew closer, I realized it was the man who had posed with Walter in the photograph.

He was about to pass me when I stood and took a wild guess. "Hi." I smiled and held out my hand. "I hear you're in charge."

He threw his head back and laughed. "Boy, I'm in trouble now." He pumped my hand. "Jimmy Lightfoot. And you are?"

"Roberta O'Neill." I dragged Abe's last name out instead of my own at the last minute, following Alana's lead to stay anonymous. "So nice to meet you, sir. You have quite the establishment here."

"We do, we do. And our people benefit from it every single day. Is this your first time here?"

"Yes. I heard about the casino from Walter Russom." *Sort of.* "Is he one of your investors?"

Jimmy's smile didn't falter, but he blinked as if this was unwelcome news. "Hah, well, Walter certainly does his bit to support the cause." He pointed a finger at me. "I've gotta keep moving. Very nice to meet you, Roberta. Have fun with our little games." And he was gone.

Little games like slot machines? Or not telling me whether Walter was an investor? It was more likely Jimmy meant Walter supported the cause by losing lots of money at the poker tables.

Blond Ponytail arrived as I scooted back into my seat. My drink was among three others balanced on her tray. After she handed it to me, I thanked her and laid a ten-dollar bill on the tray.

"You don't have to tip me, ma'am." She tried to give it back.

I waved her hand away. "It's okay. I didn't pay for my drink, after all." I smiled. "Put it toward your college fund."

She thanked me and slid the bill into her apron pocket. "I do plan to go to college. I want to be an engineer."

"Good for you. I studied engineering, too. What's it like working here?" I asked before sipping the beer.

"Not bad. Close to home. I have a three-year-old who stays with her granny while I'm working. And people who hit the jackpot? They're the best tippers." She glanced toward the door. "Oh, look, there's Mr. Russom. Want me to tell him you're here?"

"No, it's all right," I blurted. "I'll, uh, find him later." He was pretty much the last person I wanted to see right now.

My server headed off to deliver the other drinks. I put my head down, studying the machine, and tilted my face away from the central aisle. But if I hadn't wanted to run into Walter, I shouldn't have come here at all. Another stupid idea. I was full of them this week. Why hadn't I listened to the detective, or to Madame Allegra?

Sure enough, a moment later a hand clapped me on the shoulder. "Is that Katherine's friend I see?" Walter asked in his reedy voice. "You must be hoping to get lucky like all the rest of us."

I glanced up, mustering a smile. "Hello, Mr. Russom. How are you?"

"Good, good. Knocked off work early, headed over here with an eye to picking up some fun money." His tone was pure joviality. The smudges under his eyes and the lines in his forehead told a different story altogether.

Chapter 39

Alana dropped me at the café at four thirty, saying she had to get back for dinner with her parents.

"And I'm afraid this is good-bye for now, Robbie. I'm driving home tomorrow."

"Already? Too soon."

"I know. I do miss Antonio, though, and I need a weekend at home to prepare for a big project meeting at work on Monday."

"I'm flying home Saturday, anyway," I said. "It's been so awesome to hang with you. You have to come and visit in Indiana. I have B-and-B rooms—at no cost to friends and family, of course—and I can show you the area. Bring the man, and you can meet mine, too."

"Deal."

"Pinky promise?" I asked.

"Always."

We hooked pinkies and went straight on to a hug.

"You have my number," she said.

"Hey, I've had your number since kindergarten!" I climbed out and shut the door. I leaned into the open window. "Say hi to the 'rents."

She gave me a thumbs-up and drove off. I watched her go, shaking my head. Why in the world hadn't we seen each other in the last decade? We had picked up this week exactly where we'd left off, except with the added richness of new experiences thrown into the mix.

I stood in front of the café and thought. It was four thirty and the sun wouldn't set for another hour. Still, it was a bit late to start a bike ride, considering I would have to change first. And I'd had a good ride early this morning. I realized I hadn't walked around the mission yet this trip. I'd only ridden by at the start of the week.

Despite the Catholic Church's sordid history of enslaving hundreds of Chumash people centuries earlier—a fact about which I'd been unaware as a child—I'd always loved walking the mission grounds and imagining the monks walking silently in their habits, hands hidden in the joined sleeves. I decided to pay a visit for old times' sake.

After I ran up to my room and used the facilities, I slid into my rental car. Soon enough, I pulled into the parking area to the left of the graceful old mission. I stared. Why was it empty? I checked the mission's Web site on my phone. Oh. Because the mission was closed for the day. It was still a working church and monastery, and the members of the religious order who lived there needed their privacy. I didn't care. I hadn't planned to go inside, anyway, and the grounds outside the walls were always open for strolling. I parked and stashed my bag on the floor, pocketing the key.

I put Paul's death, Walter's gambling, and everything else firmly out of my mind and strolled about as any Midwesterner on vacation would. I meandered along the covered walkway in front of the mission building, which featured arches ending in pillars every eight feet, typical of the colonial architecture. I imagined monks and Chumash alike being shaded by the roof. Shade was a lot more important than shelter from rain in this part of the world. The walkway was paved with antique stones that had settled, so their uneven surface now presented something of a walking hazard.

The antique *lavandería* sat on the sloping lawn in front of the mission, a long and wide water trough with outsloping sides where the Chumash women washed the monks' habits. A replica bear's head was at one end and the original Chumash-carved lion's head at the other end for the water outlet. Sadness bit at me. The creative, functional, fifteen-thousand-year-old Chumash culture had been essentially wiped out by the Spanish and their Franciscans in the eighteenth century.

I veered past the thick-trunked pepper tree in a pitifully small Chumash herb garden. I walked through a picnic area where small orange flowers popped against the green of a vine covering the fence, and then down steps into the olive grove. Along a walkway lined with round stones meandered mosaics picturing the fourteen stations of the cross. The dramatic tile panels sat atop rectangular pillars, the stones of which had been hauled up from the creek by misbehaving seminarians, according to the brochure at the entrance. The dusty gray of the spiky, thin olive leaves cast a slightly spooky light over the area, which also had pea stone paths winding through the trees.

As a chef, I brightened when I came near La Huerta—the Orchard—which was the mission's garden. Unfortunately, it was behind a chain link fence and a sign on the gate said it was only open for tours by appointment. But even viewed through a wire barrier, the tangerine tree, the soaring banana plant with its green clusters of five-inch fruit, the herbs and greens and spiky artichoke leaves made my heart happy. I could smell the citrus from here.

Wandering up and down the fence peering into the garden, I had to start squinting. I glanced up and exclaimed out loud. I couldn't see the ocean from where I stood, but I knew the sun was dipping into the Pacific, casting a sunny path into infinity. The shadows up here deepened into purple, and the rocky faces of the mountains above glowed pink only at their peaks. Time for this vacationer to head home.

My perambulations had landed me at the far end of the garden's fence, and behind me was an empty employee parking lot and utility area. I reversed direction and pointed myself toward my car.

Something rustled behind me. I froze, my heart in my throat. The sound stopped, too. I reached for my phone. No! I swore silently. My cell was safe in the car with my purse. How could I be twenty-eight years old

with a half dozen murder investigations behind me
and leave my phone anywhere except on my person?
How?

I glanced over my shoulder but didn't see anyone. I
laced my keys through my knuckles as I had after the
movie and walked briskly down the path. I headed
around the corner toward the long line of tile-topped
stone columns. Should I sprint for the car? What if I
tripped? Was I actually being pursued? Maybe a crow
had made the noise, or a rat. Maybe I'd become
paranoid. I paused for a moment and took a deep
breath, silently blowing it out, listening. I brought
my hand to my mouth when I heard a faint sound.
That wasn't the noise of a large bird on a flimsy tree
limb. It was a human sound, like a throat clearing or
a sneeze being stifled.

Why hadn't I listened to the palm reader on the
pier? I resumed my fast walk, watching my step but
moving as quickly as I could. A branch cracked behind me. I raced up the six steps to the picnic area
where I'd entered, but my toe caught on the next to
last step. I windmilled my arms, barely catching myself. As I hurried between the wooden tables, my
footsteps resounded louder on the gravel than a
hundred monks crunching popcorn.

Finally, I spied the parking lot. And my insides
turned to ice. A big SUV was backed into a spot near
the exit. An SUV that hadn't been there when I arrived. The vehicle didn't seem to be running, but I
couldn't tell for sure from here. The light was wrong
to see if anyone lurked behind the wheel.

I cursed. I had to get to my car. I heard another noise,

this time coming from the olive grove. It sounded like a shoe crunching on pea stone. Whirling, I thought I caught a glimpse of light-colored pants moving fast in my direction. Time for me to get out of here. I aimed for my car and sprinted for all I was worth.

Chapter 40

I drove more desperately than a white-tailed deer racing to beat a forest fire. Breathless, I pulled into a space in front of the library's main branch, the same place I'd met Detective Gifford earlier. I hadn't been followed here, not that I could tell. I pulled out my phone finally. I knew I should contact the detective, but I called Jason's number instead. I needed the comfort of an old friend more than anything. Gifford might think I was being paranoid, anyway.

When Jason picked up, I heaved the hugest sigh of relief I'd ever breathed.

"What's up, Rob?" My friend's tone was breezy, casual.

My voice came out in a sob. "I hope you're free for dinner again, because I really need to talk with you."

"Hey." Jason's voice changed to dead serious. "Are you okay? What happened? Where are you?"

"I'm in front of the central library. I'm, uh, yeah, I'm okay." I took in a deep breath to steady my wobbly voice and blew it out. "A kind of scary thing happened and I really, really don't want to be alone. And I might have been followed."

"Seriously? Somebody is chasing you?" He swore.

"No. Well, not right now."

"Good. I was going to cook tonight, anyway, and I've already shopped. You've just become my lucky dinner guest. Now, sit tight. Park as close to the building as you can and under a light. I'll be there in fifteen and guide you to my apartment. Cool?"

"Thank you," I whispered.

"On second thought, the library's open until nine. Lock your car and go inside. I'll find you."

I nodded once, even though he couldn't see me. "You're the best."

He disconnected. I was already parked under a streetlamp near the entrance. But Jason was right. I needed to be inside where it was light and where other people—safe people—would surround me.

It took me a minute to summon my courage, though. I climbed out, pressed the lock button on the key fob, and hurried toward the door. An ample-figured woman carrying an armload of books ambled in front of me as if she never moved faster. I did a quick recon over each shoulder, terrified my pursuer would spot me out here.

The woman with the books started to open the door.

"Let me help you, ma'am." I reached over her shoulder and pressed the door open ahead of her.

"Thanks, dear." She gave me a wide, lipsticked smile and headed for the counter with a RETURNS sign hanging above it.

I slid through the door, sinking into a cushioned armchair opposite the main desk, relaxing a little. I felt, what? Normal. It seemed normal to be in a busy city library on a winter evening. Normal to watch teens slouch past in leggings, Uggs, and earbuds. Normal to see a dad ushering his toddler son toward the children's room. Normal even for the librarian to hold a finger to her lips when two men in suits started speaking in tones too loud for a library. The air smelled of books and paper and new carpet, exactly as it should.

As my breathing returned to a calmer pace—a more normal one—I pondered my earlier panics. What on earth had come over me this week? I'd acted the fool, the foolhardy, and the irrational being. Why? Such behavior wasn't like me. Maybe it was being back in the place where I'd been a child. When I wasn't expected to act like an adult. When nobody thought I needed to be anyone more responsible than a girl—albeit a smart and well-loved girl—my age, whatever it was at the time.

"Face it, Jordan," I mutely scolded myself. "You're no girl anymore. You own a business, a successful business. You are closer to thirty than any other age. You can't go around prying into people's lives without expecting consequences. And you definitely can't be leaving your phone in the car at the end of the day while roving about a historic property alone."

I'd also totally ignored the fortune-teller's cautions. This was the second time I'd felt in danger. On the other hand, she'd said I would survive to return to the love of my heart. Abe. I closed the idea in my hand and held it tight, determined for it to be true. As I calmed, my posture sagged. I'd had a day way too full of discoveries and tensions. And then my stomach growled so loud the librarian across the way glanced up and smiled knowingly. It was definitely dinnertime.

My gaze whipped to the front door next time it opened, a smile already creeping over my face. But the slender young man who entered was not my buddy Jason, Cybercrimes Detective Wong. It was Tommy Moore. And he wore light-colored chinos.

Had it been Walter's intern following me at the mission? Katherine had been wearing light-colored pants earlier, too. It was also possible nobody had been after me. Perhaps Tommy was merely here returning a library book. Did people his age even check out books from libraries?

Still, my heart rate revved up again. My chair was behind the copy machine, and I shifted in it so I wasn't facing the door. Maybe Tommy wouldn't see me.

"Hey, Moore," Jason's distinctive voice said.

Whew. He'd arrived. And . . . he knew Tommy? I twisted back to see them high-fiving.

"What are you doing here?" Jason asked him.

Tommy rolled his eyes. "Returning my mom's books for her. See you on the field Saturday?" He laid three hardcovers on the Returns counter.

"You bet."

Tommy headed out. Jason glanced around and crossed over to my chair. He squatted in front of me. "How's it going, my friend?" He kept his voice to a murmur. "You had me worried."

"How do you know Tommy?"

"Moore? He's the newbie on my Ultimate team. He's not bad, actually."

I gave my head a little shake at this unexpected news. "Let's get out of here."

Chapter 41

I perched in Jason's kitchen on a wooden swiveling stool with a back. A glass of a very nice pinot noir sat on the counter in front of me, and I watched an aproned Jason wield a sharp chef's knife. It wasn't a big workspace, but he seemed well equipped with good implements. An array of high-quality saucepans hung from hooks above the gas stove and the sink was bare of dirty dishes. Not like some bachelor pads I'd seen.

"Are you sure I can't help?" I asked.

"No. You relax. Nainai, my Chinese grandma, taught me this years ago. I can stir-fry in my sleep."

My fingers were itching to do some cooking, but I'd have plenty of culinary fun after I got back to my restaurant. I crunched on a few wasabi-coated roasted peas as he chopped pungent ginger and cut a head of broccoli into bite-sized pieces.

He glanced over at me. "You okay with tofu?" he asked.

"Sure, love it."

"So many people claim they dislike it. They don't realize it's a vehicle for other flavors. Like garlic, for example." He used the flat of the knife and the heel of his hand to whack three fat bulbs, a trick that makes the skins slide off, one I'd learned long ago.

He had also set a bowl of skinny jicama spears on the counter to munch on.

"These are so good," I said, savoring the crisp, slightly sweet root. "We can't get jicama in Indiana."

"Your loss, Rob."

"I know. We have other positives out there to make up for it, though." I took a sip of wine.

"What, like ice, snow, and tornadoes?"

"Yes, but also stunning springs and heartbreakingly beautiful falls. Listen, I'm sorry for alarming you earlier."

"No worries. It's a fraught week, isn't it? I was waiting for you to be ready to talk about why you got spooked."

"The thing is, the detective interviewed me today. At the library, in fact. He warned me not to pursue the investigation. And later I kind of didn't follow his advice."

Jason peered at me over his glasses. "Kind of?"

I ticked stories off on my fingers. "First, I went with Alana to meet with Katherine about how she handles weddings. No, wait. Something happened earlier." I told him what Luisa had said about Walter.

"I might have heard about Russom's predilection for gambling." He drained off the water the tofu came in, cubed the firm block, and drizzled tamari generously over it.

"Oh?" I asked.

"You know what I do, right?"

"Internet crimes."

"That's the ballpark. It's not illegal to gamble on-line in California, but it is against the law to start your own private betting site. I shouldn't tell you this, but Russom has been attempting that and trying to hide it."

"Interesting," I said. And maybe not paying the taxes on what he made, either.

"He's been on our radar for a while."

"Well, while Katherine and Alana were talking, I happened to see a photograph in the hallway of Walter looking very friendly with someone in front of a casino," I went on. "After we left Katherine's—and no, she isn't going to hire Ms. Control Freak Russom to run her wedding for a zillion dollars—we drove up to Santa Inez to check out the casino."

Jason gaped.

"Okay, it was my suggestion. Alana was happy to go along. Neither of us had ever been inside one, and it's a pretty drive."

He made a scoffing sound, but didn't speak.

"While we were there, I met the manager, Jimmy Lightfoot. He was the one in the photograph. I also talked with a waitress, who said Walter plays high-stakes poker."

"She happened to tell you Walter plays poker?" He cocked his head and squinted through one eye at me.

"I might have referred to him as an acquaintance I was looking for." I cleared my throat. How could my old classmate be making me squirm like this? "Walter

himself came in a little later. The waitress made it
sound like he was a regular."

He nodded. "But you weren't threatened at the
casino." He focused on nicking the ends off a pile of
snow peas.

"No, not at all, and we drove back. After Alana
dropped me off at my room, I decided to visit the
mission. It was closed, but anybody can walk around
outside, so I did. Except I stupidly left my phone in
my car, and I got distracted checking out the grounds
until it was almost dark." I told him about the noise,
about thinking someone was after me. "I was nearly
to the parking lot when I swear I saw someone wearing light pants following me on the pathway along
the stations of the cross. I ran for my car and drove
like a maniac to the library, where I called you." I
blew out a ragged breath.

"Hey, girl. You're safe. Okay?"

"Yeah. Thing is, when I arrived at the mission, the
parking lot was empty. When I got back to the lot, a big
SUV was parked near the exit. Katherine drives one,
and so does Walter, or he owns one, anyway. Plus, you
saw what Tommy was wearing at the library."

He gave me an incredulous look. "You actually
think I notice what another dude is wearing, like,
ever?"

I laughed. "I suppose guys don't pay attention to
that kind of thing. Although you *are* a detective."

"Cyberdetective, Robbie. *Cyber* being the key word."
He measured rice wine, soy sauce, cornstarch, and
hoisin sauce into a small mixing bowl and whisked
them together.

"Anyway, Tommy was wearing light chinos in the library." I got back to my story. "Earlier, Katherine had on a pair of cream-colored pants, and she's definitely in good enough shape to give chase. Either of them could have been after me. Or maybe it was one of Walter's bodyguards."

"Russom has bodyguards?"

"It looked like it when I heard him speak last night. Big guys in shades acting like Secret Service agents."

"Okay. But why would Moore be chasing you? I can kind of see Katherine doing it, or the dudes hired to protect a company president under threat. Maybe. But a kid barely out of high school who lives at home?"

"Because he's an eager-beaver intern who seems completely taken with his boss? Because if Walter is suspicious of my asking questions around town, he could have asked Tommy to help put me out of commission. Or Katherine, as you rightly point out."

"I don't suppose you wrote down the SUV's plate number," Jason said. "Or noticed the make?"

I shook my head.

"See, women notice clothes. Men notice cars." He held up a hand when I opened my mouth. "Gross generalization, I know. Forget it."

"What about this?" I went on. "Suppose Katherine killed Paul to help her gambling-addicted father, and Walter wasn't in on it? She knows he needs money. She knows Paul was leading the effort to basically put Agrosafe out of business. She puts Paul permanently out of business instead."

"Paranoid much?"

"Hey, I thought you were my buddy." I pointed at him, at me, back at him.

"You know I'm your friend." He didn't smile, though, and continued slowly and carefully. "You need to tell Gifford everything you've told me tonight." He set a wok on the stove and lit the gas burner under it. "But be aware he won't be happy you just happened to be wandering unaccompanied in Russom's house. Or that you went to the casino and asked questions about the man."

"I'm aware of that. And I will call him."

He poured sesame oil into the pan. "This is going to go fast, and we'll eat in minutes. I'm going to stop talking. I have to focus."

He ignored me as he deftly wielded long cooking chopsticks, stir-frying one ingredient after the next. The last to go in were the tofu cubes, which he laid in the middle of the pan and slid a wide lid over the wok. He hurried around the counter to a small table and laid it with place mats, napkins, and chopsticks. He set an empty wineglass and the bottle at one place, then returned to the stove. Lid off, he stirred in the sauce, sprinkled on sesame seeds, and stirred another minute before turning off the flame.

"Voilà!" He spooned white rice into two wide shallow bowls, topped each with a generous portion of the stir-fry, and brought them to the table.

I joined him with my glass. "If only assembling a homicide case was so easy."

Jason gazed at me, finally saying, "No kidding." He poured wine into his glass and topped mine up.

"I wonder if they'll find out about Paul's death before I leave. I can't do anything about it one way or the other," I mused. "Hey, thanks for being here, Jase." I lifted my glass. "And for asking me over."

He clinked. "Here's to friends. It'll all be fine, Rob. You'll see."

I sure as heck hoped so.

Chapter 42

Our fabulous meal was a mere memory an hour later, with only a few grains of rice left in my dish and an abandoned cube of the savory, soy-soaked tofu on Jason's. I sat back in my chair as he regaled me with funny, sometimes poignant, stories of his father's Chinese relatives. Jason's grandparents had come to the States as adults, which had been tough, but they'd forged a successful life for themselves and their children. His dad played first violin with the Los Angeles Philharmonic and his mom, also of Asian ancestry, was a full professor in physics at UCSB. Other relatives who'd come for visits had experienced pretty severe culture shock.

He was in the middle of a tale about forks, knives, and boneless chicken when my cell buzzed in my back pocket.

I checked it and glanced over at Jason. "I'm sorry. It's Alana. Okay if I take the call? She's going back to Berkeley tomorrow."

"Of course."

Jason was about to pour me more wine, but I covered my glass with my hand. I still had to drive home. He stood, gathering up the dishes.

I connected the call. "Hey, Al. I'm at Jason's. The man cooked me the best dinner. I'm putting you on speaker so he can listen in if he wants, okay?"

"Sure," she said.

"Hi, Alana," Jason piped up.

"Hey, Jason," she replied.

"What's going on?" I asked.

"I talked to Mommy about the Moores."

I smiled to myself at my friend continuing to call her mother "Mommy"—an appellation I had never abandoned for my mom, either, for as long as I'd had her.

"Sydelle is a widow," Alana went on. "Her husband died of a massive heart attack ten years ago. But he left a whopping insurance policy and some valuable investments, so she's able to live in the style to which she was already accustomed and not have to find a pesky day job. She does play tennis with Katherine's father."

And more than tennis, according to Katherine. I glanced around Jason's living room as she spoke. The decor would be called male minimal, with a gray sofa, a desk in the corner, and a gray recliner facing a shelving unit holding a big screen and a gaming console. A floor-to-ceiling bookshelf was crammed with books, except for a portrait of Jason, his parents, and his sisters. A framed calligraphy of a few Chinese characters hung from the wall next to the books.

"Tommy Moore is the older child and his little sister is a sophomore at Chumash," Alana finished.

"Any history of homicide in the family?" I asked.

Jason shot me a chin-back-frowning-brows-half-smile look of incredulity.

She laughed out loud. "Yeah, like my mother would know about homicide."

I laughed, too. She was right, of course. "Can't hurt to ask. No wonder Walter gave the kid a gap-year job. Maybe Tommy hopes if he behaves he'll have a new dad at home. He's been without a father for a long time."

"True," Alana said. "From what you said, Robbie, and based on what we saw at the casino, seems to me Mrs. Moore might not be getting the high-power second husband she expects, not if Walter's in a lot of debt from gambling." A background noise came through Alana's call. "Sorry, guys, I have to go. Great to see you both this week."

"Love you," I said. "Be in touch."

"Bye, Alana," Jason added. "Let me know next time you're back in town."

"You got it." She disconnected.

I set my phone on the table and stared at Jason. "Do you think it means anything? Tommy's mom and Katherine's father being an item?"

"I don't know." He sat again, wiping his hands on a dish towel. "But I did learn something today you'll want to hear."

I waited. "And?"

"I actually shouldn't be telling you this. But I will, mostly because you alerted us to look for it. Mel's lab tests found a neurotoxin in Paul's system."

"So it was murder," I breathed, eyes wide.

"From all reports he was neither suicidal nor suffered from clinical depression. So, yes, they're calling it a homicide."

"Wait. You've known about this since before I got here, since before I saw you at the library. Why didn't you tell me?"

"I didn't want to spoil dinner," Jason said. "Plus, you were ever-so-slightly freaked out by your experience at the mission. Talking about homicide over dinner wasn't going to help."

I thought. "I guess you're right. Thank you." I swished the last bit of wine in my glass, then set my chin in my hand with my elbow on the table, my mom's manners lessons tossed to the side. "Now what?"

"Now they have to figure out who gave it to him, and how."

"Right." I tapped my glass. "Paul's housemate, Grace, told me the police took his takeout lunch box. Do they think the poison was put in his food?"

"I'm really out of the loop for that kind of detail, Rob. Sorry."

"And I suppose you don't know about anyone's alibis, either. Walter's, Katherine's, Tommy's. Heck, even Sydelle. If she's so taken with Walter, maybe she did his dirty work."

He raised an eyebrow. "Maybe, but I haven't been apprised about alibis or the lack thereof."

"It's okay. I didn't expect you had."

"The only reason I know about the autopsy results is that Mel slipped me a text from her personal phone to mine."

"She did?" I asked. "She's awesome. Wasn't telling you kind of risky?"

"Yes. But we're good friends." He cleared his throat. "Also, and this is strictly unkosher, she said she would be willing to talk with you about it."

"Wow. She told me a few days ago she wouldn't be able to, since I'm not family."

"If Mel says she'll do something, she'll do it. And she won't use her work phone."

"Okay, thank you. I'll look for her message. I won't tell a soul." I wanted to rub my hands together, though. "Did I tell you about the alpaca farmer I met? Her name is Ceci Shaterian."

"The name sounds kind of familiar, but I can't place it."

"She had to sell out of her property in Oxnard at a loss because of Agrosafe spray drift."

"Ugh," he said. "Selling must have been hard on her."

"For sure, and she hates Walter for it," I said. "If he had been the murder victim, Detective Gifford would want to look into Ceci's alibi, for sure."

"What happened to her animals?"

"They got sick from the spray but survived. Ceci and her husband have new property in the foothills now. Liz and I went up there this morning to visit the alpacas."

Jason peered at me.

"Ceci invited me."

"Now you're going to tell me it's a pretty drive."

"It is! Anyway, it turns out Paul's sister, Taylor, volunteers with the animals there."

His mouth dropped open. I hurried on.

"Which I swear I did not know. Taylor said Paul had been trying to befriend somebody he worked with, asking her over for meals, trying to look out for her. It had to be Zoe."

"Because of her addiction."

"Yeah," I said. "They both work—or worked—at the Green Artichoke. But Taylor told me the person wasn't really having it."

He blinked, as if processing this new bit of information. "You're thinking Zoe might have poisoned a meal Paul took home from the restaurant. But . . . why, Rob? Why would she want to kill him?"

"I don't have a clue. But if I dig some more, maybe I'll find one."

Jason set his forearms on the table and leaned toward me. "No digging. Call Gifford. Let him dig. Okay?"

"I guess." I drummed my fingers on the table.

"No guessing, Rob. I really, truly don't want you to get hurt. One of the people we've been talking about is capable of taking another person's life. Which is a step way, way beyond where pretty much any of us would ever dream of going."

"I know. I've had contact with other killers, remember. You're right. I'll leave it to the cops." A yawn escaped me. "And right now I'm going to leave you to your bed and go find mine."

As I drove home, blessedly without anyone following me, I thought about Zoe. I hoped she wasn't involved in Paul's death. I couldn't figure out why she would be. If Zoe had crossed that line Jason spoke of, if she'd taken the one extra step to end someone's life, Zoe's life would also be ruined. And it would devastate Liz.

Chapter 43

Back in my lovely room by nine, I did my due diligence. I found Nolan Gifford's card and tapped his number into my phone.

"OMG, thank goodness he didn't pick up," I said to the walls. I'd had entirely enough chastising today to last me the rest of the year—and it was only February. I sent a quick text saying I was e-mailing him. I was just as happy typing what I'd promised Jason I would tell the detective.

> *Detective Gifford:*
> *I ran into Paul E's sister, Taylor, at Ceci Shaterian's alpaca farm today. Taylor said Paul had been befriending a dishwasher at work lately, asking her home for meals. Paul and Zoe worked together at the Green Artichoke, as I'm sure you're aware. I didn't mention what Taylor said when we talked earlier because I didn't think it was important, but I'd rather let you decide if it is or isn't.*

I also went with my recently engaged friend, Alana Lieberman, to Katherine Russom's wedding planning office today. Katherine works out of her father's home. I happened to see a photograph of Walter Russom and Jimmy Lightfoot of the casino in Santa Inez on the hallway wall. I'm sure you already know of their connection.

I stared at the screen. Gifford surely didn't need to know Alana and I had also gone to the casino. Was there anything else I owed him? My mission adventure? Probably, for what it was worth.

I walked around the mission grounds in the late afternoon today after the museum closed. While I was there, a dark SUV parked in the lot. I believe someone in light-colored pants was following me. I felt threatened and finally made it to my car and drove away. Sorry, didn't get a plate number of the vehicle. Katherine Russom drives an SUV and was wearing light-colored pants earlier.

Oh, and Alana's mother says Walter is dating widow Sydelle Moore, mother of his intern, Tommy. This might sound like gossip, but again, better to let you decide. FYI, I saw Tommy Moore at the library wearing light-colored chinos. Walter Russom's bodyguards also wear khaki pants.

I hope you are able to resolve the case soon.
Best,
Robbie Jordan

There. I tapped Send and was done with it. If that wasn't acting like a responsible citizen, I didn't know what was. I opened the window, poured an inch of bourbon with a splash of water, and settled in on the bed to call Abe. I missed him wicked bad, as a college friend from Massachusetts used to say.

Strike two. He didn't answer. *Rats.* I didn't bother with a voice message and shot him a text, instead.

Miss you. Call me before seven your time? Can't wait to see you Sat!

I hit Send on the message. Now what? The other night I had thought of making a crossword puzzle. Now that I knew for real that Paul was murdered, my itch to put all the facts in order was stronger. And hey, who needed graph paper when there were free online apps for creating crosswords? Jason and Detective Gifford couldn't fault me for digging when it was entirely a cerebral exercise executed in the privacy of my own room.

I hunted on my iPad until I found some free software that looked user-friendly, then I organized my thoughts. My clues were going to involve making assumptions and leaps of faith. As far as I could tell, real detecting made a lot of assumptions and leaps, too. And then backed it up with actual evidence, of course. I started typing in the Clues section.

In debt from gambling
Loyal to father
Needs money for drugs
Eager to please potential stepfather
Widow with romantic interest to encourage

Hmm. This was going to be a pretty small puzzle at this rate. But it was only the Suspects list. What did

Kinsey Millhone look for? Motive, means, and opportunity. Or was my Suspects list really a Motive list? I
forged ahead.

Access to Agrosafe neurotoxin
Able to dose Paul's food

Speaking of opportunity, I'd asked waitress Debbie if Zoe had been at work the night before Paul
died. What had she said? I squinted, searching my
memory. Yes, she'd said Zoe was washing dishes.
That was also when Debbie had mentioned they took
their smoking breaks together.

But had anybody else had opportunity? The house
Paul and Grace lived in was old. I doubted it had
good locks. Anyone daring could have sneaked in
and put the poison in Paul's food. Except that would
have risked killing Grace instead. And was breaking
and entering means or opportunity? An alibi, if it
stood up, would equal lack of opportunity. But what
was the lack of means?

I stamped my foot. I didn't know what Walter,
Katherine, Tommy, or Sydelle had been up to the
night before or the morning of Paul's death. And I
didn't think I had any way of knowing. I pictured
Walter's home and my eyes flew wide. Unless Cody
knew. He lived there, too. I'd seen his room.

Wait. Alana and I had eaten at Boathouse on Monday at five or so, and Cody had been working. He'd
likely been on shift until they closed.

I opened a new tab on the browser and checked
the Boathouse hours. They closed at nine on Mon-

days. Would Cody have noticed his dad or sister leaving the house or coming in that night or the next morning? Cody himself was a strong ally of Paul's—if what he'd told Alana and me was true—and wasn't on the Suspects list. But I didn't have his cell number and it was too late to call the restaurant. Besides, there was no way I could pose a question about his closest relatives' whereabouts without him knowing what I was doing. I swore in frustration.

I took a deep breath. And a sip of whiskey. Impatience would get me nowhere. Maybe I was going about this the wrong way. Or maybe I simply didn't have enough information or sufficient facts at my disposal either to design the puzzle or solve it.

And speaking of information, this morning at breakfast Hector had hurried off saying he had to make a call. He'd said he might know something. But what? Carmen had given me his cell number. I might as well ask him. I texted,

Hector, this is Robbie. This morning you said you might know something in regard to Agrosafe and Paul's death. Willing to share?

I tapped Send and stared at the phone for the next minute. No reply. He was probably out dancing. Strike three, unless he got back to me later. I really should give up on this amateur-sleuthing thing. Not my circus, not my monkey. Except I felt it was, and I'd never been known as a quitter. Well, except for fishing.

Saved from my confused stewing by the literal bell, I smiled at Abe's ringtone and connected. "Hey, sweetheart," I said. "How's my favorite Hoosier?"

"Missing you, but otherwise I'm well. A dude was giving a talk in Nashville on spelunking and I wanted to hear it."

I frowned at the sketchy connection. "What the heck is 'speedlumping'?" I asked.

He roared with laughter. "Do you know I love you?"

"Um, yes. Please answer my question."

Abe recovered enough to say, "SPEE-lunking, sugar. It's exploring caves."

"Oh! I know what spelunking is. I just couldn't hear you. Indiana has caves?"

"Sure, lots of them, especially down here in the southern part of the state. I've always wanted to get into exploring the caves, but never made the time. We'll go together this spring or summer."

I cleared my throat. "My dearest darling Abe. Do you not remember I tend to panic in small, confined spaces? Didn't I ever tell you?"

He groaned and waited a beat before speaking. "Well, shoot. Of course I knew. That thing with the tunnel."

"That thing with the tunnel." The time when a killer had invaded my private property through a tunnel I hadn't even known existed. Through a narrow, confined space I'd had to traverse more than once. Yeah, that thing. "Geez, it happened already a year ago."

"I'm sorry, honey. Don't worry. I'll go caving with a group, or maybe take Sean, if he wants to try it."

"Yes, you will." I put a smile in my voice to soften the message. "So what have you been up to?"

"Working, picking banjo, cooking for my boy. The usual. How about you?"

I was about to launch into the whole story, then swerved down another conversational path. We could talk about this mess on Saturday. "Seeing old friends and old haunts, eating great food. I'll tell you all about it when I get back."

Chapter 44

I dragged myself up out of sleep the next morning. Right before I awoke, I'd been alone and in the passenger seat of a huge van, which was backing up slowly with no one at the wheel. Through crowded urban streets. In the dark. I couldn't maneuver my foot far enough to reach the brake pedal, and somehow I could barely see. I've never been so glad to awaken to a nominally safe reality.

After I washed up, a little online digging landed me the location of the tennis courts nearest the Russom home. I figured Walter and Sydelle for early-morning-tennis types. Granted it was winter, but habits were habits. And in a place like southern California, even the northern reaches of the region, playing early in the day to beat the heat was always a good idea.

By six thirty I'd made myself ready for my last Santa Barbara day in capris, T-shirt, light sweater, and Keens, sandals so well engineered you could jog in them. I grabbed a takeout cup of coffee from the carafe downstairs on my way out. I needed it, having slept worse than restlessly.

"Robbie, you eating?" Carmen called from the pass-through window.

The air smelled of crispy sweet pastries, a hint of chiles, and the heavenly aroma of cured meats on the grill. I nearly plopped into the closest seat and gave myself up to it. This kind of deliciousness in the early morning, and I hadn't had to prep and cook it? Nirvana.

"Yes, but later," I replied. "I have to run do something. I promise I'll be back to eat."

My host gave me a thumbs-up. "Mamá's got a yummy special waiting with your name on it." Luisa's smiling face appeared behind her.

I waved at both women, then headed out. Immediately after I got on the freeway, I passed the gigantic Moreton Bay Fig Tree, whose canopy spanned a hundred and seventy feet. At nearly that many years old, it wasn't as ancient as the giant Sequoias in the Sierra Nevada mountains that Mom and I had camped among when I was young. Still, the Moreton was an impressive sight.

Esmeralda, the name I'd christened my phone's GPS, directed me in her usual no-nonsense way east several exits on the 101. Alana had driven to the Russoms' neighborhood yesterday, but I hadn't lived here in so long I was a little at sea, geographically. I passed the zoo and wished I'd paid it a visit this week. Maybe somehow I could squeeze in a walk there later today.

This exit had me driving through the late Ms. Grafton's stomping grounds on my way to Montecito

Lite. The homes along here were large, tastefully lovely, and protected by master-gardener landscaping, walls, and locked gates. *Good.* Sue had deserved some luxury and privacy as a reward for all twenty-five of her brilliant mysteries. She'd died not so long ago, only in her early seventies, and had firmly declared there would be no *Z Is for Zero* ending to the Kinsey Millhone series. I blew a kiss in homage, even though I didn't know which estate had been hers.

Esmeralda directed me to turn left. "You will arrive at your destination in a quarter mile," she pronounced, sounding way too smug for seven in the morning. I slowed, watching out for tennis courts.

"Your destination is on the left," Es said. "You have arrived," she announced in triumph.

I wasn't sure how they'd made the GPS voice sound weirdly both human and robotic. Didn't matter. She was right. On my left were six well-appointed tennis courts. Nice pavement, newly painted tall fencing, well-stretched nets, lights on tall posts for night play.

Now that I was here, I found myself with an attack of nerves. I wanted to talk with Walter and his girlfriend. But how to accomplish a conversation without looking as if I were digging, as the cops so elegantly put it, my buddy Jason included? Did I have a premise, an excuse? I could, I supposed, claim I was also a tennis player and say Sydelle's son, Tommy, had told me about these courts. Which was true. And if they asked me to hit a few balls, well, I was wearing sandals, wasn't I? I couldn't possibly.

I decided to navigate the situation as I went. I parked and climbed out, bringing my coffee as a se-

curity blanket. Or, more important, as a caffeine fix.
I followed the paths around the courts, hearing the
signature *bonk* of balls, the grunts of servers and serious backhanders. They weren't quite Venus Williams-
or Rafael Nadal-level grunts, but close. Serious
amateurs frequented these courts.

Bingo. I spied Walter in white shorts and a black
shirt. He was playing doubles with a sinewy woman,
her in a tight blue sleeveless top and a blue-and-
white split tennis skirt, her expression more cut-
throat than any I'd seen on TV. She was Sydelle, the
same person who'd driven away with Walter after the
farmers' market. Their opponents were a younger
man and woman who looked a lot more relaxed,
both wearing nylon shorts and cotton T-shirts featuring Ventura Beach in colorful printing.

None of them paid a speck of attention to me. I
sank onto a bench positioned outside the fence near
the net and watched them play. The other couple,
more my age than Walter and Sydelle's, were energetic and seemed to enjoy each other's company.
Sydelle, on the other hand, didn't crack a smile or
even speak to Walter. She was a hundred percent focused on the game. At least the bodyguards weren't
lurking here.

I had flitted by Wimbledon matches on television,
but I didn't know anything about tennis scoring or
winning, and I'd never once picked up a racket.
These players were tossing around terms like *deuce*,
fifteen, *love*, and more. Finally, the game appeared to
be over. Sydelle didn't look happy as she grabbed a
small towel before joining Walter at the net to shake
hands with the other couple, who smiled graciously.

The younger couple picked up their towels and gear and headed out through a gate in the fence.

Walter had his back to me, but I could see Sydelle's nostrils flaring even from here. I glanced at the court on the other side of my bench but kept my hearing and my peripheral vision focused on this one.

"What kind of playing was that, Walter?" Sydelle demanded. She patted her forehead with the towel, then slung it around her neck.

"You can't win every time, Delle." He bit off the words.

"Yeah, but you hardly ever win anymore." Her voice was hard, too. "Not here, not at the casino."

I peered at them again.

He straightened his back. "My company, on the other hand, is doing very well these days. One might even say winning. I mean it, one can't succeed at every turn." He cleared his throat. "And you played your usual beautiful, strong game. I love watching you on the courts, and everywhere else, too." He slung his arm around her shoulders and squeezed.

The compliment seemed to do the trick. Her posture softened and she leaned into him, murmuring.

I took this as my cue to exit stage right, making a beeline for my car. I didn't really need to talk to them. Maybe both Walter and Sydelle had a soft, affectionate side to balance their ambition. But had Walter meant Agrosafe was winning because the threats to its products had been removed? Threats in the persons of Jeanine Jordan and Paul Etxgeberria?

Chapter 45

At eight thirty, I plopped onto a stool at the counter facing the café's pass-through window, even though my feet dangled. "I am so ready for a big breakfast, Carmen." And longer legs, too, but that ferry had left the dock long ago.

"You got it, Robbie." She slid me a menu even as she tossed her scarlet-streaked braid back over her shoulder.

"Did you say you had a special with my name on it?" I asked.

"*Numero Uno.*" She pointed at a Specials blackboard a lot like the one in my restaurant.

"OMG. Chile Relleno à la Chef? Yes, please, *señora.*" I wanted to ask how Luisa—the chef—presented the cheese-stuffed and batter-fried green chiles, but I didn't. I figured I'd understand when it was on my plate.

Mamá leaned her smiling face into the pass-through. "*¿Sopapillas, tambien?*"

Now my eyes really bugged out. "Of course! *Sí, sí.*"

Now I really had died and gone to heaven. Deep-fried puffs of pastry as light as clouds served in a honey syrup were the preferred food of goddesses and were more typical of New Mexico. Another delicacy not to be found within hundreds of miles of the state I now called home. No, I wasn't about to forgo *sopapillas* simply because the calories would go straight to my already padded hips.

"*Bueno,*" Luisa said and disappeared back into the kitchen.

"Carmen, did you ever get a chance to look at your security camera footage?" I kept my voice low.

"I tried. Something's wrong with it." She pulled her mouth to the side. "Can't see anything."

Too bad.

"So you're leaving early tomorrow, right?" she asked.

"I am." I tilted my head from side to side, miming how reluctant I was to go.

"But now you know where you'll stay when you come back."

"Absolutely. Listen, you and Mamá should come visit me. I have rooms upstairs like you do. You can meet my Pajarito. I'll serve you biscuits and gravy and show you more green leaves and grass than you ever imagined could grow." The first time I'd traveled to Indiana with my mom to visit her sister, Adele, when I was six, it had been in June right after school had gotten out. I could not believe how green it was everywhere. It hadn't even seemed possible to someone growing up in a semi-arid climate like this one.

Carmen turned to face her mother and let out a

string of Spanish. All I picked up was a trilled "Robbie."

Luisa smiled broadly at me and thumped her heart twice. "*Sí,*" she said decisively.

Carmen bustled off. Her little bird-cat purred on the floor but couldn't quite reach my ankles. He coiled himself and leapt up to the stool next to mine, then commenced a serious washing. Having an animal inside a restaurant wouldn't fly in South Lick, but maybe the rules were more lax here, or maybe Carmen didn't have the health inspector dropping by on a regular basis—and breathing down her neck—like I did.

Hector stuck his head through the pass-through window. "Hey, Robbie. I got your text but it was too late to answer. Mind if I join you?"

"Please."

He emerged from the kitchen and picked up Pajarito, then sat with the cat on his lap, stroking his back, not looking at me.

I kept my voice low. "Did you find out anything?"

"Maybe." He finally gazed at me, his face somber. "Mamá told you about Walter Russom's gambling problem."

"Yes."

"I know a guy who knows a guy. The other guy isn't a particularly nice type. And Russom owes him a boatload of money. He might lose his house."

"Ouch. By 'not particularly nice,' do you mean like the Mob or something? Here in Santa Barbara?"

Hector gave me a kind but pitying look. "I think you might have led a pretty sheltered life in ways, Robbie. Yes, we have bad guys even here in paradise."

A lightbulb went on in my head, just like in the old cartoons. "Is it Jimmy Lightfoot?"

"No way. Lightfoot is a businessman and a straight one. He does a ton of good for his people, on and off the rez. No, this is someone else. Trust me, you don't want to know his name."

"That's fine. But, Hector, the detective does want it. He needs it. Will you tell him?"

He blew out a breath. The sounds of cookware clanking and pops of frying emitted from the kitchen. All around us was the hum of conversation, a laugh here, the clink of fork on plate there. Hector drummed his fingers on the counter. I sipped my coffee.

He looked at me with a slow, nodding frown. "Okay. Text me how to reach him."

"Thanks. I will."

He slid off the stool, depositing Pajarito onto it. "I have to run do prep in the truck. When do you head home?"

"Tomorrow morning. It was awfully nice getting to know you a little better this week." I held out my hand.

He shook it. "Same here, Robbie. You take care today, all right?" He still wasn't smiling.

"I promise."

He disappeared into the kitchen. The cat jumped down and followed him. Hector had looked beyond worried. The same way Madame Allegra had. I again felt the chill that had come over me at the fortune-teller's. I sat up straight, trying to shake it off. I had twenty-four hours until I was on a plane home. What could happen in this beautiful place full of light?

I sent Hector the detective's number, then burrowed into my phone. Nothing new. Except . . . Oh! A text had come in a minute ago from a number I didn't recognize or already have in my phone. I opened it to read,

Let's talk. Meet me Alice Keck west entrance ten thirty.

This must be from Mel Washington's personal phone about Paul's autopsy. I tapped out a quick reply.

Thx. See you then.

How had I nearly forgotten Jason had said Mel was willing to give me details about Paul's death? I chalked it up to an over-full brain. Was it odd she hadn't identified herself in the text? No. Jason would have told her he had let me know she'd be contacting me unofficially.

It was only nine now. I had plenty of time to eat and make it downtown by ten thirty. I had almost no time left to contribute to Paul's murder investigation—which, of course, the detective didn't want me to—but if Mel laid out the facts of Paul's death for me, I might sleep more easily. Or maybe Gifford and team would have arrested the killer by the time I needed to leave before dawn to catch my flight from LAX to Indy.

Luisa herself delivered my breakfast. She set down a steaming platter with three chiles rellenos arrayed in a triangle surrounded by avocado slices atop a mound of what had to be Mexican fried rice, with specks of red and green peppers, a smattering of black beans intermingled with bits of scrambled eggs, and covered with melted cheese and salsa. I'd eaten avocado every day of my trip and wasn't a bit tired of its smooth, rich taste and texture. Yep, I was in heaven.

Carmen handed me a small plate holding two glistening *sopapillas* and set down a hefty bloody Mary next to it.

"Wow." I was truly stunned. *"Gracias*, Mamá, Carmen.*"* I stood and gave them each a hug. "But I didn't order a drink, Carmen."

She waved me away. "Sit, eat, drink." She leaned closer and whispered, "On the house."

All I could do was smile as Luisa headed back for the kitchen. Carmen tended to other customers. I blissed out on my meal.

Chapter 46

I pulled into a parking space on Santa Barbara Street near the west entrance to the park at a few minutes before ten thirty. Despite the size of my filling breakfast, I'd wisely taken only a couple of sips of the bloody Mary. The last thing I needed was an arrest for DUI the day before I left, or worse, hurting someone because I'd been driving impaired. I'd promised Carmen I would stop in for a drink tonight before I went to bed instead.

I put down the windows and let the sunny air fill the rental. I couldn't see Mel strolling, perched on a bench, or sitting in a car, so I stayed put behind the wheel. My Spidey sense came back to remind me she hadn't identified herself, which was odd. I gazed at her text again. *Huh.* I copied the number and texted it to Jason's personal phone, hoping he had it on him at work. I added a message:

Is this the number I should expect to be contacted from?

Despite the vagueness, he would know I meant Mel.

His reply dinged seconds later.

No! I'll run a search. Stay safe. Or better, leave the area.

Staying safe was definitely the plan. I didn't leave, but I clicked the doors locked. Just in case. Just in case of what, I didn't want to think about.

The sidewalk here was full of briefcase holders walking briskly. Parents meandered with strollers and toddlers in tow. A few down-on-their luck people huddled under blankets on benches, while others sat mutely on the ground holding hand-lettered cardboard signs asking for a day's work or food for their six kids.

Not a tall, stylish, obsidian-skinned pathologist among them. But as I watched, I did spot someone familiar. Cody Russom hurried toward the entrance wheeling a bicycle, giving me a sad déjà vu from my meeting with Paul only five days earlier. Cody wheeled the bike into the park, then halted next to a cactus with spiky red flowers and pointed twisting tendrils that reminded me of an octopus.

He shed the bike helmet and started to do a slow 360. I slid down so my head was barely visible above the steering wheel. When he faced away again I straightened. Had *he* texted me and not Mel? I'd never given him my cell number. Was Cody trying to trap me? Or had he contacted me to hand over a piece of evidence that would incriminate Paul's killer?

Jason texted me.

Number not Mel's. It belongs to Walter Russom's multi-line account. Leave, Rob. Drive to police station. Or anywhere, please. And let Gifford know.

I could drive away now. I could head over to Mr. Straight Arrow Gifford and report the text. But I didn't want to leave until I understood what was going on. Maybe Cody needed help. Maybe his text had been because he'd learned something important. About his father's culpability in Paul's death? Or Katherine's?

On the other hand, he could be on their team. He was family, after all. He could have lied to Alana and me about his anti-Agrosafe activism. I hit the steering wheel, wishing I had a partner in crime-solving at my side. But surely I could get out and talk to Cody. There were so many people around, and it was a sunny public space.

I had my hand on the door handle, but pulled it away. No. It would be just my luck to get into some kidnap scenario or another equally bad ending. Instead, I took a deep breath and found Detective Gifford's number on my phone.

By some miracle, he answered with a terse, "Gifford."

"Detective, this is Robbie Jordan. I got a text from someone this morning who wanted to talk to me at Alice Keck Park. I didn't know who it was. I am here in my car with the doors locked at the west entrance to the park. Cody Russom arrived a minute ago, and he's looking around for someone. I expect it's me. Maybe he knows something about Paul's death."

"Thank you. Please drive away now, but stop after a block and text me the number. Did he arrive in a vehicle?"

"No, by bicycle."

"I'll send someone over ASAP."

He disconnected before I could even say okay. Cody had now perched on a bench, but he was tapping his thigh in a nervous gesture and he kept glancing around. I focused on my phone and sent Gifford the number Cody had texted me from. There. Now I was supposed to drive away. But what if Cody left? Someone should tell the police which way he went, and it seemed obvious I was the one to do it.

I glanced back at him. The bench was empty. *Shoot.* Where had he—?

A noisy breath of relief escaped my lips. A group of tourists passed by on the sidewalk to reveal Cody walking his bike. Straight toward me. I peered at him. Or not walking toward me, per se. I didn't think he'd seen me.

Now what? I still didn't think I should get out of the car, but I didn't want to lose the kid, either. The street had too much traffic to follow him slowly in my vehicle if he started riding. Instead, I leaned over on the passenger seat and lowered the window.

"Cody," I called.

He glanced around, but didn't seem to see me. I tapped the horn quickly and leaned closer to the window.

"Cody, hi."

He bent down. "There you are. Thank God." His face was a portrait of Worried Young Man. He crouched, resting his bike against the side of the car. "Did you get my text?"

"I got a text from somebody, but I didn't know who it was. How did you know my number?"

"Oh, that." He shot a glance at the park and back at me. "I hacked my sister's reunion account. Your number was in your registrant's data set. Katherine has, like, zero security on the database."

The kid was smart, for sure. Well, he had said he was studying computer science. "What did you want to talk about?"

"It's bad. I mean, like, really bad." He sounded as if he was about to start crying. "It took me forever to decide whether to tell someone or not."

Ugh. Now I had a bad feeling, too. He was going to tell me his own father was guilty of murder. Poor Cody.

He shuddered, but shook it off. "It's just that Katherine, she—"

"Ah, Cody Russom." Noland Gifford materialized at Cody's side.

Cody glanced up with eyes widened in alarm.

"Exactly the person I've been looking for." The detective laid a hand on Cody's shoulder, then leaned down to give me a look through the window. His expression telegraphed his disapproval that I hadn't followed instructions and gotten myself out of there five minutes ago.

"Why are you looking for me?" Cody shrugged off the hand. He stood and gripped his bike like a shield.

I slid out of the car and hurried around the front. At this point, I didn't care what Gifford thought. I suddenly cared about Cody a lot more.

"Yes, why?" I asked Gifford.

"I'll simply say we're curious about your recent communications, Mr. Russom." The detective kept his voice low and firm.

A patrol car pulled up and angled in front of my rental, blocking me from leaving. At least the police car wasn't broadcasting its presence with lights or siren. Two shorts-wearing patrol officers on bicycles rode up and dismounted, too. The male officer held the bikes and the female stood with her hands on her belt. A couple approaching arm in arm on the sidewalk halted, staring, then hurried across the street.

"Do you have any objection to coming to the station so we can record an informational interview with you?" Gifford asked Cody.

Cody looked more like a scared puppy than a college student. "Um, I don't know. What do you think I should do, Robbie?"

"He's not being charged with anything, right, Detective?" I asked.

"No, he's not."

"You should go, Cody. Go and tell them whatever you were about to tell me. And didn't get a chance to," I added for Gifford's benefit. Or maybe my own.

"All right," Cody whispered. "What about my bike?" He searched Gifford's face.

"We'll bring it with us." Gifford signaled to one of the bike cops. The woman stepped forward and ushered Cody toward the police car, where an officer waited at the open passenger door. At least they weren't locking him in the back.

"Cody, do you want me to call anyone for you?" I called out.

Desperation washed over his face. "Not Katherine! Not my dad, either." He swallowed. "But could you tell Boathouse I'm, um, sick, and won't make the noon shift?"

"Of course," I assured him. "Call me when you're done at the station if you can."

Within a minute the patrol car was gone, Cody's bike in the back seat.

Gifford turned to me. "What did he tell you?"

"Nothing, unfortunately. Seriously, I stayed in my car, texted you his number, and was watching so he wouldn't leave the park. When it looked like he planned to, I spoke to him through the window."

"I still wish you had left." He folded his arms.

"You might have lost him!" I cleared my throat, giving myself a moment to calm down. "He started to say something about Katherine, and then you arrived and interrupted him."

The detective nodded once. "Had you given him your number?"

"No, but he's in computer science at the college." I told Gifford what Cody told me about hacking into Katherine's account.

"Okay. Good to know. I have to get over to the station. Thanks for alerting me about him. When did you say you were going back to Indiana?"

Had I said? "Tomorrow morning."

"Have a wonderful last day of vacation in our lovely city." He stressed the word *vacation* as he gave me a grim smile.

"I'll try, thank you." I watched him amble off, hands in pockets. A vacationer was the last thing I felt like, especially after seeing Cody's nerves and his fear. His mention of his own sister in association with the word *bad* was even worse.

Chapter 47

I sat stunned in my car with the windows still open. It seemed like hours had passed since I parked here, but it had been only fifteen minutes. I squinted at the winter light. I sniffed the air smelling of pungent eucalyptus leaves and the sweet perfume of oranges. How could it be so sunny, so fragrant, so California, when darkness was the backdrop? Murder. Poison. Lies.

Cody had been about to tell me something—something really bad—about Katherine. He'd hacked into her reunion database to find me. He might have also dug into her personal e-mail and read an incriminating detail about Paul's death. But incriminating who? Walter and his thugs, or maybe Sydelle? Or Zoe. Tommy. Katherine herself. I only hoped Cody would call me after Gifford finished with him so I could learn what he'd found.

Speaking of calls, I needed to phone Boathouse for Cody. I searched for the number and hit the phone icon. The manager didn't sound very convinced, but I said I was Cody's aunt visiting from back east and my nephew really was under the weather. I mustered a weak smile after I disconnected. Yeah, his very young aunt.

Now what should I do? I assumed Jason would learn what had gone down. Just in case, I shot him a quick text.

All's well. Det. took Cody to station to talk.

He returned only a *K.* I sat behind the wheel, gazing out the window, thinking. Foot traffic had resumed on the sidewalk, now that the commotion the cops had caused was gone.

I guessed I could go back to my room and pack. I could take a last walk on the beach. I could shop for fresh tortillas, dried ancho chiles, and See's peanut brittle—the best in the known universe—to take home. Maybe find a mission ornament for Abe's parents' Christmas tree and a surfing T-shirt for his son, Sean. What kind of souvenir should I bring Abe, besides the alpaca mittens? I could probably find him an artichoke cookbook at Chaucer's Bookstore, or even a cookbook from Gilroy, Garlic Capital of the World, two hundred fifty miles north of here near the coast.

Before I had a chance to turn the key in the ignition, my phone dinged with another text.

This is Mel W. Meet me at library in ten?

Whew. Much better than packing. And I'd have time for shopping later.

Yes, thx.

I saved *Mel W Personal* into my contacts list, locked the car, and set out for a five-minute walk. My Friday was looking up, if you can call learning about a poisoning an ascent.

She was waiting on a low white wall outside the fifteen-foot-high arched windows of the library when I arrived, swiping through something on her phone.

"Hi," I said, sitting a few feet away on the same wall. "Thanks for contacting me." A bottlebrush tree nearby dangled its poufy red brushes, and a calla lily boasted creamy white trumpet blooms curling around suggestive tangerine-colored protuberances. A tall white fountain burbled gently, but the sound didn't calm my racing heart.

"Sure, Robbie. This conversation is strictly in the shade, you understand." She waited for me to agree.

I nodded. "You said earlier you wouldn't be able to tell me anything."

"I'm aware of that. But I thought you deserved to know we detected methyl iodide in Etxgeberria's body. I wouldn't have known to look if you hadn't alerted me to the possibility. It's a neurotoxin and is a chemical so reliably carcinogenic it's used to create cancer cells in laboratories."

My mouth fell open. "You're kidding."

"I'm not. Here's the list of effects." She read off her phone. "Irritation to the eyes, skin, and respiratory system. Nausea, vomiting, dizziness, ataxia."

"Wait." I held up a finger. "What's ataxia?" I should know the meaning from doing crosswords but was having a sudden—and hopefully temporary—case of amnesia.

"Impaired balance or coordination. Shall I go on?" Mel asked.

"Please."

"It can also cause slurred speech, drowsiness, and dermatitis. Toxicity includes metabolic disturbance, renal failure, venous and arterial thrombosis."

"Thrombosis is blood clots, right?"

"Yes. Here's the kicker. The chemical can cause encephalopathy, with seizures and coma." She gave me a sorrowful look. "That is, it includes a characteristic pattern of brain injury."

"Wow." And I'd thought I was stunned before. "How can such toxins even be sold and used?"

"Mind you, these effects would be caused by direct ingestion of a heavy dose, either through the air or orally."

"Like in food."

"Yes. Exactly like in food."

I thought. "Did Paul experience all that external stuff? Dermatitis, vomiting, irritated eyes?"

"The EMTs didn't report evidence of vomit, and I didn't see issues with his skin or eyes. But a large enough dose of the stuff administered by mouth all at once? It could have gone straight to his basic life functions. His body wouldn't have had time to react in other ways."

I stared at her. "Did you find it in his blood or in his stomach?"

"Both, Robbie." She kept her voice gentle. "And I didn't see any injection sites."

"So it got into his blood from what he ate. And you found it in his lunch container."

"The container goes to their lab, not to me. I deal only with human remains."

Ouch. That word again. I folded one arm across

my stomach and sank my forehead into my other hand. Finally, I straightened.

"Paul was a lively, passionate soul. He didn't deserve this end. And I don't think he ever would have ingested a toxin like that on purpose."

"He didn't deserve it." She gazed straight at me, her glistening eyes matching my own. "No one deserves to be murdered. I am going to declare the manner of death a homicide."

I blew out a breath. "You probably know what my last question is."

"Could this fungicide have caused your mother's rupture? I truly doubt it, Robbie. I think she died of some really rotten luck Mother Nature dealt her. I believe Jeanine had a weak spot in a cerebral blood vessel, which had probably been there since she was born. I'm sorry. If it's any comfort, I do not believe anyone killed her."

Chapter 48

After the library, I kept walking. Downtown Santa Barbara wasn't all that big. Not far from the public library was the impressive county courthouse built a hundred years earlier. I gazed up at the eighty-five-foot-high clock tower and decided to climb to the top.

I hadn't been inside the courthouse in years. The smooth tile floors were cool and quiet. Arches topped doorways and windows, and mosaic tilework decorated the walls. Still in use as the Superior Court, lawyers, judges, and plaintiffs bustled here and there. Did they become accustomed to working in such a beautiful building?

I headed up to the tower. One hundred and twenty-nine steps later, I stood on the observation deck. Even it was beautiful, with a red tile floor, pillars topped by arches, and a metal grill fence all around. I did a slow 360. The Pacific Ocean stretched out to China, with the five closest Channel Islands in clear relief today, even tiny Anacapa. A half turn and I gazed up at the mountains. When would the next wildfire strike? How would I feel back home, where all I could see were low hills and hollows instead of western ridges always high on the horizon to comfort me?

Mel had seemed pretty clear she didn't think Mom had been poisoned. I supposed I should feel comforted by that. Knowing that Paul had definitively been murdered cast a black shadow on my feelings.

I stood back when five schoolchildren burst onto the deck, panting with flushed cheeks from the climb.

"I won!" a little boy exclaimed.

"Only because you pushed in front of me," a red-haired girl objected.

An adult woman appeared with ten other kids and corralled them all for a geography lesson. I aimed myself at the stairs. On the way down, I paused at the glass wall separating the clock room from the stairwell. The recently restored Seth Thomas green metal mechanism was a work of art, with an intricate system of weights and pulleys. Too bad murder investigations didn't tick along as smoothly.

Once outside, I remembered I'd never gotten that ice cream cone I'd wanted. McConnell's was only a few blocks farther over on State Street. I crossed over and pointed myself down Anacapa Street, which was one-way in the direction I was walking. I passed Carrillo Street. Kinsey Millhone's office was supposed to have been only a block away. I wished I could mosey over there and ask the fictional PI for assistance.

A few cars drove by. After a minute something alerted me, raising the hair on my arms. I whipped my head around to the left.

And swore. A black SUV with tinted windows followed several yards behind me, driving only as fast as I was walking. I froze even though I wanted to run. I made myself move, picking up my pace. My stomach roiled. It was hard to swallow. Who was following me? I reached the grand old Lobero Theatre. I could dash in, pound on the door, but the box office wouldn't be open at noon on a Friday. I could turn around and run up the street. The SUV wouldn't be able to get to me without crashing into other cars obeying the one-way signs.

A beep sounded from the street. The vehicle was next to me with the passenger window down. Tommy Moore leaned over.

"Can I give you a ride somewhere, Irene?" He wasn't smiling, but he didn't look malicious, either.

A breath whooshed out of me. "Uh, no thanks, Tommy." I mustered a faint smile. "Have a good day."

He waved, then drove on at a more normal pace. I stood in place and stared after him. Had the kid seriously been following me? Something was definitely off about him driving so slowly behind me. I hadn't been able to see if either of Walter's bodyguards had been in the back seat, or Walter himself, for that matter.

I guessed it didn't matter. I was safe for the moment. And now I needed that ice cream more than ever.

Five minutes later I surveyed the array of flavors in the storefront shop. The big arched window facing the street let in sunlight that further brightened the white subway-tiled walls.

The teen behind the counter smiled. "You get two scoops in a small, and you can have different flavors if you want."

"How can I possibly decide?" I walked up and down the case full of delectable-sounding flavors. "I'll have a small Dark Chocolate Chips and Nibs, plus a scoop of Whiskey and Pecan Pralines."

"That's a popular combo. In a cone or a cup?"

"A sugar cone, please, with the chocolate on the bottom."

"You got it."

After a quick minute she set the cone in a holder on the counter so we both had hands free to exchange money. I thanked her and took my first nibble. The smoky taste of bourbon was a perfect match for a rich and creamy base.

I wandered down to the end of the counter to grab a couple of paper napkins. An upright freezer was just beyond, full of prepacked pints and quarts. I shuddered.

I'd never told Abe, but the reason I was claustrophobic stemmed from an adventure gone bad when I was eight. Alana and I had been out riding bikes around the neighborhood. Our moms had agreed to let us be free-range children within the boundaries of a certain number of square blocks.

This sunny day we'd dared each other to explore the backyard of an abandoned house, the kind everybody gave a wide berth to on Halloween night, convinced it was haunted. Neither of us knew why the place was unoccupied, but the front yard was unkempt with high, dry weeds and trash, the screen door hung by one hinge, and the cracked driveway was empty. We'd dropped our bikes and crept around to the rear. Someone had once nurtured fruit trees and they were still bearing among the weeds and abandoned household items. A rusty washing machine had been discarded, along with an ancient fridge on its back and an abandoned dishwasher. Next to the high wall an orange tree's branches leaned toward the ground from the weight of overripe fruit. The brambles of neglected raspberry vines protected the back of the property.

We'd decided to play hide-and-seek. Alana covered her eyes and counted out loud. I tiptoed to the fridge, which was missing its shelves, and closed myself in, hearing the door click shut. The walls were so thick I could barely hear her voice.

Time went by. I heard a sound like a clunk, but Alana didn't pull the door open. Where was she? Why didn't she find me? I pounded on the walls. I yelled with all my small-girl might. *Nada.* And I couldn't push the door open because it had latched.

My breathing grew shallow and fast. I wanted Mommy. I wanted out. I needed to pee. I curled into myself, weeping. What if no one ever came for me? Was this going to be my coffin?

With a wrenching sound the door pulled open. The light hurt my eyes. I squinted to see my mom standing there with concern on her face, a crowbar in her hand, and sawdust in her hair. Alana stood behind her looking scared. Mom dropped the tool and reached out her arms. I climbed out and let her envelop me in her comfort.

"Why didn't you find me, Al?" I asked in a small voice.

"I tried to open the door, but the handle broke off. I rode to your house and got your mom. I'm sorry, Rob. Were you scared?"

I could only nod.

Chapter 49

A solo walk on East Beach was exactly what I needed after this morning. I didn't need lunch, not after the breakfast I'd had, now topped by the ice cream. I didn't need bad news. I certainly didn't need a big, dark vehicle tailing me, whether from malice or by coincidence, or scary memories from the past. I didn't even need a bike ride, for once. Scrunching sand under my bare toes, accompanied by the music of waves and gulls screeching, with salt air filling my lungs? A beach on the Pacific Ocean was the only prescription for me.

Breathe in, breathe out was my mantra for the hour. Bad thoughts out, fresh air in. And the shore was full of fresh air. The wind had picked up since earlier. The pelicans were all hunkered down on the breakwater stretching into the harbor. Several wet-suited kite surfers rode the waves, gripping lines leading to brightly colored arches of nylon. I stopped to watch them. The fearlessness the sport required, not to mention arm and upper torso strength, was impressive. The water temperature couldn't have been above sixty degrees. Regular surfing in the winter was crazy enough. To me, these guys and gals were lunatics as they sped along the surface of the water. For them, it must provide sheer exhilaration. Otherwise, why risk injury or death to do it?

I shook my head at the kite surfers' bravado as well as their foolhardiness, and walked on. I supposed I myself had been braver in the last year or two than I'd ever been. I had taken on a sole-proprietor business back in my adopted town. And I'd confronted a few bad guys—and women—and lived to flip pancakes the next day. I wouldn't have it any other way.

When my phone buzzed in my back pocket, I almost ignored it. What if it was Cody, though? Or Abe? I gave up speculating and pulled it out to see Liz's name. I could use a last visit with her before I left. She would want to know about Mom's death being from natural causes, too. I felt bad I hadn't already thought of telling her, but I got over it. I'd only really had the facts confirmed by Mel less than an hour ago.

I connected and greeted Liz.

"Robbie, aren't you leaving soon?"

"Yes, tomorrow morning early."

"That's what I thought. Do you want to have dinner tonight?"

I laughed. "I was about to ask you the same thing. Of course I do. Where?"

"How about the Green Artichoke? I have a few things I want to give Zoe, and I think she works on Fridays. Meet me there at five thirty?"

"Great. And I have something I want to tell you, but in person."

She waited a beat before speaking. "Okay. I'll make a reservation. Otherwise on a Friday evening we'll be in the bar and it'll be nutso noisy."

We said our good-byes and ended the call. Even if I departed not knowing who killed Paul, touching base again with my mother's best friend would mean a lot.

Interesting that she said she was going to make contact with Zoe. Somehow I'd gotten the impression Liz had given up on being in touch with her, not that I believed a mom could ever really give up on her daughter and her only child. Liz had said she couldn't allow Zoe to live at home. Maybe that was why I'd thought they didn't speak. I was glad Liz was still looking out for my former classmate. In the perfect future, Zoe would get the help she needed, stay clean, and find happiness in work, love, and family. If this made me sound like Pollyanna, so be it. I was well aware futures were rarely perfect.

My energetic striding slowed to a toe-dragging mosey. Out behind the Green Artichoke the other evening, Zoe had called Katherine a witch. This morning, Cody had mentioned Katherine in the same breath as "really bad." My nostrils flared and I halted so suddenly a man nearly clipped my elbow as he passed me.

"Move out of the way next time you stop so suddenly, okay, sweetheart?" he tossed over his power-walking shoulder.

Zoe had cautioned me to keep my distance from Katherine. I swore under my breath. Sure, Katherine could be difficult. But what if, in an effort to save Daddy's finances, she had tried—successfully or unsuccessfully—to rope Zoe into poisoning Paul?

As a person living with an addiction, Zoe was extra vulnerable. I wouldn't be surprised if Katherine or someone else had preyed on her. I sent out an intention for Zoe not to be involved in Paul's death. It truly would kill Liz, or close to it.

Chapter 50

All beached out, I plopped down on the bed in my room at a little after two. I had a ten o'clock flight out of Los Angeles International tomorrow morning, which meant I'd have to get up by five at the latest and drive out of here shortly thereafter to get to LAX on time. When I came back after dinner tonight, I needed to remember to ask Carmen if I could get a quick cup of coffee super early and take it in a disposable cup.

I'd successfully executed a fly-by shopping excursion to several tourist shops on my way back here, picking up every item I'd thought of earlier, plus a T-shirt for yours truly. I rarely bought things for myself at home, so these were guilt-free purchases. I hoisted my suitcase onto the bed, even though I'd never fully unpacked it, and started layering in clean clothes, gifts, my laundry bag, and everything else I wouldn't need in the next fifteen hours.

It was a good thing my purple carry-on had a zipper allowing for a few more inches of expansion. I had to pay to check the bag anyway, so I could carry home the olive oil. My flight was direct from LA to Indy, and I was going home. I could easily do without all this stuff if it got lost for a few days, unlike when bags went missing at the start of a trip.

As I folded and organized and stashed, I thought about Cody. Why hadn't he called? Surely he wasn't still at the station talking to Gifford? What had he been poised to tell me about Katherine? I stopped short. Did she have any idea he was revealing something about her to the authorities? Worse, would Cody be safe when he was released? Maybe they were keeping him for his own safety.

For the umpteenth time that week, I swore out loud, not something I normally made a practice of. Whipping out my phone, I texted Gifford.

Please keep Cody safe from Katherine and Walter.

I sent it. Maybe my message was a stupid impulse. Maybe the detective had already thought of protecting his witness, especially if Cody had revealed his sister— or his father—to have done something tragically criminal.

I had few blood relatives. I could never conceive of hurting Adele or Roberto, and I knew they felt the same. By the same token, none of us would ever commit murder. Perhaps once a person crossed such a line, nothing was off-limits. If Walter or Katherine was nasty enough to have pulled off Paul's murder, they were surely dastardly enough to wipe out an informant, too, even if he was related by blood.

From mysteries I'd read, I knew poisoning was considered a "woman's crime," maybe because it was tidier. Guns and knives produced a lot of blood, and knives and strangling needed someone strong enough to kill by that means. Would Walter have poisoned Paul? And why use the very chemicals his own company manufactured? That was too stupid to contemplate. On the other hand, if he was at risk of losing his house and his livelihood, he could have been desperate enough to act stupidly. Katherine was the calculating type. She wasn't personally desperate, I didn't think, but she might have been willing to commit an extreme act to save her father. It was possible they'd acted together, too.

I laid down the shirt I'd been folding and set my elbows on the windowsill. Through the screen I breathed in a hint of rosemary layered with the aroma of bread baking and the ever-present scent of the sea. It helped to soothe the turmoil of feelings this week had brought up, the suspicions and murky facts.

I was going to miss being here. This room, my hosts and old friends, the city, this breathtaking region, with or without wildfires. Something about home always drew me back.

Sighing, I returned to the job at hand. My gaze fell on the iPad. I'd never gotten around to digging into Agrosafe's finances. Because I'd learned they were privately held? Still, it was worth a try, if only to confirm Walter was in need of money. I sat at the desk and got out my virtual shovel. The going was slow at first. As it was a company not being publicly traded, Agrosafe had no filings of profit and loss statements, no registrations of investors or expenses, no annual reports.

Half an hour later I sat back. Very interesting. I'd finally found a recent news article in the financial section confirming an S. Moore being an angel investor. *Sydelle.* She was dating Walter *and* also rescuing him. What people wouldn't do for love. But what else had she done for Walter? Katherine wouldn't have cooperated with her to kill Paul, I was sure. Katherine had been clear she didn't like Sydelle. Maybe she wasn't involved at all but had discovered Sydelle had poisoned Paul. And that was what Cody had learned.

I slammed my fist on the desk. I wished I knew what he'd been about to tell me. I stared at my phone. I found Cody's number and texted him.

Pls let me know how it went with Gifford. And stay safe.

I didn't hold out much hope of him replying, and he didn't. Back to packing for me. Murder or no murder, I was getting on that plane tomorrow, homeward bound.

Chapter 51

After I finished packing, I took myself for a stroll around Carmen's neighborhood, soaking up the sight of flowers and other plants that simply didn't grow outdoors in Indiana. I returned to change into the dress I'd worn to the reunion, plus leggings and a sweater. The wind from earlier hadn't let up, and it felt like the milder weather of this week was about to take a more wintery turn. California winter, that is.

I didn't see Liz's VW in the parking lot of the Green Artichoke, but I went in, anyway. I was a little early. She'd been right. The bar was hopping. No hostess stood behind the counter in front, but I thought I spied a familiar face on the other side of the bar area and headed there. Sure enough, Grace Fujiyama stood around a beer-glass-filled high-top table with a half dozen men and women, all in snug yoga clothes. Paul's roomie caught sight of me and waved.

"Hey, Robbie."

"Hi, Grace." I smiled. "Is this the beer-and-yoga group?"

"You got it. I teach an extra-strenuous Bikram class on Friday afternoons and then we head over here to reward ourselves."

"And reverse all the benefits," a lithe man said, his tan the dark golden color of wildflower honey.

"Not all of them," Grace objected. "Do you want to join us?" she asked me.

"No, thanks. I'm having dinner with a friend, but she's not here yet."

Grace turned her back on the group and took a step away, motioning me to accompany her, lowering her voice. "Have you heard anything else about . . ." Her voice trailed off.

I shook my head. "Not really." I didn't think Paul's poisoning was public knowledge yet, and I couldn't break Mel's trust, at least not with Grace.

"They questioned me some more today, the Gifford dude and another guy."

"Really?"

"Yeah." She rolled her eyes. "The detective wanted me to go to the station, too, so he could record the interview. He was totally pressing me about who could have gotten into the apartment, about Paul's friends, about how I knew him. It was crazy."

"How did you come to share the place with Paul, anyway?"

"I've been friends with Taylor, his sister, for years. She comes to my classes and stuff. He told her he was looking for someone to share his apartment. I'd recently gotten divorced. It worked out fine."

"The house where you live does seem a little, well—"

Grace laughed. "Shabby? It is. The landlord doesn't care about the condition of the building very much, unfortunately. And frankly, the door locks and the windows aren't very secure, but it's also cheap rent. The place has always felt safe to me, but if somebody wanted to get in through the back or the side, I'm sure they could. You can't see a thing through that huge firethorn hedge between the houses. Which I told the detective. He wasn't very happy about it."

She might have been at the station at the same time as Cody. "Did you happen to see a kid there, I mean, a college-age dude, longish blond hair?"

"In uniform? Like a cadet or something?"

"No, he was being questioned, too. He's, uh, an acquaintance of mine." I didn't need to go into who Cody was.

She bobbed her head once. "Maybe I did see him. When an officer was showing me to the interview room, another one was taking a guy who looked like the one you described to the men's room. He wasn't in handcuffs or anything, but it looked like the officer was making sure he wasn't alone in the hall, either."

Whew. At least Cody hadn't been arrested. I caught a movement in my peripheral vision. Liz was waving at me from the hostess station. I waved back.

"There's my friend. Good to see you, Grace."

"You, too. Enjoy your dinner." She turned back to her friends.

Liz was now following the hostess to a table. I

walked slowly to join her. Someone could have broken into Grace and Paul's kitchen and put the stuff in his food. Someone who knew what Paul's lunch box looked like. *Zoe.* This must have been why Gifford was asking Grace about the locks.

I reached the table where Liz had just sat and summoned a smile I wasn't feeling. I slid into the chair opposite her.

"Hey, Robbie. I'm glad this worked out."

"Me, too." I took a second look at her. Liz's silver hair looked tired tonight, and her slender shoulders slumped under a rainbow-striped knit tunic.

"Did you see somebody you knew in the bar?" she asked.

"Sort of. It's Grace Fujiyama. She and Paul shared an apartment."

"How do you know her?" Liz looked confused.

"I stopped by there the other day and we had a little chat. I don't know her any more than that." I focused on the menu. "I ate at the bar here with Jason Wong earlier this week. This looks like a more extensive selection. What do you recommend?"

When she didn't answer, I looked up.

"You've been investigating, I can tell." Her gaze was intent. "Does Grace know something about Paul's death?"

"Actually, not a thing. Except she said the apartment's locks and windows aren't very secure."

"So somebody could have broken in. But did the police ever figure out if he was poisoned?"

Our server showed up. I smiled to see it was Debbie again.

"Ladies, good evening," she said.

"Hi, Debbie," Liz said, clearly also acquainted with her. "This is my friend Robbie."

"We actually met a few days ago. Hello, Robbie. Can I start you both with drinks tonight?"

I gave the drinks menu a quick once-over. "It's my last night in California for a while. I'm going to go all out and have the grapefruit margarita with Milagro tequila. And salt on the rim, of course."

"You got it. Frozen or not frozen?"

"Liquid, please." Frozen made the flavors harder to taste, and who needed an ice cream headache with a cocktail?

"I might as well have the same," Liz said. After Debbie left, she went on. "You said you had something to tell me in person. I'm anxious to know what it is."

"I'm sure you are." I spoke in my softest voice. "I feel like you should know, although you have to keep it completely confidential until you see it on the news." Where I expected it would appear one day soon.

"Of course."

"You put me in touch with Paul. It was you who told me he thought someone might have killed Mom. Well, I told you I'd learned my mom's death probably wasn't homicide, but today I found out Paul's definitely was."

Liz gasped. She propped her elbow on the table and covered her mouth, staring at me.

I nodded. "And it was the chemical Agrosafe makes. Someone put it in his food. The pathologist told me it was such a big dose it probably killed him pretty quickly without any external signs."

"The poor, poor man. Killed for doing what was right, for seeking a cleaner, safer environment." She shook her head in disgust.

Debbie arrived and set down our drinks. "Enjoy. Are you ladies ready to order some dinner or do you need a few more minutes?"

"I haven't even looked yet," I said. "Do you have specials tonight?"

The server blinked. "Heck, did I forget to tell you those? Sure we do. A king crab ceviche appetizer using local limes, garnished with kumquat skins from the owner's own trees. A Carpinteria greens-and-avocado salad with Cachuma goat cheese. Avocados also grown in the owner's backyard. Grilled locally caught red snapper with a wasabi-lime treatment served with Manchego risotto and baby haricots verts sautéed in garlic butter." She checked her list. "Oh, and the San Andreas triple-chocolate cake."

"Otherwise known as the earthquake cake," Liz added.

"Precisely." Debbie looked pleased.

"I want all those," I declared. "Liz, split the app and salad with me?"

"You bet, and the dessert, too," Liz agreed. "And I'll have the regular grilled salmon for my entrée. Oh, and an order of the deep-fried hearts, of course."

"Excellent choices." The server beamed. "I'll go put in those orders."

Liz's smile disappeared. "Debbie, wait. Zoe's on tonight, isn't she?"

Debbie's expression went somber, too. "Yes."

"Thanks. I have a few things for her. I'll take them around back later."

"That's fine," Debbie said, gazing into Liz's face with concerned eyes. "You're a good mom."

Liz looked down and murmured, "I try. But it's not enough."

Chapter 52

"This ceviche is brilliant, isn't it?" I asked Liz. The lime juice had essentially cooked the raw crabmeat, and the slivers of kumquat skin were sweet and crunchy. A sprinkle of finely minced red onion contributed a touch of sharpness, and I also detected a dash of a back-burner hot pepper.

"It's superb."

"Do you ever make ceviche at home? I mean with fish, not crab."

"Never have. I don't cook very much anymore." Liz took a sip from the huge stemmed bowl the margarita was served in.

"I do cook, of course, every day, but mostly not for myself. And the only local fish I'd be able to make ceviche from would be freshwater bass or catfish. I should give it a try sometime when I'm making dinner for only Abe and myself."

"You sounded happy when you mentioned him earlier." She tilted her head. "Tell me more about this man of yours."

"I kind of got lucky. He's smart, cute, and a great cook. He supports himself and his teenage son as an electric lineman. Plays banjo and can accurately shoot a bow and arrow." I'd seen him do exactly that to save our lives last winter. "And he can track animals in the woods."

"Does the son live with him?"

"Not full time, because he mainly lives with his mom, Abe's ex. But Abe has the boy regularly. He's a good kid, and he spends a lot of time with Abe's parents, too. Sean and I get along great, which helps."

"Most important in all that, Abe adores you, am I right?"

"You are correct." I blushed. "And it's obviously mutual."

"Then you are exceedingly lucky." Liz straightened her knife and spoon. She took a sip of water. She blew out a breath.

I watched her, my heart tearing apart. "I'm so sorry about Zoe," I finally said. "I hope she'll find the help she needs, Liz."

"You and me both, Robbie."

"When I was on the beach this week, I remembered all the sand art she used to make, and some of her creations in high school. She's so talented."

"She is." Liz shook herself a little and changed the subject. She started talking about a weaving class she was taking. I mentioned a podcast I was following. I'd finished the last artichoke heart when my phone buzzed. I pulled it out of my bag and checked the display, eyes widening to see Cody's name. "Excuse me," I murmured. I held the phone in my lap and slid open the text.

Finally out. Told cops Katherine's messages showed she bribed a Zoe Stover to poison Paul's food. Where R U?

My heart sank to my toes. A frigid stream of dread washed through me. I read the message again. I'd been afraid of this. I could not tell Liz. No way.

I tapped back a reply.

Thx. Out to dinner. Stay away from your sister, K?

But would he? With any luck, Gifford already had Katherine in custody. Cody's text was time stamped 6:10. He'd been at the station for eight hours. Had he overlapped with Katherine? Seen her in the hall, like Grace had overlapped with him? I kept the phone hidden and sent a quick message to Jason.

News? Cody texted me KR bribed Z to . . .

I sent it, not wanting to be too explicit. There was nothing else I could do right now. My hands were virtually tied from being an outsider, albeit an interested one. After making sure Jason didn't text me right back, I stashed the phone and glanced up.

"Anything happening?" Liz asked. "Was it news about Paul?" She searched my face.

I prayed she couldn't read my thoughts. "No, no. Airline changing the departure time by four minutes." I picked up my margarita and finished it instead of telling her the awful, terrible, dreadful truth.

Debbie appeared at the table. She'd said Zoe was here working. Why hadn't the detective already come and taken her away? I stared at her, but I couldn't broach the question in front of Liz.

"Guess you didn't like those appetizers much," Debbie said, gathering up the plates. "I'll bring your salads right out."

"Thanks," Liz said. She also drained her glass and

edged it toward Debbie. "Can I get a glass of the Fire-stone pinot grigio, please?"

"Of course." Debbie glanced at me.

"I think I'd better stick with water, thanks." The margarita was already going to my head.

"You got it." She headed back to the kitchen.

Zoe wouldn't have any idea she was washing her mom's plate. Or that Cody might have just changed her life irrevocably.

Debbie came back with our salad split onto two plates. Except my stomach roiled like a rowboat on a white-capped ocean. I wasn't sure I could eat.

Should I tell Liz what I'd learned? I wasn't positive if she would forgive me if she found out later what I'd kept from her while sitting only feet away. But what if the whole thing was a mistake? Maybe Katherine had tried to bribe Zoe and she'd refused. Maybe Cody was lying to protect his father, and Zoe had nothing to do with the murder. I would have ruined Liz's dinner for nothing.

Chapter 53

With full stomachs and me holding two takeout bags containing half a piece of the San Andreas cake each, Liz and I exited the restaurant. Both of us had realized halfway through our main courses that ordering the cake had been overambitious.

"Seven o'clock is when Zoe takes her smoke break," Liz said. "Come on back." She carried the cloth shopping bag she'd brought in with her.

I didn't say I already knew what time she had her break. "Don't you want to see her by yourself?"

"Actually? No. Please come with me?" Her voice shook a little.

We walked around to the back of the restaurant, as I had on Tuesday. The screen door to the kitchen whapped and a lighter flared. The cigarette tip glowed red in the darkness. I stayed a few steps behind Liz.

She approached her daughter. "Hi, Zoe honey." She held out her arms, but Zoe took a step back.

"What are you doing here, Mom?" Zoe's tone was harsh, accusing.

"I wanted to see you."

"But you didn't want me living in your house. In *our* house."

Liz waited a beat without speaking. "I brought you a few things I thought you might need." She held out the bag.

Zoe folded her arms instead of reaching for the bag. "What kind of things?"

"Stuff you like. Your favorite shampoo. Power bars. A couple of new packs of underwear. Even black nail polish."

What a thoughtful thing for Liz to do. Give her stuff rather than money to buy it with—which Zoe might have used for drugs instead.

Liz set down the bag in front of Zoe's feet. "How are you, sweetheart?"

Zoe looked away and blew out smoke, then gazed at her mom. "Life sucks. That's how I am. But I've been clean for fifty-two days."

Liz held her hand to her cheek. "I'm grateful for those fifty-two days, honey, and I'm pulling for you to keep it that way tomorrow, too."

"And the day after, and the day after that." Zoe sounded tired, even though I couldn't really see her face. "I know the one-day-at-a-time routine, Mom." She caught sight of me. "Great. You brought Miss Success Story, herself. Hey, Robbie Jordan."

"Hi, Zoe." I spoke softly.

Zoe puffed on her cigarette, not looking at either of us.

"We'll go now," Liz murmured. "There isn't an hour in the day when I don't think about you, Zo."

Two cruisers roared around from the front, police lights strobing but *sans* sirens.

No.

Liz sucked in a breath, wide eyed. Zoe muttered an expletive.

The police cars pulled up in a V, creating a barricade. A spotlight came alive on top of one cruiser, bathing Zoe in bright light. She raised a forearm in front of her eyes. Two uniforms poured out of each vehicle, hurrying toward us. Detective Gifford suddenly slid around in front of me. I had a very bad feeling about this, but I wasn't surprised.

"Zoe Stover?" Gifford asked her.

"Yeah." She threw her cigarette on the ground and folded her arms over her chest. "What's going on? I didn't do anything wrong."

"I'm Detective Sergeant Gifford of the SBPD. I'm here to arrest you for the murder of Paul Etxgeberria." He nodded to the closest officer, who drew out handcuffs.

"What?" Zoe cried. "No! It's not true."

"She would never hurt someone," Liz protested, rushing toward Zoe. "You can't."

"Ma'am, please step back." Gifford blocked Liz with his arm. "Ms. Stover, your co-conspirator signed a sworn statement."

Katherine.

"My . . ." Zoe gaped at him, jaw dropped in disbelief.

Liz clutched my elbow in a death grip.

Gifford went on. "She told us she paid you to put a large quantity of methyl iodide, otherwise known as a widely used Agrosafe fungicide, in the victim's food. The dose was enough to kill him. We found traces in his lunchbox and in his stomach. Your fingerprints are also on the food container."

Liz drew in another sharp breath.

"I did not do it. Katherine is lying if she says I did." Zoe's voice grew low and furious. "She wanted me to kill Paul, sure. She asked me to. She bugged me on Messenger. She said she was going to give me a lot of money to support my drug habit. Sir, with all due respect, you can check with the halfway house I now call home. I have been clean for fifty-two days. I no longer need her dirty money." She lifted her chin. "I refused that witch. You want to arrest a murderer, arrest Katherine Russom. She acted on her own."

"We do have Ms. Russom in custody," the detective acknowledged.

"Sir?" The officer holding the handcuffs looked at Gifford, who gave a little shake of his head.

"And the fingerprints?" the detective asked Zoe.

"Paul brought the container to work dirty and was going to put his dinner in it. I washed it and handed it to him. I hate dishwashing gloves, so I don't wear them. That's how my freaking fingerprints got on the container, I swear. I'm telling the truth."

The detective lowered his chin, as if he didn't believe her.

"Look, sometimes Katherine texted me and she kept those kind of clean," Zoe went on. "For explicit stuff, she used Snapchat, and she's dumb enough to think the messages disappeared. They don't if you save them right away. I copied all of them instantly and saved them on a thumb drive. I can prove it."

Gifford gazed at her. "Ms. Stover, are you willing to accompany us to the station to give a statement?"

"If I have to."

"We would appreciate it. I withdraw the accusation regarding arrest. For the moment."

The officer gestured toward the nearest cruiser. Zoe turned a pleading face toward Liz. "You believe me, don't you, Mom?"

"Of course, sweetie. I'll be there at the station when you're done."

Zoe gave her a sad smile. "Tell my boss I won't be back tonight."

I watched as the officer shielded Zoe's head from the top of the opening into the back seat. The door clicked shut.

Gifford turned to me. "I'm not going to ask why you're here, Ms. Jordan. And I gather you, ma'am, are Zoe's mother?"

Liz nodded, her eyes full. "I'm Elizabeth Stover."

"Did either of you have any inkling about what Zoe said?" he asked.

"Are you kidding?" Liz asked. "Of course not."

"Me, neither," I added. "Seriously, all I knew was what I told you this morning, what Cody didn't finish telling me." I was sure he couldn't see my crossed fingers behind my back.

Chapter 54

After the cruiser drove off with Zoe, and the other officers left, too, I gave Liz a long, hard hug.

She finally pushed back and wiped her eyes. "Robbie, you believe her, don't you?"

"Yes," I said. It was the only answer I could give her, and it was a true one. "I do. I hate to think Katherine is that evil, that manipulative, but between her and Zoe? It's Katherine all the way. Heck, for all we know, Walter and Katherine worked together to murder Paul."

"Zoe's been through some tough stuff." Liz stared at the ground. "I had no idea she'd been clean so long. I mean, it's not even two months, but I don't think she's let off using for more than three weeks since she started." She looked up. "Maybe she's on her way back?" Her voice shook.

"I'm sure she is, and she sounded determined to stay that way. Come on, let's go around front where it's light." I picked up the bag Liz had brought for Zoe and handed it to her. "I'll tell the manager Zoe won't be back tonight. You take this to your girl and wait for her."

As we walked, Liz said, "I need to call a lawyer, too."

"That's probably a really good idea." I stopped. "Wait a sec. You *are* a lawyer, Liz."

She shook her head. "Robbie, I write wills and do estate planning. I don't practice criminal law, but you can bet I know some excellent people who do."

"Good."

Liz gazed at the ground for a moment, then looked up. "Robbie, would you come to the police station with me? I'm not feeling very clearheaded at the moment."

"Of course. I'll meet you there, okay?"

"Thanks." After another quick hug, she climbed into her VW and putted off.

I glanced at my hand, still clutching both dessert bags. *Oh, well.* I went inside the Green Artichoke and spied Debbie. She hurried over to where I stood in the entryway.

"Everything okay? We saw police lights out back."

"I think everything's going to be fine." I worded the next part carefully. I didn't want talk to start up among her coworkers about Zoe almost being arrested. "The authorities simply want to ask Zoe a few questions about something she witnessed regarding Paul's death. She asked me to let her boss know she's sorry, but she won't be back tonight. Can you tell the manager, please?"

"Sure. You be well, now. And come again soon."

"Thanks. You take care, too. I'm going home tomorrow, but I'll be back, for sure."

"Good." She turned away.

"By the way, Debbie, they have Paul's killer in custody. I thought you'd want to know."

She turned back. "Really? Who is it?"

"I can't say." Or didn't think I should right now.

"Whatever. Bless you, Robbie. I'll let the gang know."

Chapter 55

Fifteen minutes later I sat with Liz on a bench in the police department front lobby. It being Santa Barbara, this was no stark, depressing space. Instead, every doorway and window was arched, reminding me of the county courthouse. Mosaic tiles lined the peach-colored walls, and several tall plants decorated the corners.

Still, the window to the interior was thick, and visitors needed to speak through a slatted metal disk in the middle of the tinted glass to communicate with the uniform inside. The air in here smelled faintly of cleaning solution mixed with traces of fearful desperation. Of all the reasons to be in a police department lobby, few were happy ones.

"Are they going to let you go in to see Zoe?" I asked Liz.

"I think so. I don't even know why they're still holding her." She worried a cuticle on her thumb.

"I'm sure they have more questions for her, and

Gifford is going to need to see that thumb drive, where she saved Katherine's messages."

"I guess." She rose and paced to the door and back. "I'm worried that my lawyer friend hasn't returned my call. Even though the detective didn't handcuff Zoe, he did take her away."

In the back seat of the cruiser, too. I kept that thought to myself. "I hope the lawyer contacts you soon. I still think it's a good idea to hire one." When my phone vibrated in my bag, I checked the display. "It's Jason. I'll take his call outside, but I won't be long."

Liz nodded, and I connected as I hurried out onto a well-lit front walk.

"Hey, Jason."

"I'm glad I reached you."

"Did you hear what went on a little while ago?"

"A bit of it," he said. "I have some news, too."

"I'm at the police station right now with Liz, waiting to see Zoe. So what do you know?"

"I got your text and poked around a little," Jason began. "You were right about Cody ratting on his sister. Good thing he did. This afternoon Giff finally roped me in for my cyber superpowers. Cody had dug into his sister's messages, and I did, too. By the way, I want to hire that kid. But, yeah, Katherine's in big trouble. So what happened at the 'Choke?"

"Liz and I ate dinner. She'd brought a care package for Zoe and we went out back to give it to her during her break. Two cruisers blasted in, and Detective Gifford said he was there to arrest Zoe for the murder. He told her Katherine had signed a sworn accusation against her. He called Katherine Zoe's co-conspirator, and said he had Katherine in custody."

He whistled. "How did Zoe react?"

"She stood up to Gifford. She said Katherine lied, that she'd tried to pay Zoe big cash to poison Paul. Zoe had refused. Katherine apparently used the messaging app where the texts are supposed to disappear. But Zoe saved each one to a thumb drive."

"Is she credible?" Jason asked. "Is she still using?"

"She said she isn't." I shook my head. "She told Liz and me—and Gifford—she's been clean for fifty-two days, and that he could verify it with the place she's been living."

"Maris House, I think."

"Right."

"So Zoe not only has a decent set of ethics," Jason said. "She also didn't need Katherine's money for drugs."

I nodded, even though he couldn't see me. "Exactly. Did Katherine try to get out on bail? I mean, I hope she's not going to come after anybody with a gun." The thought made me shiver.

"No bail," he said. "She's a dangerousness risk. Even without Zoe's statement, we now have plenty of communications evidence that Katherine had intent to commit homicide, whether by hiring Zoe to do it or carrying it out herself."

"Whew. Was she working with her father to do it?"

"We don't know yet."

A silver Lexus pulled to the curb. A disheveled-looking Walter climbed out of the passenger side, and a man in a suit hurried around from the driver's side.

"Here comes trouble," I murmured to Jason. "Walter and a dude looking like a lawyer just drove up.

They must be here to see Katherine, or maybe Gifford wants to question Walter. I'd better get back to Liz. I don't know how she'll react when she sees him."

"Text me when you leave, all right?"

"Deal." I disconnected just as Walter started up the steps. He saw me before I had time to go inside. Had he collaborated with Katherine to kill Paul? If he had, I wouldn't put it past Katherine to accuse him, her own father, of murder. Right now I was glad of two things: that I stood outside a well-lit police station, and that the guy in the suit was close by.

Walter halted and pointed a shaking finger at me. "How do you keep popping up?" he snarled. "If you had something to do with my little girl being falsely accused, I'll sue you up one side and down the next. Or worse."

"Now, now, Mr. Russom." The suit laid his hand atop Walter's and gently pushed the accusing arm down. "Threats are not advisable. Let's go in."

Walter gave me one more glare but complied, pulling open the door.

The lawyer mouthed, "Sorry," to me as he passed.

I stood rooted in place. I wanted to get back to Liz, but didn't care to be accosted like that again. What a relief Katherine wouldn't be getting out, and that they had the cyber evidence that she'd planned Paul's murder. With any luck, Zoe's thumb drive would be the other piece of evidence that would lock the case up tight and prove her innocence. After a moment, I headed back into the station.

Walter and the lawyer weren't there, but neither

was Liz. My phone dinged with an incoming text from her.

They said you wouldn't be able to come in with me. I'll let you know once I have her home.

That was that, then. I blew a kiss toward the innards of the station, to Liz and Zoe. I got a funny look from the uniform behind the glass and gave a little wave. My work here was done.

Chapter 56

I drove back to the café slowly, pretty sure I wouldn't be pursued on my drive tonight. It must have been Katherine who'd tried to sideswipe me after the movie and who had chased me at the mission. Or one of Walter's thugs.

I looped around on Cabrillo to drive by the beach. The rising full moon climbed up its arc, already shining a glistening stream on the waves. I idled the engine in the parking lot with my window down. I savored the sound of the waves, the smell of the sea, the sight of the silvery orb, and my relief that the week's tension was deflating as fast as a party balloon. I wished I could see one last pelican, but I knew they were all at roost somewhere. I blew the Pacific Ocean a good-bye kiss.

I'd barely made it through the outside door of the café when Carmen's voice came from the pass-through window.

"Robbie, come on back," she urged. "Your friend is here."

"Which friend?" *What?* I wasn't expecting a friend. My tension ramped back up to high. For a second I dreaded what I would find. Was this a false friend? Had Katherine gotten out, after all, and taken Carmen and Luisa hostage? I just left Walter and his lawyer at the station, so it wouldn't be them, but it could be one of his thugs. I yanked out my phone.

And heard Jason's voice from the kitchen. "This friend."

Oh. Silly me. I'd texted him I was headed back here. Sliding my finger off the 911 button, I peered through the window. Carmen, Luisa, and Jason sat on stools around the stainless-steel island, their beer bottles already half empty. Jason rattled off something in Spanish to Luisa, making her laugh. All normal. All safe. All as it should be.

I went around into the kitchen and jutted out my chin, squinting at him. "*¿Tu hablas?*" I asked in a less-than-stellar accent, pointing at him.

"Yeah, he speaks fine," Carmen said, wearing her signature broad smile.

"Speaking Spanish comes in handy on the job, plus nobody who speaks it expects a Chinese-looking dude to understand what they're saying," Jason said. "Anyway, I thought we might have more to talk about before you leave. I didn't realize these lovely ladies were throwing a party."

I slid onto the last stool and thanked Carmen for the Anchor Steam beer she handed me. It had been one of my mom's favorites. She'd told me long ago it was one of the earliest of the modern microbrews, first appearing in San Francisco in the seventies. It was still a darn good libation.

No tortilla-making was going on here tonight, and the kitchen was clean and wiped down. Still, it smelled of peppers, lime, masa, and all the other yummy foods Luisa and Carmen conjured up. I spied Pajarito snoozing inside a cardboard box in the corner.

I held up the beer. "Here's to Paul."

"And to Zoe," Jason added.

"*Y* Jeanine," Luisa tacked on.

Here's to Mom. She would have so loved to be with us right now.

"And, may I add, to Cody, who acted with courage today, turning in his own sister," Jason said. "It couldn't have been easy for him."

"I'll say. He did the right thing, though." I raised my bottle higher. *Thank you, Cody.*

"Cheers," Carmen said. "*Salud.*"

I let the cool hoppiness slide down my throat.

Carmen bustled around, setting out homemade tortilla chips and two bowls of chunky salsa on the island. "This one is *caliente*," she pointed, "this one not so much." Luisa pointed to the hot one and made a quick fanning motion with her hand in front of her mouth to illustrate.

"Got it," I said.

"We learned today that Katherine Russom killed Paul," Jason told the women.

I nodded. Carmen was doing a whispered near-simultaneous translation to her mom. Carmen crossed herself, and after she told her mother what Jason had said, Luisa did, too.

"What's even worse is that she tried to get Liz's daughter, Zoe, to do the dirty work for her." I dipped a chip in the milder salsa, which still packed a wallop of spice.

Carmen translated, then asked, "Why did she do this evil thing?" She gazed from me to Jason and back.

I swallowed. "Katherine is close to her father. As Mamá reported," I pointed to Luisa, who grinned, "Walter has a gambling addiction and is losing money. In fact, this morning Hector told me Walter owed some Mob guy so much money he might lose his house."

Carmen's eyes went wide.

"Hector promised me he would tell the detective who it was," I continued. "Katherine lives in that house, too, and runs her business out of it. She'd be nowhere without Daddy's support."

"Yep," Jason agreed.

"Paul was working hard against Agrosafe, as you know. Getting their main product banned would have put the company out of business." I waited until Carmen's translation to Luisa caught up. "Katherine must have figured killing Paul would at least let her father stay solvent."

Carmen rattled off more Spanish. Luisa shook her head sorrowfully.

"That's the thinking," Jason said. "Was Zoe still at the station when you left, Robbie?"

"Yes, but Liz had gone in and texted that I might as well leave, because they weren't going to let me in with her. She called a criminal lawyer friend, too." I explained to Carmen about Zoe saving the messages from Katherine. "Jason, Gifford would have sent someone to the place where Zoe lived to get the thumb drive, right?"

"Yeah."

"She at Maris House?" Carmen asked.

"She is." I cocked my head. "How did you know?"

Carmen threw her hands in the air. "Had a nephew who lived there for a while."

"Zoe said she's been clean for nearly two months," I said.

Carmen translated, then said, "I'm glad to hear it. They do drug tests on the residents, like, every day. Hard to avoid getting found out."

"Liz, ¿*cómo está ella?*" Luisa asked.

"It's a long story, Mamá." I blew out a breath. "I think they will heal now, Liz and her daughter." I waited for Carmen to translate.

"*Bueno, bueno.*" Luisa stood. She came over and embraced me, kissing me on both cheeks. "*Voy a mi cama.*"

"She says she's going to bed," Carmen said.

"Good travel," Luisa said to me. "*Cuídate.* Take a care."

"*Gracias*, Mamá." I smiled at her. "*Ven a visitar* Indiana."

"*Voy.*"

"She says she will," Jason said. He got a kiss on both cheeks from her, too.

Luisa disappeared out the back door as Carmen popped a few chips into her mouth.

She surveyed our beers, which were all empty. "Kahlúa, anybody? With coffee, with cream or whole milk, with vodka?"

"Man, I haven't had a White Russian in a million years," I said. "Hit me up with Kahlúa and milk over ice, please, but hold the vodka. I have to drive out of here at five-dark-thirty."

Jason shook his head. "Not for me, thanks. I'm not on call, but I have to head home pretty soon."

Carmen poured the same for herself as for me. "I think we need a little music, no?" She pressed a few buttons on an iPad on the desk. A danceable Tex-Mex rockabilly tune blared. I couldn't help moving to the rhythm even while seated.

"Now," she said. "We got one more question, I think."

"How Katherine got the poison into Paul's food," Jason said.

Carmen nodded. "Zoe worked with him at a restaurant. So, like, that would have been obvious, if she'd actually done it."

"Yeah," I said. "And his sister said Paul had been trying to make friends with Zoe, to help her."

"But if Zoe didn't administer the poison, why did the detective think she did?" Carmen asked.

I raised a finger. "And along those lines, why did Gifford come to arrest Zoe for the murder when his evidence wasn't foolproof? Doesn't it seem odd, Jason? When did he bring Katherine in for questioning, anyway?"

"It was pretty early in the afternoon," Jason replied. "It took them a while to find her after Cody spilled, which was at around eleven, I think. Gifford's people finally tracked down Katherine showing a wedding venue up the coast to prospective clients. At the time, it was her sworn testimony that sent him after Zoe. But with the messages Zoe saved, Katherine's in big trouble."

I sipped my cold, sweet drink. "I hope she's locked up when that wedding date comes around."

"I don't think Katherine's going to be helping anybody else get married," Carmen said. "It's a relief and a half to think of her behind bars."

"As to how she dosed his food, Gifford's team is on it," Jason continued. "Katherine easily could have broken into the kitchen. Cody told us she was always hanging around Paul, trying to get him to stop his protests, so she likely knew what his lunchbox looked like."

"Right," I said. "Grace told me the apartment's windows aren't in good shape. The landlord doesn't care much about the building. And there's such a big hedge at the side of the property no one would have seen somebody breaking into a side window or the back door. Do you think Katherine did it overnight?"

"She could have done it then, or the next morning when Etxgeberria was in the habit of going for a long bike ride and his housemate had an early yoga class," Jason said. "Not sure Gifford knows, exactly."

"I think I told you I saw Katherine walking on the beach with Paul on Monday night," I said. "They were arguing."

"She would have had no trouble obtaining a lethal sample of the fungicide from her dad's company. Katherine always did like to be in control." Jason's tone was wry.

"She was the first to admit it." I tapped the kitchen island with a finger, thinking. "Poor Cody. His sister is a murderer. His father's a sick gambler. And Cody's opposed to his father's livelihood. I hope the kid makes it."

"He was a good worker when he washed dishes for me back a few years," Carmen said. "Nice boy. Honest."

"That he is," Jason said. "I was serious about hiring him, Rob. I'll look out for him, make sure he gets some counseling. He'll be all right."

Carmen regarded him with a thoughtful expression. "You're a good guy."

Jason blushed and batted away the compliment.

"Jason, what if Walter knew what Katherine was up to?" I asked. "Maybe he helped her, supplied her with the chemicals. How can Gifford figure that out?"

"They have ways. Basic evidence gathering, communications, witness interviews. If Walter colluded with his daughter, Giff will nail him, I promise." He stood. "I need to get some sleep. I drew the early shift tomorrow."

"On a Saturday?" Carmen asked.

Jason threw back his shoulders and gave a mock salute. "The criminal world never sleeps, ma'am." He grinned, pushing up his geeky glasses.

Carmen extended her hand. "You come back to eat, *hijo*. First meal is on the house."

"I will." He shook her hand with both of his.

"You're the nicest cop I ever met." She wagged her head in wonder.

"Hey, we're not all bad. I am happy to know you, and your lovely mother, as well." He glanced at me. "Rob, let's not wait another ten years before hanging out again, okay?"

"You got it." We executed our ritual fist bump.

After he left, I sat with Carmen another few minutes while we finished our drinks. We talked shop about running a restaurant and a B-and-B. Even though our establishments were more than two thousand miles apart, we had tons in common—reservation systems, food-ordering software, getting reliable help, health department regulations. Finally, I rose. I gave the kitty one last pet, then straightened.

"I'm on the early shift, too. Carmen, this has been wonderful. I don't mean the murder part, but getting to know you. I feel like I've made a new friend."

"*Amiga.*"

We exchanged a hug. "You have my credit card on file," I said.

"I'll e-mail your receipt for the room in the morning. You travel safe, now."

I thanked her and trudged upstairs. This small corner of the world, nestled between mountains and sea, had justice restored once again. The Wicked Witch was behind bars. And this Dorothy was heading home. I didn't even have to click my heels.

Recipes

Mexican Chocolate Almond Cakes

Hector makes these easy mini-cakes as a dessert at his food truck. They're like eating Mexican hot chocolate in a cake.

Ingredients
  1 cup almond flour
  ⅓ cup unbleached flour or rice flour (for gluten free)
  ½ teaspoon kosher salt
  1 stick unsalted butter
  ⅓ cup dark cocoa powder
  ½ teaspoon cinnamon
  ¼ teaspoon chipotle chili powder
  1 tablespoon baking powder
  4 large egg whites
  1 tablespoon dark rum or bourbon
  ¾ cup sugar

Directions
Preheat oven to 375 degrees F. Spray a 24-cup mini-muffin tin with oil.

In a small saucepan over medium heat, melt the butter, then continue to cook, swirling the pan often, until fragrant and deep golden brown, four to five minutes. Remove from heat and let cool for a few minutes, stir in cocoa powder, cinnamon, chipotle powder, and rum. Set aside.

Whip egg whites on medium high until light and foamy. Don't overbeat or they will become dry and stiff. With mixer running, slowly add sugar and continue to whip until thick and glossy and holds soft peaks, two to four minutes. Reduce to low and gradually add flours, baking powder, and salt until incorporated, about ten seconds.

With the mixer still on low, slowly pour in butter mixture until integrated. Remove bowl from mixer and, using a spatula, fold the batter by hand a few times, then divide evenly among the muffin cups.

Bake until toothpick inserted into the cakes at the center comes out clean, ten to twelve minutes. Cool on a wire rack for five minutes in the pan before removing, then cool completely before serving.

Flaky Chicken Empanadas

These yummy bits are served at the Chumash High School reunion.

Ingredients
    1 large boneless chicken breast
    1 tablespoon ground cumin
    1 teaspoon chili powder
    1 teaspoon salt
    ½ teaspoon ground black pepper
    1 tablespoon olive oil
    6 ounces grated Pepper Jack cheese (or regu-
        lar Monterey Jack)
    4 ounces cream cheese, softened
    ¼ cup finely diced red bell pepper
    2 puff pastry sheets, thawed
    1 egg plus 1 tablespoon water whisked together
        in a small bowl

Directions
Preheat oven to 400 degrees F. Line two baking sheets with parchment paper.

Combine cumin, chili powder, salt, and pepper in a small bowl.

Slice the chicken lengthwise into inch-wide strips. Rub all surfaces with the spice mix.

Heat oil in a skillet at medium high. Lay in chicken strips not touching each other. Sauté for two to three minutes until brown on bottom, then flip them over. Sauté for one more minute. Lower heat to medium low and cook until chicken is done, about ten minutes in all.

Remove from heat and cool for an hour. Dice the chicken, ending up with about two cups.

In a large bowl, combine the chicken, cream cheese, grated cheese, and peppers. Use your hands to mix well.

Lay out one sheet of puff pastry on a lightly floured surface. Lightly flour the top of the dough and roll out to an approximate dimension of 11" x 15". Cut 3 ½" circles in the dough with a biscuit cutter, a glass, or a bowl. Repeat with the other sheet of puff pastry. Gather dough scraps and roll out to dimensions to fit additional circles.

Place one tablespoon of the chicken mixture in the center of each circle. Lightly brush the edge of half of a circle with egg wash and fold over, then pinch edges tightly to seal. Place on prepared baking sheet. Repeat with remaining circles, but DO NOT dip your brush in the egg wash again until your brush becomes dry because too much egg wash will prevent the dough edges from sticking.

Check each empanada to make sure there is about a finger's width of dough sealed together before the filling starts. Crimp the edges together with a fork. Pierce each empanada two times with a fork so steam can escape while baking.

Spread empanadas apart so they are not touching on the baking sheet. Brush the tops/sides evenly with egg wash. Bake until golden brown, approximately fifteen minutes. Serve hot.

While empanadas are lined on the baking sheet before baking, transfer entire baking sheet to the freezer. Once frozen, add individual empanadas to a freezer bag or glass container with lid.

When ready to bake, line desired amount of empanadas on a parchment-lined baking sheet, and bake at 400 degrees F. for twenty minutes or until golden and cooked through.

Avocado Huevos Rancheros

Carmen serves these for breakfast at the Nacho Average Café.

Ingredients
8 fresh corn tortillas
Refried beans
4 eggs
Oil or butter for frying
Salsa, fresh or from a jar
Monterey Jack cheese, grated
1 ripe avocado, peeled and sliced
8 ounces sour cream

Directions
Warm refried beans in the microwave in a glass or ceramic bowl and set aside. Wrap tortillas in damp paper towels and heat in the microwave for fifteen to thirty seconds until warm and soft. Wrap in a clean dish towel to stay warm.

Lay a stack of two warm tortillas on each plate. Spread the top one with a layer of refried beans. Sprinkle with cheese. Keep warm in a low oven.

Gently fry eggs sunny-side up or over easy, to your preference.

Lay two fried eggs on top of the tortillas on each plate, cover with sliced avocados, and top with salsa and a dollop of sour cream. Serve immediately, with additional warm tortillas rolled in a cloth.

Orange Scones

Carmen and Luisa make these at Nacho Average Café. Perfect with coffee or as part of a hearty brunch.

Ingredients

Scones
⅓ cup sugar
Zest of one large orange
2 cups unbleached flour
1 teaspoon baking powder
¼ teaspoon baking soda
½ teaspoon salt
½ cup unsalted butter, frozen
½ cup sour cream
1 egg

For the glaze
1½ tablespoons unsalted butter
½ cup powdered sugar
½ teaspoon vanilla extract
2 tablespoons freshly squeezed orange juice
    (squeeze the orange you just zested)

Instructions

Preheat oven to 400 degrees F. and set oven rack to the middle position. Line a baking sheet with parchment paper and set aside.

In a medium-sized bowl, gently toss flour, baking powder, baking soda, and salt. Set aside. In a separate small bowl, whisk sour cream and egg until completely smooth. Set aside.

In a large bowl, stir sugar and orange zest together until sugar is moistened and zest is evenly distributed. Pour in flour mixture and toss to combine. Grate frozen butter into mixture using a medium grater. Using your hands, work in the butter until the mixture resembles a coarse meal. Gently stir in sour cream mixture until just about combined. Do not overwork the dough. Very gently press the dough against the sides of the bowl a few times and form a ball. The dough will be sticky at first but will come together as you form it.

Place dough on a lightly floured surface and gently pat into an 8" circle about ¾" thick. Use a very sharp knife to cut into eight triangles (like a pizza). Transfer triangles onto prepared baking sheet, leaving about 1" between.

Bake scones for fifteen to seventeen minutes or until the tops begin to turn golden. Don't take them out too early or they will be too soft. Allow them to cool for ten minutes on the baking sheet before transferring to a wire rack to finish cooling completely.

While the scones bake, prepare the glaze. Melt butter in a glass dish in the microwave for thirty seconds. Whisk in powdered sugar, vanilla, and orange juice until smooth. Once completely cooled, drizzle the glaze on the scone tops and sides with a spoon.

Broccoli Tofu Stir-Fry

Jason Wong whips up this easy recipe he learned from his Chinese grandmother for a dinner with Robbie.

Ingredients

3 tablespoons tamari or soy sauce
1 container firm tofu, drained
1 one-inch knob ginger, peeled and minced
1 head broccoli, cut into bite-sized pieces
1 pound snow peas, trimmed
3 fat cloves garlic, peeled and minced
2 tablespoons sesame or peanut oil
1 tablespoon sesame seeds

For the sauce

1 tablespoon cornstarch
1 tablespoon hoisin sauce
Tamari from the tofu
2 tablespoons rice wine or sherry
3 tablespoons water

Directions

In its container, cut the tofu into half-inch pieces and drizzle tamari over it. Prepare other vegetables. Drain tamari into a small bowl and whisk in other sauce ingredients. Set aside.

Heat oil in a wok at medium high until it shimmers. Add ginger, broccoli, and snow peas and stir until broccoli and peas are bright green, but not soft. Add garlic and stir for no more than one minute. Clear a space in the middle and gently add the tofu and any remaining soy sauce so it doesn't break up. Cover with a wide lid and turn down the heat to low. Uncover after two minutes, whisk the sauce again, and stir it in, integrating all ingredients.

Remove from heat when the sauce thickens and sprinkle on sesame seeds. Serve hot over rice.

Nachos

Robbie orders chicken mole nachos in Santa Barbara. These nachos are a simpler version you can make at home and enjoy with drinks, in front of the game, or as an easy light dinner.

Ingredients

Nachos
  1 tablespoon extra-virgin olive oil
  1 large onion, chopped
  2 garlic cloves, minced
  1 teaspoon cumin
  1 teaspoon chili powder
  1 15-ounce can refried beans
  ¼ cup water
  1 9-ounce bag tortilla chips
  2 cups shredded cheddar cheese
  2 cups shredded Monterey Jack

For the topping
  1 avocado, diced
  1 large tomato, diced
  Sour cream, for drizzling
  Salsa (fresh or from a jar)
  Hot sauce (optional)
  ¼ cup fresh cilantro leaves (optional)

Directions

Preheat oven to 425 degrees F. and line a large baking sheet with foil.

In a skillet over medium heat, heat oil. Add

onion and cook until soft, five minutes. Add garlic and spices. Cook for one minute without browning garlic. Add refried beans and water to skillet and stir until combined. (If you're feeling lazy, omit the onions and garlic and just stir the spices and water into the beans.)

Spread half the tortilla chips on the baking sheet and top with dollops of bean mixture. Sprinkle on half the cheese. Repeat one more layer.

Bake five minutes or until cheese melts.

Scatter with tomato and avocado, and drizzle with sour cream and salsa. Enjoy hot. Offer hot sauce and cilantro as options. You can omit the beans for those who can't digest them.

Connect with

Us

Visit us online at
KensingtonBooks.com
to read more from your favorite authors, see books
by series, view reading group guides, and more.

Join us on social media

for sneak peeks, chances to win books and prize packs,
and to share your thoughts with other readers.

facebook.com/kensingtonpublishing
twitter.com/kensingtonbooks

Tell us what you think!

To share your thoughts, submit a review,
or sign up for our eNewsletters, please visit:
KensingtonBooks.com/TellUs.

Grab These Cozy Mysteries
from
Kensington Books